Dazzler Needed To Stay Safely Hidden.

And there was no place safer than his house.

Behind locked doors.

Todd wouldn't let Frost anywhere near her.

He shoved Dazzler's bedroom door open. It banged against the reproduction cabbage rose wallpaper.

Pale skin covered a tiny waist. A constellation of moles shifted into a leaf pattern above her flared hip. He skidded to a stop at sight of her delicate shimmy, certain the only thing that kept his jaw from dropping was his tongue glued to the roof of his mouth.

"What does someone do with dirty clothes? Nurse Paula said something about a hamper, but I don't see how it cleans clothes." Dazzler tucked her body inside a cranberry-red shirt and tugged on her jeans.

Todd waited for his brain to reset. Any second now. Any second.

Also By Linda Andrews

THE DUGANS

The Christmas Village
Some Enchanted Autumn
That's Amores
A Time for Us

KNIGHTS OF THE LIVING FIVE

A Knight's Wish
A Hint of Magic
Dancing in the Kitchen

DAUGHTERS OF DESTINY

Ghost of a Chance
Gillian
Brianna
Fiona

Strange Magic

by

Linda Andrews

ZUMAYA EMBRACES   AUSTIN TX

2022

STRANGE MAGIC

© 2022 by Linda Andrews

ISBN 978-1-61271-374-8

Cover art and design © Charles Bernard

"Zumaya Embraces" and the dove colophon are trademarks of Zumaya Publications LLC, Austin TX, http://www.zumaya-publications.com/embraces.php

CHAPTER 1

Dazzler Spitfire's elven senses tingled, and her pointed ears twitched. Had her magic performed as asked? Standing on shaky legs, she slitted her eyes to peer at her surroundings. For a moment, sunlight sparked off the glitter in her lashes, blinding her, and then she saw it.

Across the two-lane road, boughs of holly climbed the sign welcoming visitors to town. Waxy green leaves and white berries complemented the cranberry script flowing across the walnut marquee: *Welcome to Holly, the Most Enchanted Town in the West.*

Yes. She'd accomplished the first step in her mission. She fist-pumped. A soft autumn breeze brushed her cheeks.

Gold, tangerine, and scarlet leaves swirled into a gourd-shape before lengthening into a mass resembling an eggplant on the ground in front of her. Two legs and two arms emerged from the torso. Moss knitted together, making a green uniform, and wild mushrooms added buttons and fleecy trim. Leaves wrapped an oval head before the newly formed scarecrow rolled onto his belly.

"Where are we this time?"

"Holly." The name sweetened Dazzler's tongue. Candy-cane lines of magic formed a ragged net around the village and blanketed the white church steeple rising above the pines. All this, and it wasn't even the official holiday season for three more days. How strong would the magic grow after Thanksgiving?

She inhaled the scent, reveled in the cinnamon-and-vanilla aroma of human magic. So imperfect, yet she was so thankful humans took the time to create it.

This place felt like home. Why had she never visited before? Why had Todd always insisted they meet in Flagstaff?

"Holly?" Stick fingers dug into the ground as Cheddar levered up. His acorn eyes blinked twice before he raked red leaves into a pile and shaped them into a Santa Claus hat. "Why did you bring us to a magical town?" Screwing the cap down on his head, he adjusted his pinecone ears to hold it up. "I thought we're supposed to be investigating why your magic always goes wrong."

Skipping to his side, Dazzler offered her friend a hand. "We are. Santa recommended I start where my magic works best."

Which was around Todd Dugan, a resident of Holly—a hub of human Christmas magic. Like elven magic, only different.

More forgiving.

And meant to be shared by all.

Cheddar's three fingers closed around her wrist. The digits were soft despite being made from twigs. Leaves rustled as he rose to his feet.

"The North Pole is full of Christmas magic. Human *and* elf. Your magic doesn't work very well there. Why would it work here?"

"That's what we're going to find out."

Dazzler hoped Todd would help her. Surely, as her friend, he wouldn't refuse otherwise she could be stripped of her magic.

She chewed on her bottom lip. Hopefully, Todd didn't hate magic so much he'd allow the North Pole Review Board to take away her powers.

Releasing Cheddar's hand, Dazzler traipsed through the dappled sunlight beneath the cottonwoods and pines lining the road. Between the evergreen boughs, she spied the snowy trunks of sycamores, aspen, and poplars. Red flashed as cardinals darted in the forest. The jingle of the bells at the tips of her pointed shoes echoed through the silent woods.

"It smells funny." Straightening, the scarecrow plucked stray leaves off his velvet vest then tucked them inside.

"It smells wonderful." Opening her arms, she spun in a circle. "The peppermint scent of elven magic is too…" She mentally fumbled for the right words. "Too harsh. This is warm. Welcoming."

Antlers gleamed in the dim forest. An ear twitched, and innocent brown eyes scanned the woods. Figgy pudding! She'd forgotten the reindeer.

Dazzler leapt behind a thick pine trunk and held her breath. Her senses strained. Had they seen her? The whole herd were notorious gossips. Tarnished tinsel! The daily reindeer report accounted for more than half the names switching from the Nice list to the Naughty one.

Cheddar's acorn eyes narrowed. "Why are you hiding?"

She flattened her hands on the trunk. Bark crackled and broke under her touch. She peered around the pine. No red glow of reindeer noses illuminated the shadowy forest. She was safe. For now. But she had to be careful. Sighing, she dusted her hands on her velvet pants.

"Dazzler?"

"Hmm?" She glared at the bells on her shoes. If she wanted to avoid the gossipy reindeer, she'd better ditch the shoes. She closed her eyes and summoned her magic. Her soles tingled, then her toes. Her heart quickened. *Please, work. Please…*

"Dazzler." Cheddar grumbled in a voice sounding like two stones rubbing together.

She lost focus. Magic drained down her legs and filtered out of her toes. She shivered at the loss.

Planting his hands on his hips, Cheddar stared up at her. "Did your magic cause letters to disappear again?"

"No." She clucked her tongue. Just because one sack of mail went astray, everyone blamed her.

She bent over and plucked the bells off her shoes. The breeze caught the green thread and whisked it away.

"Good, because there aren't any departments left for you to join if you knot ribbons in the mailroom."

Dragging her heel across the dark loam, she dropped the bells inside the furrow and buried them. Rich soil sucked at her fingers as she changed the bells into truffles. The peppermint scent stung her nose, and she waved it away. The reindeer *couldn't* know her location.

Straightening, she smoothed her red vest. "I didn't screw up sorting letters in the mailroom."

The job was practically Dazzler-proof. Everyone said so. It wasn't her fault that not all the letters were sealed. Or that some wish lists fell out of their envelopes.

The scarecrow pursed his lips. "But your magic did mess something up, didn't it?"

Tucking her fingers inside her vest pockets, she crossed them. A little white lie shouldn't land her on the Naughty List.

"Not technically."

Except this time the Review Board planned an in-depth investigation into her off-Pole activities. She boxed up the thoughts, added gift wrap and a ribbon for good measure. It was almost the Christmas season. No time for negativity.

Cheddar grimaced. Sometimes the scarecrow took his role as her conscience a little too seriously. He opened and closed his mouth then huffed a breath. Two leaves flaked off his cheek and drifted to the ground.

"Are we really on a mission for Santa?"

Santa? Well, technically... Dazzler shrugged.

His eyes widened. "Does he even know we're here?"

She tweaked the pom-pom on his hat. "Not *here*, precisely. I mean, he ordered me to pull myself together, or I'll lose my magic once the Board's inquiry is complete."

Using both hands to count the days, Cheddar shuffled forward.

"So, we have three days to fix a problem you've had for nearly twenty years?"

More than half her thirty-six. She nodded. "We could have longer than three days."

They could have the whole season, if the reindeer spies didn't tell the Board where to find her. She was certain Todd Dugan would help. They weren't just ex-family but friends. She'd been told friends helped friends in times of trouble. And she was in trouble. By Kringle, he *had* to help.

Leaves swept toward Cheddar, stuffing and lengthening his limbs until he brushed shoulders with her.

"Why do you think Todd will help? The man hates magic. Doesn't want anything to do with it."

"I helped him with his daughter." Candance was half-elf. Dazzler frowned. Of course, her help with the teenager had been more about normal-girl-growing-up stuff than her burgeoning powers. Dazzler shrugged and gift-wrapped the doubts to hide them from herself.

"I don't know." Cheddar chewed on the end of a twig. "You do remember he's in charge of Holly's Christmas display this year, right?"

"All the more reason for me to be here." She flapped a hand, dismissing his concerns. "I can help him with the lights, make this the best year yet, and free him up to tend the reindeer."

Since the town of Holly was one of the way stations for Santa's midnight ride, its herd needed to be in tiptop shape. She could stop Todd from splitting his focus. The town might depend on the lights, but the world depended on Santa.

Skipping ahead, Cheddar pivoted. He walked backward, facing her.

"If you're here in hiding, the reindeer can't be allowed to see you. Just one report, and news of your location will spread among the elves before first cocoa is finished."

She opened her mouth then shut it. She knew firsthand how much elves loved gossip.

"Don't worry, I won't let the reindeer see me."

A white tail flashed in the woods. So, how was she to prevent it?

"Good." Cheddar nodded then turned his body but not his head. "I was afraid you'd want to help him. The last thing we need is a repeat of last Christmas Eve."

Heat flamed in Dazzler's cheeks. "I didn't know the magic corn had turned bad."

"Santa nearly passed out from the fumes." Cheddar faced front. "As it was, he had to backtrack to Boise because his eyes teared up, putting him behind schedule."

And elves loved their schedules.

And order.

And discipline.

And rules.

"That wasn't my fault." Despite the cool breeze, sweat beaded Dazzler's forehead. Would she ever escape her reputation? Glancing down, she glared at the cranberry tunic and tights. Not in this uniform.

She zigged to the side of the road and pushed aside the drooping branches of a willow. Brown grass crunched underfoot as she leapt a drainage ditch. Planting her feet on a carpet of leaves, pine needles, and bark, she closed her eyes and inhaled.

A dollop of magic would fix her clothes.

She tapped into the leylines running underfoot. Leaves rustled. Grass whispered. Peppermint scented the air. A soft breeze picked up the forest offerings and swirled them around her. Her soles tingled; then the sensation climbed her legs, hit her torso, and radiated out her arms and head. The debris knit together, flattened, then stretched. Bark-brown pants wrapped her legs. Sleigh-red and pumpkin-orange colored her new sweater. The lemon-yellow collar of her undershirt hugged her neck.

Cheddar's nose crinkled. "No jacket?"

Dazzler shrugged. Northern Arizona was warm compared to Santa's place. "You know elves are quite at home in subzero temperatures. Why do you think Santa picked the North Pole?"

Cheddar scratched his chin. "You do seem to be able to control your magic here. Perhaps, we can solve the mystery after all."

"I dress myself every day." Dazzler tapped her toes as her shoes changed into sturdy boots. Changing clothes required minimal energy. Her unique magic traces were practically invisible in Holly's fabric. She tilted Cheddar's hat rakishly over his acorn eye. "Come on. Let's go to town."

Grumbling, he pushed back the hat.

She reached the side of the road and stomped her boots. Spare leaves and twigs dropped to the asphalt. The church spire rose above the pines.

"The town is this way."

"I can't believe Santa would approve of you coming into the human realm to solve your magic problem." Cheddar's attention snapped to her so fast two leaves fluttered off his neck. "Your ex-cousin-in-law has a daughter who is the same age as you were when your magic started acting up."

She nodded. "Except she's just now coming into her magic. And I've had mine since birth."

Dazzler had been a master weaver at five. At seventeen, her spells had started to go awry. Hope fluttered inside her. Santa's insights wouldn't fail her.

Cheddar pushed the pompom on his hat to the back of his head. "You know Todd may not want to see you. He split with his wife at this time of year sixteen years ago. Despite your holidays together, he always makes sure to spend this time alone with his daughter and his family."

She rubbed the heart birthmark on her wrist. Time didn't matter when someone lost the love of their life.

"All the more reason for him to be supported by his friends and family."

Cheddar glanced up at her. His uniform quickly morphed into a flannel shirt and black jeans.

"Have you ever been in love?"

"No." But she knew what it was like to feel as if something was missing inside, of being incomplete.

She shook off the thought. There was nothing wrong with her.

Nothing.

Tilting his head, the scarecrow pursed his lips. "And if he asks us to leave?"

Todd wouldn't. He couldn't. She needed help.

"Then I'll take my investigation elsewhere." Stuffing her hands in her pockets, she hid her crossed fingers again. In Todd and Candance, Dazzler was certain she'd find the key to her malfunctioning magic.

They rounded the bend. On the right, a white farmhouse roosted in a meadow. Horses lipped at the yellowing grass. Pine boughs and red ribbons festooned the line of carriages parked along the driveway. On the left, pumpkins huddled in a patch where wooden cutouts of the Kringles, Santa's sleigh, and his flying reindeer encroached on the symbols of fall.

A reindeer leapt over a hedge trimmed in twinkle lights.

"Ready or not, here I come."

Antlers twinkled under the forest canopy. The reindeer loved their games.

Dazzler increased her pace. The forest gave way to bungalow suburbs. Wicker snowmen congregated on the right, taking shelter under two leafless apple trees. Lights outlined sloping eaves and spiraled down porch pillars. Oversized candy canes and ribbon candies lined walkways. The road forked near a butter-yellow Victorian offering homemade ornaments. Arrows pointed to the left, directing traffic.

"You lost?"

Standing near a compost box, an old man leaned on the rake in his hands. Leaves formed a pile by his scuffed boots. The rolled-up sleeves of his faded blue thermal shirt revealed a faded anchor tattoo on his forearm. Age pleated ruddy features trimmed by the white hair sticking out from his motheaten cap.

"No. Not at all." Her stomach cramped. She would be welcomed here. She *would*.

He squinted at her for a moment; then his attention shifted to Cheddar. Leaves from his pile formed orderly lines and slipped under the scarecrow's pants, fattening him.

"The both of you are more suited to Pumpkin and their celebration of all things Halloween than Christmas." The old man stabbed his rake tines into the leaves, stopping their exodus.

Gasping, Cheddar shifted behind her and set his hand against her back. His shudder of fear transmitted through his twig fingers to her.

Dazzler straightened. No one would harm her friend. "I'm Dazzler Spitfire, and this is Cheddar."

"Ole Henderson." The old man rubbed his cold-kissed nose and cheeks. "I knew you was magic, but you're an *elf*."

"Of course." She tucked a black curl behind her pointed ear. Not many magical creatures had ears like hers, even in Halloween towns.

"If you're one of Santa's helpers, how come you have a scarecrow with you?"

"Cheddar is my friend." She raised her chin.

The old man grunted. "You ain't got a real friend, so you had to make one? I thought everyone was friendly at the North Pole. What kind of elf doesn't have friends at the North Pole?"

Black trimmed her vision as his words hit too close. She forced herself to breathe.

"Cheddar was a gift. We don't return gifts at the North Pole."

Especially after the great cookie fire a decade ago. Not that she'd tell the old man that. Humans needed to believe Santa's place was perfect and magical.

Ole gathered the remaining leaves before resting the rake against the compost bin. "Thought you elves were supposed to be all white and silvery, like winter? You're more like bark and leaves. You'd kinda stand out and all, up in the frozen north."

Dazzler stumbled back a step. Her vision shimmered. "I'm a perfectly good elf."

Most of the time.

Ole rubbed his chin. "I ain't saying you're not, just saying it would be easy for folks to see you from up high. Thought you'd be silver and white to blend in with the snow."

Cheddar set his chin on her shoulder, stopping her retreat.

"Santa only works with Sylvan elves. *Sylvan* means *woods*." He pointed a knobby twig finger toward the bare trees overhead. "Do you expect that tree to be like all the others? No. You want some trees for shade, others for fruit, and the evergreens for Christmas."

Ole Henderson's snowy hair twitched under his knit cap, and he raised his hands in surrender. "Just so long as you can do magic, you're welcome."

"Magic?" She blinked. "Holly has the strongest kind of magic outside of Santa's realm."

"You obviously have to be filled in about the town." He removed his fleece-lined jacket from a bent nail on the compost bin and shrugged into it.

"I know all about Holly. The town was founded during the Gold Rush but didn't really begin to attract a lot of settlers until after the wars that followed." Dazzler smiled. She was good at research and remembered every bit of the history she'd looked into eighteen years ago. "After the First World War, Santa's reindeer were exhausted by the time they hit the western US. He feared he wouldn't keep Christmas for those in the newer states, but thankfully the settlers had a magical background and helped him corral enough elk to fill the team. The way station was created, and the townsfolk started raising reindeer."

Ole shook his head. "I'm not talking about the town's history. I'm talking about the man in charge."

"Todd Dugan?" He was about as perfect as a human could be. Dazzler raised her chin. No one would besmirch her friend.

Ole set his hand on the small of her back and guided her down the lane.

"Guess I should have trusted the mayor to have a backup plan."

Backup plan? Why would they need one? Dazzler blocked the old man's view as Cheddar dove into the compost bin. The scarecrow muttered and hummed to the rotting vegetation, offering comfort.

"I know Todd Dugan."

"Of course you do. He married one of your kind."

The houses lining the lane grew closer together, then morphed into portly Victorians with white picket fences holding up garland bunting.

Dazzler mentally recited her favorite types of cookies in alphabetical order to cool her temper. At sugar cookies, she found her tongue.

"Todd has been nothing but kind. Why would the mayor need a backup plan?"

"Because of the curse."

"What curse?"

"Todd is the only Dugan to divorce his mate. Ever." Ole nodded slowly as if weighed down by the importance of the revelation.

She shrugged. "I have met many humans. Divorce is common in families." And a little magic went a long way to healing their broken hearts.

Ole tugged his hat off his head and wrung the knit material between his arthritic hands.

"Do you know why we teach science in high school and not magic?"

Dazzler squirmed. This had to be some kind of test. "Magic can't be taught. It's felt—in here." She tapped her chest.

"Exactly." Ole beamed as if she were a slow student who'd finally understood the lesson.

Except she didn't understand. Not even a little. Still, she nodded as they turned down Main Street.

Garland arched overhead. Ribbons perched atop globe street-lamps. A man in a white apron scratched an advertisement for pumpkin pies and muffins off the bakery windows. A sandwich board in front of a red-brick diner counted the days remaining of pumpkin spice until the arrival of everything peppermint. A woman fiddled with a display of Santas at the souvenir shop but stopped to stare at them.

Dazzler waved at her, then at the man hanging wreaths on the signposts.

Carolers in street clothes paused at their marks on the corners and went over their playlist. On the marquee above the Art Deco theater, black letters listed the times classic holiday movies would play and boasted free popcorn.

Ole huffed. "You don't see the problem at all. When a Dugan meets his match, the lights go out in Holly. Once a Dugan wins the love of his mate, his heart overflows, causing every light in town to blaze. What if Todd can't hold enough magic in his broken heart, and the town stays dark? A lot of folks's holiday will be ruined. Heavens to Betsy, some might stop believing and dim the fat man's power. We don't even know if evicting Todd from town would fix the problem."

Dazzler caught her breath. Evict Todd, tear him away from his family and friends at the holidays? Surely, no one would be so cruel. She glanced at her human companion. From the set of his jaw, that's exactly what Ole would do.

Well, not on her watch.

She cracked her knuckles. She'd protect Todd. "Everything will go off without a hitch. You'll see."

Ole pursed then flattened his lips. "But…"

"Todd's heart is here in Holly. His family lives here. His daughter lives here. Everything he loves is here."

Ole harrumphed.

Voices swelled from the town's center. Men, women, and children poured out of the businesses lining the square. Ribbons of lights wrapped the lampposts. Clusters of red and green bulbs streamed from the pines lining the walk to the Greek revival courthouse in the center. A marching band practiced Christmas carols in the snow-white gazebo on the right. Around it, wrought iron cafe tables and chairs waited to be filled.

Dazzler floated on a cloud of vanilla and cinnamon. Inhaling deeply, she filled her lungs. Warmth radiated from her center and infused her fingers and toes. Such strong magic. It was wonderful. Amazing. She spun in a circle taking it all in.

"Not bad, eh?" Ole rubbed his hands together. "For those that don't believe, there's a logical reason for everything. But for those who do, it's pure magic."

A lump formed in her throat. Her feet left the ground, and sugar plums circled her, tickling as they twirled.

"I love it."

A crowd gathered in the square. Steam danced above mugs of coffee, hot cocoa, and tea. A few reindeer gathered near a grass patch behind the gazebo. Returning to earth, Dazzler shifted into the center of the crowd, glad she was short enough to hide from the four-legged snitches.

The mayor bounded into the gazebo. The crowd quieted. He straightened his suit jacket, pushed up his wire-rim glasses, grinned, and then addressed the crowd.

"I'll save my speech for Thanksgiving and the few polite citizens who'll pretend it's not the same one I give every year."

Dazzler chuckled along with everyone else. This camaraderie was nice.

"And now for the man to help us usher in the season for ourselves and so many of our town's visitors." Mayor Browning pointed to a dark-haired man at the front of the crowd. "Please welcome Todd Dugan."

The crowd clapped. A few cheered.

Todd climbed the steps two at a time. Cold brushed color on his high cheekbones and crooked nose. His cobalt eyes crackled with energy and enthusiasm. Rolling his broad shoulders, he tugged a tablet from his fawn-colored jacket.

"As we all know, the spirit of Christmas is strongest in the heart of a child."

He beamed. She smiled back. Joy was so infectious.

Shifting to the edge of the gazebo, he turned the tablet toward a little girl drowsing in her mother's arms.

"Can you tap that button here?" He pointed to a green box on the screen.

The girl nodded and sucked her thumb. The crowd twittered in sympathy.

But Dazzler sniffed acrid notes of unease. Everyone knew the importance of the Christmas spirit in Santa's magic. She muttered a little calming spell—everything would be perfect.

The mother removed her daughter's thumb from her mouth with a pop and pressed it against the box. Magic filled the nooks and crannies of the square. Lights twinkled in trees and on eaves. Pixie-dust trails wrote welcoming messages above the courthouse. An animated Santa and workshop elves danced and hummed as they worked on toys for good boys and girls.

Wonderful. Amazing. Dazzler clapped until her palms hurt. Why had everyone been worried? Todd Dugan could do anything.

Todd straightened. His gaze fell on her, and his eyes widened with shock.

Then he smiled.

Her joy increased. Everything was always better when it was shared.

His lips parted as if he were about to speak.

A voice rang across the square. "It certainly says Christmas."

Dazzler froze. No. No, this couldn't be happening. Her cousin Willa couldn't be here. Then she spied it. The sparkle of glitter on snow-white hair. Elven hair.

Todd tore his attention from Dazzler and pinned his ex-wife with a stare.

"Willa."

And the lights went dark.

CHAPTER 2

"The lights are out."

Ignoring the mayor, Todd Dugan ground his back molars. The legend of the connection of the lights and the Dugans was magic. Just like the two elves in the audience. He'd learned long ago magic didn't apply to him.

"I know the lights are out."

He'd been there before when everything had gone sideways. So had most of the town.

The crowd's murmurs lapped at the gazebo. He knew someone wanted him kicked out of town before too much damage was done. A baby cried. On the lawn behind him, the high school marching band hit a discordant note.

Todd's skin prickled from the accusation in their eyes. This wasn't his fault. It was a glitch, pure and simple. He turned the tablet in his hands, and his fingers flew over the keyboard. But where was the glitch?

He'd checked and double-checked every connection with the lights. This really shouldn't be happening. This *couldn't* be happening. He checked the signal from his device to the receiver that controlled the lights in the town square. Five bars. Sour eggnog!

In front of him, the townspeople shifted.

Old man Henderson muttered under his breath, "The boy is a disaster with magic."

The prim librarian nodded. The baseball coach crossed his arms, pecs rippling under his sweatshirt.

"If you'll bear with us." Stepping forward, Mayor Browning raised his hands, a silent plea for calm. "I'm sure everything will be under control soon."

Todd grunted. Nice to know one of them was sure. But even in high school, Paul Browning had always been the confident one.

Browning nudged Todd and lowered his voice. "I guess now isn't the time to tell you I invited your ex-wife to emcee the festivities."

Todd blinked. He'd known there had to be a reason for his ex to show up. Still...

His fingers hovered over the screen. "Is this about the bet?"

Ducking his head, Browning hid his grin from the restless crowd. "Magic, one; technology, zero. And I get your sleigh all winter."

"You have coal for brains. And keep your mittens off my ride." Todd didn't need magic. Not at all. He just had to get his technology working. He ran a diagnostic and tapped his foot as the progress bar started to glow. Any second now. Any second...

Someone cleared her throat. The crowd parted, opening an aisle between the silvery elf and the gazebo. Todd didn't bother glancing up. He knew that sound. His stomach clenched, waiting for the lecture on what he was doing wrong.

"I think I have an explanation." Willa Sparkles nodded to people in greeting as she glided forward. Sunlight glinted off her snowy hair. Her alabaster skin glowed, revealing iceberg-blue veins at her temples. Sooty lashes framed her pale-blue eyes.

A little girl stroked a chubby finger down the crisp white velvet of Willa's jacket. Rainbow sparks took wing at the contact. The townsfolk oohed and ahhed. Santa's elves had that effect on most people.

Thankfully, Todd wasn't most people. He'd tired of such perfection a decade and a half ago. He preferred a warm soul, not an ice queen.

His tablet finished its diagnostics with a chime of bells. No error found. *That can't be right.* Digging his finger into the power button, he rebooted the tablet. As the wheel spun down, he scanned the crowd.

Brown eyes caught his. His ex-cousin-in-law Dazzler Spitfire smiled from behind the burly baker. With a twinkle in her eye, she flashed him a thumbs-up.

Todd's chest constricted. Why was she here? No doubt his daughter had invited her. And Dazzler, being Dazzler, was always willing to help. He hoped she wouldn't use her magic to assist him. He could handle a little glitch. Just as soon as he figured out where his tech had gone wrong.

"Pardon me, but perhaps I should have said *who* is responsible." Willa's voice was a cold splash of water.

Mayor Browning stiffened, and his gaze cut to Todd. "*Who* is responsible?"

Todd shifted his attention to his ex-wife, and he clamped his lips together. Naturally, she'd blame him. She'd never liked his technology.

She arched an eyebrow. "My cousin Disaster, er, Dazzler."

Todd gripped the tablet until it shook in his hands. He refused to look in Dazzler's direction—his ex would notice.

"Mom." Candance tugged on Willa's sleeve. Their seventeen-year-old daughter's chestnut hair was streaked with white. Her green eyes shimmered into blue. Sparkles faded her summer tan. Soon, his baby would resemble one of Santa's elves and head off to her job at the North Pole.

And he would be left alone. He forced a smile.

Candance picked at the dry skin on her fingers, a nervous habit from when she was five. "That's not a nice thing to say."

Browning whistled low under his breath. "I can't believe she's your ex-wife," he muttered to Todd.

Obviously, the mayor saw the initial appeal of the elf. Heck, from the number of open mouths in the crowd, most of the town did, too. Even old man Henderson had nearly lost his dentures.

"I'd marry her, lights or no lights." The ex-quarterback muscled aside the librarian. A few of the men nodded; two women glared.

The librarian, Mrs. Martin, dug a bony elbow into the quarterback's side, stopping his progress. "The matter of the lights is not a joke. Where is this Disaster woman? Let's ask her if she's responsible for them going out."

"Her name isn't 'Disaster'. It's Dazzler." Light flickered over Todd as his tablet started up. "And she isn't a woman."

Mayor Browning cocked a brown eyebrow.

"She's an elf. Like Willa." *But warm, and kind, and always smiling.* Todd's skin heated.

His ex-wife squinted at him.

Deer droppings! He was glad she couldn't hear his thoughts.

Ducking his head, he entered his passcode and reconnected with the computer coordinating the light display. He waited for the app to open and peeked toward Dazzler. Her spot was empty.

"And she isn't here. She's also not responsible for the lights."

"So, it *is* you!" Old man Henderson jabbed a gnarled digit at Todd.

He tamped down the feeling of abandonment. His ex-cousin had been there during his divorce, the insanity of raising his daughter, and helping Candance transition from human teen to newly empowered elf. He exhaled slowly as the tablet reported it couldn't connect with the control panel. Relief bowed his shoulders.

"It's just a technical glitch." He flashed the screen with its scarlet bars at the crowd.

Mrs. Martin tugged her readers out of her flame-red hair and perched them on her nose. "I hope you can fix it, young man. We can't have Christmas ruined on a technicality."

Hashmarks appeared on his ex-wife's alabaster forehead. "I won't allow Christmas to be ruined. I—"

A little girl squealed then clapped. Candance pointed to the columns of the Greek Revival courthouse plopped in the center of the town square.

"Some of the lights are back on."

"Maybe it was a short." Returning her glasses to her hair, Mrs. Martin pursed her lips as if the admission tasted tart.

Todd's nose twitched with the scent of peppermint. One bar turned green. It wasn't a short. His tech was starting to work again, just like he'd known it would.

Old man Henderson snorted. "There's a more likely explanation."

A reindeer galloped across the flat roof of the courthouse, a string of lights tangled around his antlers. He took to the air with another reindeer hard on his hooves. Two more played tug-of-war with a strand of red bulbs near the fountain.

Todd eyed the first reindeer. He knew his family herd; none had markings like that. And was that a maple leaf tail? Where had that creature come from? There could be only one place—the North Pole. Willa must have ridden it down.

Old man Henderson scratched the ring of white hair circling his pink scalp. "When are you going to corral them reindeer? You know how they love their games."

The crowd peeled away in threes and fours. Youngsters chased the strings of lights the reindeer had trailed across the ground. Teens scrambled up bare trees and retrieved snowmen, elves, and reindeer lawn ornaments. Adults collected bouquets of glowing candy canes and lollipops before drilling them into the ground to light the sidewalks.

His ex-wife stomped her foot. Bells jingled at the tips of her boots. "I'm telling you this isn't the work of playful reindeer."

Todd shook his head. Willa could never admit to a mistake. Well, none besides the mistake of marrying him.

Old man Henderson hunched over, blew on the plug of the lights outlining the gazebo, then plugged it into an outlet. Todd held his breath. The lights had to work. The curse couldn't be responsible. It just couldn't.

After a moment, red lights trimmed the white woodwork. Old man Henderson grunted at the success then shuffled off to the next outlet. Across the cobblestone street, the lights on the barber shop, drugstore, hardware store, and candy store glowed brightly in the afternoon sunshine. Half the town was lit.

Todd switched off the power on his tablet. He'd best help gather the lights.

Mayor Browning clamped a hand on Todd's shoulder. Willa planted two ivory boots on the bottom step of the gazebo. The jingle bells glinted at their pointed tips.

"I'm telling you, it's not a short. This has Disas—Dazzler's magic written all over it."

"Why don't you tell us about it?" With his free hand, Browning gestured toward the wooden benches lining the gazebo before taking a seat in the back.

Todd shrugged off his friend's grip. The man was determined to win the bet. There wasn't enough icing in Holly for that to happen. Dropping to a bench, he tucked the tablet inside his jacket and turned the collar up against the arctic breeze his ex always brought with her.

Like a fluffy white cloud fleeing a winter gale, Willa sailed into the gazebo. She ignored him and focused on the mayor.

"My cousin Disaster—"

"Mom." Candance flopped onto the bench beside Todd. She smiled at him before dipping her hand in his pocket to hold his. Todd squeezed her fingers like he had when she was younger, except now they didn't need warming up. Her elven nature was making her immune to the cold.

Willa rolled her eyes. "*Dazzler's…*" She stressed the name. "…magic always goes awry. Things happen. Bad things. Like the lights going out for your important season."

"Auntie D means well, Mom." Candance rested her head against Todd's shoulder. Removing his hand from his pocket, he looped an arm around her shoulders. No matter how she changed, she'd always be his daughter.

Willa's mouth firmed; a heartbeat later, she shook herself. "Dazzler always *means* well. Unfortunately, she doesn't *do* well. She's been kicked out of one department after another at the North Pole. And let's not forget last Christmas, when she nearly messed up Santa's midnight ride."

Browning arched an eyebrow, then stared at Todd.

Todd shrugged. He had no idea what event Willa spoke about. Heck, there hadn't even been a rumor about last Christmas. Then again, elves were notoriously close-lipped and clannish. He might never have found out about Willa's affair if humans hadn't also worked in Santa's workshop.

"Dazzler has been nothing but kind to our daughter. She was always here for Candance's plays and sporting events. Even when she delivered her first reindeer calf, and lost her first tooth."

Of course, he'd asked her to stop visiting him once he'd moved out of Flagstaff and back to Holly. Yet, she was here. He shook off his doubts. Dazzler knew his thoughts on magic. She wouldn't use it around him.

Willa's nostrils flared, and her jaw clenched. "I have a very important job at the North Pole, Todd. I can't just leave willy-nilly. Despite what people think, we work twelve months a year just like everyone else."

Mayor Browning cleared his throat, interrupting the brewing squabble. "The lights went out due to the reindeer games. And I'm certain someone would have noticed another elf like you in town."

"Dazzler isn't like me." Willa sniffed. "She's dark, like the woods outside in winter. All browns and greens. You might not recognize her because she can change her appearance like the Earth does from one season to the next."

"Auntie D resembles the Sylvan elves before they followed Santa north." Candance sat up straight. "Now, almost all of them use winter magic exclusively."

"Disas—Dazzler's coloring allows her to tap into all the seasons' magic. A magic she cannot control." With a toss of her head, Willa flicked a lock of white hair over her shoulder while glancing around the town square. "At least at home we can contain her damage. But she insists on wandering around, violating the Starlight Treaty, and causing problems everywhere."

Starlight Treaty? The words niggled Todd's memory. If he remembered right, the agreement had nothing to do with magic, but with humans and elves mingling outside of Santa's realm. He shut down the thought. Time to get his ex-wife to leave.

"Either way, Dazzler's not here. It's just a loose bulb."

Willa's eyes narrowed. "Oh, she's here. After her last outing, I had no choice but to call an inquiry by the Review Board. This time, they'll take her magic. They'll have no choice."

"Mom. Auntie D helped that family." Candance pushed to her feet, her fists curled at her sides.

"She broke the rules, Candance." Willa raised a finger; snowflakes swirled from the tip. "Those rules protect all of us. Do you know what would happen to us if people found out we really existed? They would hurt you."

Candance clamped her lips together. The resemblance to her mother caused Todd's stomach to clench. He shook off the moment of unease. Candance was still his daughter; he'd protected her his entire life. So had Dazzler. As usual, his ex was overreacting to get her way.

"While this is interesting, it doesn't alter the facts." Mayor Browning checked his watch before rising to his feet. "This Dazzler isn't here, and we have a lot of reindeer damage to undo."

Willa crossed her arms over her chest. "Then I guess I'll just stay and emcee the festivities as you asked me, Mr. Mayor."

Browning slanted Todd a glance. A winning glint shone in his eye. "That sounds fine to me. Todd?"

Todd forced a smile. If his friend thought that would roast his chestnuts, he was in for a surprise.

"Candance, why don't you take your mom to Patience and Charity's Bed and Breakfast. I'm sure they'll make room for our honored guest."

Candance opened and closed her mouth. "Allright."

"We'll need two rooms." Willa hooked her arm through her daughter's and glided down the steps. "Sterling Frost will be joining me."

Todd sagged on the bench. Sterling Frost. If he never heard that name, he could have died a happy man.

Applause washed over him as the bakery, hair salon, and clothing store lit up.

Browning kicked Todd's boot. "Do you think this Sterling elf will be as good-looking as your ex?"

"Sterling Frost is not an elf." If he had been, Todd would have punched him in the nose for sleeping with Willa. "Sterling is a descendant of the original Jack Frost."

And his heart was twice as cold.

"Too bad, for you." Browning paused on the top step of the gazebo. "Of course, if there were two elves in town, and the lights went out again, proving the curse extends to you, then you could have your choice of elves to marry."

Todd shook his head. "It was a technical glitch. Nothing more. Magic doesn't apply to me."

"We shall see." Browning rubbed his hands together. "I think I'll ask Santa for a new set of gloves. Ones thick enough to handle sleigh reins."

Todd rubbed his eye with his middle finger.

Clomping down the stairs, Browning chuckled. "I look forward to seeing you win your ex-wife back."

The mayor wouldn't live long enough to see that day. No one would. Todd would prove to them all that technology performed just as well as magic. As for Dazzler...

He sighed as another item joined his to-do list. A simple warning that others were looking for her should convince her to leave town. He didn't need another distraction.

And Dazzler was always distracting.

CHAPTER 3

*Dazzler ducked down a side street. Victorian homes rose grace-*fully from lawns, decked in Christmas decorations. Spiral tur-rets and gothic towers were painted in Jordan almond colors and trimmed with crisp white and gray. Along the white picket fences lining the streets hung garland and gold ribbons. Laugh-ter emanated from the village green one street over.

Flying above her head, a handful of reindeer chased a maple leaf-tailed one with a candy cane ornament in his mouth. The lead reindeer tossed the decoration to the one closing in on his left and the herd veered after the new quarry.

Maybe she had overdone it by inciting the reindeer to play.

She checked over her shoulder. No one followed. Her cousin Willa only *thought* Dazzler was here, she didn't *know* it. Daz-zler's stomach clenched. She smoothed the flannel covering her belly.

How could Willa have shown up in Holly?

Her cousin must know how much her presence affected Todd. He didn't need his ex-wife reminding him of his failed love life, not when the Holly festivities depended on his undivided at-tention. Just look how the townspeople had turned on him when the lights fell dark.

He was doing the best he could. That should count for some-thing, shouldn't it?

Fisting her hands, she squared her shoulders. She would find a way to stay and help him.

The maple leaf-tailed reindeer circled the herd before diving low and buzzing the street. Autumn leaves trembled on the trees and skittered along the cobblestone road in his wake. He spun and collided with a sycamore tree.

Leaves showered down. They condensed into a ball and eventually transformed him from a reindeer to a scarecrow. Cheddar stuffed leaves into a pair of jeans. Wiggling four stick fingers, he held them up for her to see.

"I always like it when I get improvements." His smile crinkled his acorn eyes. As he walked, leaves solidified into boots. "It's a shame to be leaving so soon."

"Leave?" Dazzler blinked. Was the human magic affecting him? He'd never had problems remembering after so short a time between stuffings. "Why would we leave?"

"Because your cousin is here and is looking for us. With her lapdog Sterling in tow. They won't allow you to finish your investigation."

"We have to stay and protect Todd. Now more than ever." Dazzler turned right onto Yule Street. "Didn't you see his face when Willa appeared?"

She was sure his heart had broken, just a little. She scratched at the birthmark on her wrist.

Cheddar shrugged. Leaves fell out of his shirt and tumbled down the street. "I wasn't paying much attention."

Youngsters of all ages played tag on brown grass in front of a lavender Victorian. A woman rocked on the violet-trimmed wraparound porch. With an excited yip, a spotted dog joined in the children's fun.

Dazzler's footsteps slowed. Should she go to another street? From the corner of her eye, she watched the kids and their babysitter. No one paid attention to her. For once, she was thankful for her coloring. Here, she could blend in.

Her attention cut back to Cheddar. "Todd was horrified and devastated to see his ex."

Her chest tightened at the memory. She had to find a way to mitigate that.

Cheddar tapped a stick finger against his stitched mouth. "If you really want to help, why not present yourself to your cousin, and the both of you return to the North Pole? She'd leave Todd alone then."

"Don't be ridiculous," Dazzler snapped. Sometimes his stuffing got in the way of logical thought. "If I turn myself in, and Willa takes me to the North Pole, then who will make certain the festivities go off without a hitch and Todd gets to spend the holidays with his family? No one, that's who. And that would ruin Christmas for everyone. It is our duty as Santa's elves to do all we can to promote the spirit of Christmas."

Cheddar's fingers ticked against wooden slats as he ran them along the picket fence. "What if Todd turns you in?"

Her breath hitched in her throat. She coughed to clear it. "He had a chance back at the square and didn't."

"Maybe he didn't see you."

"I'm not invisible, Cheddar. He *pretended* not to see me." She was familiar with the technique. Most elves adopted it when she entered their department at the North Pole. She didn't mind. Much. Besides, Todd had done it out of kindness, not because of her reputation.

Children screamed with delight as a new person was dubbed "it" in their game of tag.

Keeping her head turned away, Dazzler studied the homes on her side of the street. A buttercream-yellow Queen Anne, the third one from the end, drew her eye. Her skin itched at the neatly trimmed hedges, the even pile of the carpet of brown grass, and a tamed rosebush on the right. Just a little magic would free the vegetation. Flowers would cover the rose trellis and the bushes could reach the railing of the wraparound porch. Planting beds could break up the grass, giving homes to all sorts of woodland creatures.

Cheddar stopped trailing his fingers along the fence. "What about that old man, Ole Henderson? He could turn you in."

"He could, but he didn't." Her steps slowed in front of the house.

"That house is sad. There are no Christmas decorations like the others."

There was that. Her fingers curled into fists at her side. She daren't do magic, fix the house and make it happy, not with Willa nearby.

"We need someplace to stay out of sight. The town has a bed-and-breakfast. Perhaps we should check in and consider the best way to help Todd over a cup of hot chocolate."

"Chocolate solves a lot of problems." Cheddar wrapped his fingers around the pickets in the gate. "But we can't go to Charity and Patience's bed-and-breakfast."

"We can't?"

"No, Willa said she was going there." Cheddar lifted the latch and pushed the gate open. "Since this place looks deserted, we should hide here." He shuffled down the flagstone path.

"Cheddar!" Dazzler hissed. Figgy pudding! He was going to get them caught.

The scarecrow increased his pace.

A house door slammed across the street. The skin between Dazzler's shoulder blades tingled. They'd been spotted.

Slipping into the yard, she shut the gate behind her. Her heart thudded in her ears. If they were caught...

Cheddar ignored the porch and veered right onto the path leading to the backyard. Her legs trembled with the need to run and hide. She shouldn't do anything to give herself away.

"Martha! Martha Dugan!" a woman called out.

Dazzler bit her lip. Martha was Todd's mother. Was this her house? Would they take her in? Should she embroil them in her mess? She couldn't.

"Cheddar."

He opened the wrought iron gate and strolled into the back yard.

"Mrs. Crumbie," another woman answered. "How are the children this morning?"

"They're fine, but your reindeer are not. They've completely destroyed the light display and—"

Dazzler winced. Stuffed stockings! Had she solved the problem of the lighting glitch by causing another problem for Todd? She latched the gate behind her, shutting out their conversation.

After a short walk along the side of the clapboard house, the yard unrolled before her. An oak tree spread branches over the neatly trimmed lawn. Lemon-yellow and pumpkin-orange leaves clung to the black limbs. Fifty feet away, Cheddar plucked a few red ones from the ground and stuffed them into his shirt.

Her heart thudded at the pools of vegetation—isolated bushes and segregated annuals rooted in puddles of red bark mulch shivered in the autumn breeze. Knees trembling, she resisted the urge to drop to the ground, dig her fingers into the soil, and use magic to fill in the empty spaces.

As she tore her attention away, her gaze stuttered on the pristine swing set. Sleigh-red poles formed the A-frame and supports. For a moment, she pictured dark-haired girls and pointy-eared boys filling the marshmallow seats of the swings and air glider. She shook the nonsense from her head. When she dared to let herself dream of her forever home, she saw lush gardens bustling with wildlife.

Stick fingers raised, Cheddar raced after a falling leaf.

Dazzler turned and scanned the porch. She smiled at the rocking chair near the two-seater porch swing. That was a step in the right direction. She skimmed the Dutch back door; her breath caught in her throat. There it was. Right out of her dreams —an evergreen hammock. Two candy cane pillows topped the head and a fluffy throw blanket at the foot was perfect for snuggling and relaxing. She stumbled over the even grass. Would the chains squeak or be well-oiled?

Cheddar nibbled on the leaf he'd caught, watching her. Her boots were silent as she climbed the five steps to the porch. She trailed her fingers along the glossy white railing.

Leaves rustled behind her. Cheddar scaled the railing and flung a leg over to land on the porch.

"Well, that's a relief. We can sleep out here under the stars."

Nodding, she reached out. Her hand shook before she touched the gold braid running down the side of the hammock. By Kringle, she hadn't imagined it. As she shifted her hand, her fingers dug into the white blanket.

Cheddar flopped into the hammock. The chains jangled softly as they adjusted to his weight. He patted the fabric beside him.

"This is comfortable. Not practical for the North Pole, but quite right here in the warmer climates."

"Perfect." Dazzler removed the blanket and raised the cable knit to her nose. Cedar and sunshine tickled her senses. It smelled like Todd. But how could she have picked his house out of everyone's in town?

"Cheddar, did you happen to see whose name is on the mailbox?"

Cheddar shrugged. "I don't recall."

Cradling the throw against her chest, Dazzler crossed to the nearest window and pressed her nose against the pane. Dried-up sticks were all that remained in the pots on the windowsill. Cherry cabinets hung on the walls, and sparkling appliances gleamed on the cream granite countertops. Faces smiled at her from the photographs stuck to the stainless steel fridge. Cool air filled her mouth. *Beauty and the Beast*'s Belle took center stage between her, Todd, and Candance.

"This is Todd's house."

"It is?" Cheddar clasped his fingers behind his head and crossed his feet at the ankles. "Then he won't mind if we take a little nap. Reforming myself multiple times takes a lot of energy."

He snuggled deeper into the pillow, and his eyes drifted closed.

"I don't think Todd would mind if we rested here for a minute or two." At least, she hoped not.

She yawned. It had been a long day, but they were safe. Placing her hand on the hammock, she steadied it before lowering her bottom. That hadn't been so bad. Raising her legs, she swung them up. The hammock tilted left then right, nearly dumping her on the ground. She hung on.

Cheddar snored, but his chest squeaked and a fuzzy nose and twitching whiskers poked out of his shirt. The squirrel chittered and shook his finger at her before leaping to the ground.

"I'm sorry. I didn't mean to upset you." She relaxed her hold as the hammock steadied. "I promise you that you are safe."

Tail twitching in annoyance, the squirrel thundered across the porch then raced across the yard.

Dazzler spread the blanket across them and sank into the candy-cane pillow. Her eyes flickered close. Only a moment. Just a short nap.

Her eyes flew open. The sun was lower on the western horizon than it had been a moment ago. Hours ago, she mentally corrected herself. She'd slept for hours. Her senses reached out, picked up the squirrel inspecting his new home in the tree. A cardinal perched on a branch. Her muscles relaxed, and she inhaled a calming breath. This was Todd's house. She should be safe here.

Cheddar sat up. His pinecone ears twitched. "Somebody's coming."

Her breath caught in her throat. Who would be coming? And why would they be coming into the back yard? She scanned the area. No hiding place in the well-tended space. And if she used magic, Willa would find her. Tarnished tinsel!

Rolling off the hammock, she landed on the porch with a thud.

"Cheddar," she whispered, scrambling under the hammock. Her nails dug into the painted slats.

The scarecrow landed beside her in a flutter of leaves. Fabric rustled as he took up space beside her. "I don't think this is a very good hiding spot."

The latch on the gate clicked. They were in the side yard.

"Shhh." Her ears pricked in the silence. Who was it? It had better not be Willa. Her cousin needed to stay far away from Todd.

Cheddar rolled on top of her and dissolved in a heap. She blew a leaf out of her eyes.

"I understand, Nonna." Candance's voice filtered into the backyard. "I just had my headphones in while listening to my music. I'll keep them out in the future."

Footsteps crunched on the dying blades of grass. Not Willa's, someone heavier, bigger. Afternoon sunshine glinted on a head of brown hair. Her heart raced. Todd.

"Dazzler?" he whispered. "Are you here?"

"Da-ad." Candance's singsong voice rose at the end. "You told Mom Auntie D isn't here."

"She wasn't at the time I answered your mother," he shot back.

Sloughing off her blanket of leaves, Dazzler rolled out from under the hammock. "I'm here."

"Auntie D! You came!" Candance squealed and rushed forward. Peppermint and sunshine preceded the seventeen-year-old. A smile lit her heart-shaped face as her thin arms wrapped around Dazzler. "I missed you. I wanted to visit you once I got up north, but Mom said it was best if I didn't."

Candace rested her chin on Dazzler's shoulder. Dazzler ruffled the girl's hair, enjoying the silky feel of the white highlights.

"Your Mom was right." She closed her eyes and tamped down the pain as the admission shredded her throat. Willa never acknowledged their relationship unless pushed. "We'll make plans while I'm here, and you can sneak away so we can enjoy cocoa and cookies."

"We better." Leaning back, Candance shook her finger at Dazzler. "I think you got me in trouble with Nonna. She said I ignored her when I was sneaking in the backyard."

"She didn't call out." Dazzler offered in her defense. After planting a quick kiss on Candance's cheek, she tucked a white lock behind the girl's ears. The little girl was growing up—her ears were starting to gather into points at the top. "And I'm sorry I got you in trouble. Cookies and cocoa are never to be used to make amends. They are to be enjoyed whenever you are with those you love."

Candance squinted. Her cobalt-blue eyes shifted to silver. "Even when you're mad at that someone?"

Dazzler nodded. Friends and family were to be cherished, always. "Even then."

"Then my stomach will soon be as big a bowl of jelly as Saint Nick's, because everyone has been very welcoming at the North Pole." Candance beamed. "I have so many cousins."

Forcing a smile, Dazzler tucked her hands in her pockets. "Everyone at the North Pole is related."

Todd cleared his throat. "Candance, honey, why don't you get the grilled cheese sandwiches and tomato soup cooking while I talk to Dazzler for a minute."

Dazzler's stomach clenched. He sounded so serious. Was he upset at her arrival? Did he blame her for the failing lights?

"Sure, Dad." Candance hugged Dazzler quickly before skipping into the house. "I'm glad you're going to spend the holidays with us. It was something I've dreamed of since forever."

Dazzler glanced down at her boots.

Twig fingers raked the leaves into a pile and slid back under the hammock. Too bad she couldn't hide like Cheddar. Still, if Todd was going to ask her to leave, she'd best get it over with. She could be in Flagstaff before the hospital closed. Nurse Paula was bound to still be working. And the kids always welcomed her visits. She glanced up.

Todd raked his fingers through his dark-brown hair. "I wish you'd told me you were coming."

Knees trembling, Dazzler rested her hand on his forearm. Was he going to turn her away? "I'm sorry. It was kind of a last-minute thing."

Covering her hand, Todd tugged her down onto the top step. A moment passed. Then two. He stared at his back yard; his thumb swept back and forth across her knuckles. "Since you're here, I won't turn you away. But I have one condition. No magic."

"No magic?" Dazzler's insides did a funny dance. Hunger was getting to her. She studied his profile, the jutting of his chin, the firming of his lips. Had he heard the rumors? Did he believe them? "Why?"

"With Candance coming into *her* magic, I'm losing her to your world." He shifted so his thigh pressed against hers.

"My world." She rubbed her sternum with her free hand. He didn't consider her part of his world. Did that mean he didn't consider them to be friends?

"I need Candance to see that human Christmases are great even without magic. That it's the loved ones you surround yourself with that matter, not the ability to create something from thin air or have pointed ears."

Scooting closer, she forced a smile. "But don't you see, love *is* magic? It's—"

"My house, my rules." His eyes glinted with determination. "Besides, you don't want to disappoint Candance. Actually, your being here might work to my advantage. She'll see elves don't need magic to be happy."

Not need magic?

"I see." On one hand, Dazzler would be wanted, needed. Just not her magic, a magic she'd come here to save. Still, she could be with Candance, observe the teenager, and maybe find the root of her own magical mishaps in the process. Maybe even perform a little magic when no one was looking. "What do you want me to do?"

"Do? You can't do anything. I don't even think you'll be able to leave the house." Todd shook his head, shifting away from her. "Willa and Frost are looking for you. If they find you, then Candance's Christmas will be ruined, and everything will be for nothing."

"Not leave the house?" Dazzler groaned. There had to be a way around that caveat.

Todd glanced at her ears. "People will notice two elves in town."

Cheddar slid out from under the hammock and stared at Todd with unblinking acorn eyes. "Dazzler is a Sylvan elf. She gets her power from the woods. If you keep her locked up inside, she could get sick. Do you want that?"

"No. Of course not. I..." Color flushed Todd's cheeks, and he dropped her hand. "This was a bad idea. I should have stuck with my original plan. You'll have to leave. Elves and humans shouldn't mix."

"I have it!" The heart-shaped birthmark on her arm tingled. "Since everyone has already seen Willa and are expecting to see her, I'll change my appearance to look like her. Problem solved! It's brilliant!"

CHAPTER 4

*"Have you lost your ever-loving mind?" The words were ra-*zors in Todd's throat, but taking them back would only hurt Dazzler more. He scooted backward on the stoop, creating distance between them. How could she believe pretending to be his ex would be a good idea?

Dazzler's heart-shaped face tensed. Her brown eyes widened, and she bit her trembling bottom lip. Leaning against the porch railing, she collapsed into a ball.

"I...I'm sorry?" Her voice cracked at the end.

Tearing his gaze away, Todd stared at his empty hands. Calluses rose in ridges as he curled his fingers around air and emptiness. He had to take control of the situation. But how? Kicking her out wouldn't help him convince Candance being human was better than being an elf.

"Having Dazzler look like your wife might work." Crawling out from under the hammock, Cheddar raked up his scattered leaves and stuffed them into his shirt. "Since so many people think the Dugan curse is real, it'll look like you're doing everything to make sure the lights stay on."

"Cheddar." Dazzler's voice broke over the sharp edges of the scarecrow's name. Fabric rustled as she rubbed her hands along her arms. "Todd is right."

Todd winced. *Was* he right? He could see the advantage of Cheddar's plan. The idea burrowed deep inside his brain and took control of his vocal cords. He could use her help. With this curse business hanging over his head, folks weren't volunteering as much as they did when others chaired the committee. No. No, that would be using magic. Magic never worked in his favor.

He cleared his throat, stripping away the desire.

"Dazzler stays as herself. She spends the holidays with Candance and me in Holly as herself." He shifted, angling his body on the stoop so his knees brushed hers. His chest tightened. "I could really use your help making this Candance's best Christmas ever."

His gaze locked on her face, waited for the change he knew would come. She'd liked being needed. And he needed her. For Candance's sake.

Her lips parted before tilting up at the edges. "Oh, well, if you need a friend to help you."

He ignored the tightening of his gut. He couldn't ask so much of her without offering her something in return. "I could use your help with sprucing the place up."

"I do love Christmas and decorating and lights and..." Her smile widened. The air twinkled around her. A wisp of exotic spices scented the air. Magic. Dazzler's special kind.

He inhaled deeply as if to catch it and keep it for himself, then shook himself. What was he doing? Magic wasn't for him. Still...

He glanced around the porch. No decorations appeared out of nowhere. She had accepted his bargain.

"You can't seriously be considering this arrangement!" Planting his stick fingers on his hips, Cheddar narrowed his acorn eyes. "You are. You are seriously considering this idea. I want no part of this, Dazzler."

With a stamp of his boot, the scarecrow dissolved into a puddle of leaves and twigs. An arctic breeze swept the lot across the browning grass and gathered them into a pile at the base of the oak tree. A squirrel clambered down from the third branch, dug through the debris, and fished out the acorns. It flashed the nuts at Todd before scampering to its limb and carefully placing them on the bark.

Todd wasn't fooled. Cheddar was watching just in case Dazzler needed him. Silly scarecrow. Dazzler was safe with Todd. He'd never let anything happen to her.

Dazzler wiggled her fingers at the squirrel. "There are more acorns near the neighbor's shed."

The squirrel chittered; then, with a swish of its tail, it disappeared down the trunk.

Leaning back, Todd braced his elbows on the porch floor and waited. Dazzler moved like the seasons she drew her magic from, sometimes rushed, sometimes slow, but always arriving in her own time. Meanwhile, he could just sit beside her. The lights were on. Candance was home for the holidays. He had her favorite aunt to prove magic wasn't needed to make Christmas special. His plan would work out better than he'd anticipated.

Dazzler folded her legs and braced her chin on her knees. "Autumn is my favorite time of year."

"I thought you loved summer."

"I do." She smiled. "But in fall, I can hear Gaia tucking all her creatures into bed on this side of the world while rousing the sleepyheads from the other side. If you listen close, you can hear her whisper bedtime stories to the trees and animals around us."

Sound rumbled in Todd's chest. For a moment...

Nah, magic wasn't for him. He was just hungry. And speaking of hungry...

A flash of a fluffy tail drew his attention to the wooden fence separating his house from the neighbor's. "Are there enough nuts to see the squirrel through the winter?"

He might be able to dumpster-dive some out of old man Henderson's compost bin. The furry creature had just moved into his new digs and was a bit behind in stockpiling for the long freeze ahead.

"I told Pip where there's some unclaimed stashes."

Pip? Squirrels had names like Pip? A single snowflake swirled on the autumn breeze. Todd caught it on his finger. It stung his skin before melting.

Dazzler shivered.

Todd mentally smacked himself. He was about as welcoming as a dented jingle bell. Even though she was from the North Pole, she wasn't completely immune to the cold. And he had promised her lunch.

Turning, he slipped his hands under hers and tugged them away from her shins. Warm skin. He rubbed them anyway. "Why don't we get lunch? Grilled cheese sandwiches and tomato soup should warm us up."

Strange, it didn't seem as cold as it had a while ago. The humidity must be picking up. Maybe that single flake would turn into a flurry. He pushed off the step to stand.

"And hot chocolate?" She rose at his tug on their clasped hands. "I could use a mug right now."

"Of course." She'd always had a cup of cocoa whenever they had vacationed together. She and Candance were fanatics about the stuff. And he always searched the grocery stores for exotic flavors to feed his daughter's inner elf. All part of good parenting. He just hoped the last bit didn't take her away from him forever.

Setting his hand on the small of Dazzler's back, he guided her into the house.

She paused on the threshold and inhaled deeply. Todd tensed. Was his kitchen too clean, too sparse? Her side of their shared hotel room had always been messy. He'd always assumed the clothes left on the floor had been his daughter's. The brushes, makeup, and hair ties certainly were normal accouterments of a female's mess.

"I like your use of natural materials." With a sigh, Dazzler stepped on the rag rug then kicked off her boots. She ran her hand down the curve of the coat tree before caressing the decorative knob designed to hold up the weight of wool.

Todd's temperature spiked at the erotic caress. What in the world was wrong with him? This was his friend Dazzler, not a woman. He shouldn't be thinking of such things.

"Food's almost ready." Staring at the text message on her phone, Candance poured red liquid into the bowls set on the granite countertop. Steam danced over the tomato soup. His daughter set the pot down on the gas burner with a clang.

"Everything okay?" Dazzler hiked a hip and slid onto the tall barstool. Slim fingers rubbed together, and the twinkle of magic indicated they were clean.

His fingers twitched. She'd cleaned his hands before meals on picnics and camping trips. The tingling sensation was pleasant. Still, she was breaking the rules. Clearing his throat, he glanced pointedly at her hands.

She flushed then sat on them.

"Everything's fine. It's just Michael." Propping her elbows on the counter, Candance dipped one triangle of her grilled cheese into her soup and stirred. "He heard I was back in town and wants to hang out."

Todd slapped on the tap and shoved his hands under the warm water. Michael. Michael who? There were two in Candance's senior class, and one who'd graduated last year. All of them had been sniffing around his daughter. He didn't like it. Could Dazzler give his daughter a zit so hideous they left her alone?

"Michael Thomas?" Dazzler dipped her spoon into her dish then blew the steam away from her soup. "I thought he broke up with you when you told him you were going to the North Pole to work instead of college."

Todd slapped the tap closed. How could his baby have broken up with someone she wasn't supposed to be going out with? Besides, Michael Thomas was a year older than her.

"This is Michael Johnson." Candance stopped stirring and stared off into space. Her gaze lost focus. "He was wondering if my ears are like the elves in the movies."

Todd's eyes narrowed. Teenage boys and their "wondering".

"Your ears had better be all he's checking out."

"Dad!" Candance blushed bright red. Her eyes shifted to blue, and a peppermint tang stung the air. "We've been friends since for-ev-er. He's not thinking like that."

She set another serving of soup-and-sandwich on the breakfast bar but remained standing near the stove.

Todd grunted. All teenage boys thought like that. He took a seat beside Dazzler.

She ducked her head to hide her smile. A lock of brown hair tumbled over her breasts.

Nice. Firm... Todd filtered air through his teeth and squelched the mental image. Apparently, some adult males thought like that, too.

Tearing off a bite of her sandwich, Dazzler swirled the bread to capture the cheesey strings. "I'd like to meet Michael. Thank him for helping you pass your AP English class."

Todd's snort rippled across his soup. Good luck with meeting any of that crowd one-on-one. Candance always said...

"Sure. He'd like to meet you, too." Forgoing her spoon, Candance raised the bowl to her lips and guzzled it down.

Todd blinked. Why was Dazzler allowed to meet Michael Johnson? "Just a minute..."

Dumping her empty bowl in the sink, Candance wiped the dribble of tomato soup from her chin with her sleeve. "I'll make sure he knows not to tell anyone Auntie D's here."

"Oh!" The last corner of the sandwich slipped from Dazzler's fingers and splatted in her soup. Red stained her sleeve. "Maybe that's not such a good idea with your mom looking for me. I won't feel comfortable with him lying to your mother to protect me."

Candance cocked her head. "Michael won't tell." Electricity arced between her fingers. "Not if he knows what's good for him."

Todd cleared his throat. "No magic, sweet pea."

With a flick of her wrist, Candance dispersed it. "Fine."

Dazzler pushed away her bowl.

Todd cupped Dazzler's clenched fist. "We'll find a way so Michael can meet your aunt, and so she can leave the house."

Candance snorted. "Dad, there's no reason she can't leave the house as she is. Auntie D looks more like us than an elf. She just has to cover her ears."

There was a flaw in that logic. Todd recognized the danger, even if they didn't. "That won't help if your mother or Frost starts flashing her picture to our neighbors, looking for her."

"She could glamour them. Her disguise wouldn't work on elves, but everyone else would see what she wanted. Of course, if Mom spotted her, she'd see the real Auntie D." Candance jammed the last of her sandwich into her mouth. Her cheeks bulged as she chewed. "Uncle Frost says—"

"Sterling Frost is not your uncle." Todd snapped. The only expertise the coldhearted creature had was in seducing other people's wives. He'd like to punch him right in his ice jaw. "And we don't need magic to fix this. We can do it ourselves."

Candance swallowed hard. "I'm gonna go get ready to meet Michael then dinner with Mom and Unc—er, Sterling. If that's okay?"

Todd tamped down his irritation at the mention of Frost. The man may have ruined Todd's marriage, but he wouldn't touch Todd's relationship with his daughter. Still, acting like a knucklehead wasn't helping, either.

"Of course. Have fun."

Candance swerved toward Dazzler and threw her arms around the elf.

"I'm so glad you're here." She smacked a loud kiss on Dazzler's cheek, then his, and bounced out of the kitchen. "See you later, alligators."

Todd watched the door swing shut behind his daughter. She'd be back. This was her home. She belonged here, not the North Pole. She'd see that. Eventually.

"Maybe Frost will be so busy chasing after Willa, he won't have time to look for you."

Dazzler reached for her discarded bowl. He picked it up before she could.

"You're a guest in my house today."

She nodded and stared at the floor. "I understand."

He doubted it. Nudging her shoulder, he dropped his voice. "Tomorrow, you're family, and you're gonna have to pitch in and help with chores. Which means dishes."

"Then I'll enjoy my night off." Her smile didn't reach her eyes.

His gut clenched. He had to get her to smile. She always smiled.

Adding their dishes to Candance's in the sink, he wiped his hands on a towel. "Oh, you're not getting a night off. You have to give me a chance to earn some of my pride back after you snookered me at Mexican Train."

"I didn't bring the game."

"Ha! Like that's an excuse." He pointed to the row of dusty cookbooks with a box of dominoes stretched across the top. The edges were worn, the lid cracked. She'd given the game to him when Candance was five to save him from marathons of *Chutes and Ladders* and *Candyland.*

Dazzler's eyes crinkled at the corners, and she cracked her knuckles. "Don't think I'll go easy on you."

Todd grabbed the box and ushered her into the dining room. The bare walnut table gleamed in the sunshine streaming through the window. "You'll be begging for mercy when I'm done."

"Yeah, sure." She wrapped her hand around the ladderback chair. Her sleeve brushed it, leaving a smear of soup in its wake. Nose wrinkled, she plucked at her cuff. "I need to clean up first."

Dominoes clattered across the polished wood. "No magic, right?"

Pink tinged her cheeks. "Right. No magic."

His hand stilled over the tiles. She looked so lost, so confused. Guilt spiked him. What was wrong with cleaning up the old-fashioned way without magic? His brain tripped over a stray thought.

"How do you plan to change clothes?"

Or did she? And just what would she sleep in? He tried to contain the thought, but it sprang free like a jack-in-the-box. He hated jack-in-the-boxes.

"Relax, I'm not going to walk around naked." A dimple flashed in her cheek. "I packed a bag. I just need a linen cupboard to retrieve it from my cottage. Portals don't leave traces, unless.... unless you think that's too much magic?"

His brain took a moment to restart from the *naked* comment. What had she said? Something about a linen cupboard? "Ah, um, we have a closet for towels in the bathroom. Up the stairs, second door on the right."

She glanced at the tiles. "No cheating while I'm gone."

"I won't." He had cunning.

Shaking her head, she strode from the room.

He had to get those crazy thoughts under control. He quickly flipped the tiles over before mixing them around.

No sooner had she stepped into the foyer then feminine laughter swirled into the dining room. He raised his head and smiled. What were those two up to now? He turned to spy on them.

A moment later, the oak stairs creaked, and Candance breezed into the room. Her lips were glossy and her eyes smoky. She was growing up.

"I've set sheets and blankets in the back room."

"Good thinking." He really needed to have a word with Michael Johnson, let the kid know reindeer didn't just pull Santa's sleigh but could help dispose of boys who didn't treat his daughter right.

Candance picked up a wooden domino rack and tapped it against her palm. "Dad, about Unc—Sterling Frost."

Todd clenched his jaw and glanced at her. "What about him?"

"He isn't interested in Mom."

"No?" The ice king had seemed plenty interested when Todd found his ex-wife and the icicle in bed.

"No." Candance chewed on her lip gloss. "I think he's in love with Auntie D."

Todd blinked.

"He's always going on about him and Auntie D working on the new Polar expansion. He has the models in his office of the new electronics division. Said he and Auntie D will run it together, create a whole new North Pole, like Jack Frost and Alfreda, the first Sylvan elf that lead her people north with Santa."

Rage bubbled up from near Todd's toes and boiled through his limbs.

"It's why he volunteered to search for Auntie D. To help her. Unc—Sterling keeps going on and on about the magic they could create after they're united."

No. Hell, no. Dazzler didn't deserve to be in that scumbag's presence, let alone his degenerate thoughts.

Red filled Todd's vision. He stormed out of the dining room and blew through the living room. Racing through the foyer, he took the stairs two at a time. The runner did nothing to muffle his footfalls on the scarred oak planks in the hall. Dazzler needed to stay safely hidden.

And there was no place safer than his house.

Behind locked doors.

Todd wouldn't let Frost anywhere near her.

He shoved Dazzler's bedroom door open. It banged against the reproduction cabbage rose wallpaper.

Pale skin covered a tiny waist. A constellation of moles shifted into a leaf pattern above her flared hip. He skidded to a stop at sight of her delicate shimmy, certain the only thing that kept his jaw from dropping was his tongue glued to the roof of his mouth.

"What does someone do with dirty clothes? Nurse Paula said something about a hamper, but I don't see how it cleans clothes." Dazzler tucked her body inside a cranberry-red shirt and tugged on her jeans.

Todd waited for his brain to reset. Any second now. Any second.

Stepping over her discarded shirt, Dazzler removed a stack of sweaters from the Santa sack melting on the sleigh bed. Many of them bore hallmarks of the places they'd vacationed over the years.

"It's at times like this I wish I was a house elf and enjoyed cleaning. Or knew how to clean like humans."

She straightened. Her gaze locked on his.

He struggled to breathe. Why had he come up here? Behind her, a snowflake swirled beyond the window pane. Right. Frost.

"You can't work with Sterling Frost." He spat the name to clean it from his tongue.

"Sterling's motives are as clear as a sheet of ice." She snorted. "He's being kind to me to curry favor with my parents and win their support for the new expansion."

"He's working with the review board."

She bit her lip for a moment as if pondering what to say. "If he finds anything, he'll try to use it as leverage against my parents."

Todd swallowed a litany of swear words. "What's to investigate anyway? You help terminal kids enjoy a magical holiday with their family before they pass. If magic isn't to make things better, then what good is it?"

The corner of her mouth quirked up. "It isn't that. Well, it is, but isn't. The last boy, Jerome—he took home a souvenir of the trip."

"So? You buy souvenirs all the time on our trips." He pointed to the stack of clothes in her hands. "It's a very human and elf trait."

"Yes, but I'm only allowed to lead these trips as long as the families view them as just dreams. A souvenir is a more tangible memory." She stroked the logo of the amusement park they'd visited last summer. "And this was an ornament from the eternal Christmas tree in the town square."

Todd frowned. Obviously, that was supposed to mean something, but he had nothing.

"It's enchanted." She crossed to the dresser on his right. "The reindeer ornament flies and talks. The family found it after the funeral, and now they know it wasn't a dream. Worse, it's eluding our retrieval teams."

"That's not your fault." Crossing his arms, he propped a hip against the doorjamb. "Why investigate you? Why not the team that can't wrangle a tiny reindeer?"

Sure, reindeer were tricky, but they loved carrots, would do anything to have one.

"They're being investigated, too." She paused with her hand on the drawer's antique glass knob. "And I know I'll be cleared of any wrongdoing. I mean, children are remarkably fast and crafty. It's just…"

"Just?"

"You know how some kids love unicorns and dinosaurs, wanting to visit them more than the North Pole?"

"Yeah." His arms tensed. He'd encouraged her more liberal interpretation of the board's ruling to fulfill the dying kids' wishes instead of limiting their magical journeys to the North Pole. Had his advice gotten her into trouble? If so, he'd speak to the board himself and take the blame.

"Well, there are so many who want unicorns and dinosaurs I didn't think it would be a bad thing to, you know, create a magical world and not erase it after our visit. Unicorns and dinosaurs are living creatures, after all. They deserve to have fun and play and..."

Shoving away from the door, Todd crossed to her side. "What will happen if the Board finds that world?"

She jerked open the top drawer and froze.

"Dazzler, surely, it won't be that bad." His hand shook as he cupped her shoulders. She was always so strong and sure. Only once had he seen her break down and cry. Only...

He squelched the thought. He had to find a way to help her with her current problem. "I mean, the world is in another dimension, and only you know how to craft the portal. Surely, there's no harm in it."

Her mouth opened and closed, yet she uttered no words.

Curling his body around hers, he peered down. He ignored the shadow of cleavage and stared at the open drawer. Rows and rows of hot cocoa mixes filled the space.

She plopped her stack of sweaters on the dresser then ran her fingers over the intact cellophane wrapping. Her body trembled with excitement. "Cinnamon? Pineapple? Strawberry cocoa? I've never heard of these mixes. Are these for me?"

"Yes." His skin heated. Maybe he was getting ill. Releasing her, he stepped to the side and opened the drawer beside hers. More cocoa boxes filled the interior. This time the writing wasn't in English.

"Ooohh." Her eyes lit up and her hip brushed his as she moved to peer inside. "French. Italian. Swiss. Belgian. Dutch. German. Someone's been shopping online."

"My brothers. I have one in France. One in Italy. Candance loves the stuff." The words spilled across his lips in a torrent.

Dazzler nodded. "And she won't mind if I have some?"

A snort came from the doorway. Candance rolled her eyes, the whites flashing brightly against her darker makeup.

"They don't pick it up for me. Dad's been having them pick it up, and he picks it up when we visit, and he has a catalog that specializes in the stuff. He's like a dragon, except it's cocoa he hoards, and I don't get to drink a drop."

"Well, you two can drink it now." Todd's ears tingled with embarrassment. The unbroken seals provided their own evidence. Better to change the subject and hope for an empty drawer. Bending, he yanked out the bottom one. More cocoa. Slamming it shut, he tugged open the middle one. Free. Thank God. He didn't want to check the remaining two on Dazzler's side.

She reached for the second drawer on her side.

He didn't want to see. "If that's not enough space, there's the closet. For dresses and stuff."

Dazzler glanced up. "Dresses?"

"After the lighting ceremony, there's a dance." Candance plucked a tin of pumpkin spice cocoa from the drawer. "You have to go, Auntie D. There's a live band, fairy lights, and the Bakers provide lots of treats. It's magical. I can loan you a dress, if you don't have one."

He pictured himself holding Dazzler as they waltzed across the cobblestone street in front of the Christmas tree. She'd fit in his arms; her face would be turned up to his. His throat tightened. Maybe his mother's tomato soup was off.

He threw open the polished-wood closet door. Inside, like a game of *Tetris*, boxes of electric cocoa makers in every size, shape, and manufacture filled the interior. By Kringle, maybe he needed help.

With a gasp of pleasure, Dazzler rushed forward. She dropped to her knees and tugged out the boxes. "It's like an elven Christmas. I didn't think you liked cocoa."

"He doesn't. Those are for you." Candance popped open the tin of pumpkin spice cocoa and inhaled deeply. "Dad picks one from every catalog he gets. I think it's an excuse for him to try the latest technology."

"But why didn't you ever give them to me?" Dazzler blinked up at him before slicing the seal on a copper brewer with her fingernail.

He rubbed the back of his neck. Why hadn't he? Why? His mind blanked so he shrugged. "I figured you didn't need one since you have magic."

"No one makes cocoa with magic. Cocoa *is* magic." Dazzler squeaked, then dove in the closet and pulled out an antique silver pot. "It's a Theobroma infusor!" She hugged it to her chest. "If these are for me, I'm taking them with me when I return to the North Pole."

Todd bit off the denial. He had bought them for her, so why didn't he want her to take them? "Of course."

Candance capped the tin in her hands. "And take some of the cocoa, too. I was afraid I would come back home and my room would be taken over by specialty boxes."

Teenagers and their overreacting. "It's not that bad."

"Not that bad? Dad, I believe denial is not just a river in Egypt." Candance flipped up the bedskirt. Boxes of cocoa filled the space underneath. "The first step in breaking your addiction is...?"

"I'm still your father, and there's time left to move you to the Naughty list."

"Ha! Elves don't go on the list." Candance stuck her tongue out at him. "I'm going over to Michael's house. He's got the latest X-box game, and we're going to play it until dinner with Mom."

Todd nodded. She considered herself an elf, not a human. He sawed for air. "Call me when you're on your way home."

Bells chimed throughout the house. Someone was at the front door, demanding entrance.

CHAPTER 5

No one in the guest bedroom moved. The doorbell rang again. Todd had no doubt his ex-wife and that buzzkill Frost wanted to search his house for Dazzler. Over his dead body.

Candance bit her lip.

Avoiding a puddle of late-afternoon sun, Dazzler scooted closer to the closet. Would she create a portal and disappear?

He couldn't let her leave. Inhaling deeply, Todd took charge. Keeping them safe was his job. "Candance, go out the back and cut through the neighbor's yard to Michael's."

He didn't want his daughter to have to lie to her mother or see him with Frost.

She nodded, turned on her heel, and thudded down the hallway toward the back staircase.

Dazzler hugged the cocoa maker closer. "What do you want me to do?"

His visitor leaned on the doorbell. The chime echoed deep in the old Victorian, then restarted on an endless loop. Knocking joined the cacophony. Impatient beggars.

He knelt on the floor in front of Dazzler. "You don't have to do anything. I won't let Willa or Frost take you."

She nodded, then shook her head. "Maybe I should just go."

He set his finger against her lips. Damn, they were soft. "You're staying. And we'll figure out something so you won't be confined to the house. Candance might be on to something."

"Really?"

Her gaze skittered away from his, but he saw the flame of hope there. He wanted to touch her, to relieve her of her burdens. Instead, he tapped the cocoa maker in her arms. "Why don't you make a cup while I get rid of our visitor?"

She glanced at the back of the closet before nodding. "Okay."

Pushing to his feet, he jogged to the hallway. Air whooshed out of his lungs as she unpacked the cocoa maker. She would be here when he returned.

Jogging down the hall, he slid along the landing and raced down the stairs two at a time. The doorbell stopped, but fists still drummed the door.

"I'm coming. I'm coming." Not that they could hear him above the racket. He clamped down on his anger. He would be polite but firm. They weren't searching his house. He would deny any knowledge of Dazzler's whereabouts. And he wouldn't punch Frost.

Nah, he wouldn't promise that last one.

Rolling the tension from his shoulders, he wrenched the antique brass knob and threw open the door.

His mother and father rushed inside, pushing him back until his knees hit the deacon's bench against the foyer wall. Leaves swirled on the cool breeze blowing them inside. Carrying two acorns, a squirrel scrambled onto the rocking chair on the wraparound porch. His brothers and their families elbowed him aside next.

Great. A family intervention was just what he needed.

Todd's father, Burl Dugan, bared his teeth in a grim smile. "We came as soon as we heard. Curse or no curse, you're not remarrying that...that she-elf."

"We're making plans." His mother Martha's white curls trembled. "Your brothers and their families are coming from France and Italy. Add their magic to the bit we have here, and we'll keep the lights on until kingdom come."

She shoved a platter of homemade cookies into Todd's gut.

"Mom." He caught the platter, balancing it before the cookies spilled.

His brother Cade held up a six-pack of pumpkin-spice craft ale. "I'm already working on a set of figurines to create your perfect match. Trust me, she'll look nothing like the snow queen."

Cade's wife Egypt snugged an infant higher on her chest while a four-year-old boy tugged on her hand. "I have friends. I'm sure one of them will make a great wife for you."

"Uh," Todd blinked. "I can pick out my own wife."

If he ever wanted to marry again. Which he did not. He had to suffer from the stigma of the curse. He wouldn't foist it on anyone else.

Still wearing his sheriff's uniform, his brother Nick swung another six-pack of beer from one hand while restraining his four-year-old daughter under his arm in a football hold. "We're not going to let that she-elf get her claws into you again. I've requisitioned four generators. The lights will stay on."

Nick's wife Lonnie stroked her swollen belly under her black-and-orange tunic. Her round brooch proclaimed that witches had better hex. "And my coven and I enchanted the generators. Since my ancestor cast the curse, I should be able to keep the spell at bay until after the holiday season."

His skin twitched at the second mention of magic. Why didn't they see he was immune?

His mom sighed as she looked around the room. "Oh, my sweet baby boy. Just look at what that she-elf did to you. There's no tree. No stockings. No—"

Burl patted his wife's shoulder. "We'll fix this."

Cheese and crackers, he wasn't a boy. Nor did he need his family's help. Todd shut the door with his hip.

"Mom. Dad." He glared at his brothers. "Guys. I've got this covered."

"No," Lonnie rubbed her hands together. "*We've* got this covered. I think I can magic up some decorations."

"No! No magic in my house." Todd's shout echoed around the room.

Silence blanketed his family.

Well, he'd gotten their attention. Now to kick them out.

Nick set the beer on the coffee table in front of the sectional sofa and his daughter on her feet. "I'll get the ornaments. I'll just look for the dusty boxes in Scrooge's attic." He shoved a finger at Todd. "Be nice."

Todd held up his hands. He was nice. *They* were the ones being difficult.

Pigtails slapping her back, the little girl zoomed to the windowseat where Todd had stashed Candance's old toys. Cade unleashed his son on the puzzles and picture books in the nook.

"I'll look outside in that pit he calls a garage for the outdoor decorations."

"You don't…" Todd dropped the tray of cookies on the table. His father clamped a hand on his shoulder.

"This is a Dugan family matter, and the Dugan family will handle it."

Lonnie plopped down on the chaise. "Oh, my!"

Nick skidded to a stop at the base of the stairs, his mouth open.

Egypt caught Cade's shirt, stopping him in his tracks.

All attention focused on the second-floor landing.

Glowing like newfallen snow, a silver elf stood at the top of the staircase. Dazzler had done it, had used magic to make herself look like his ex-wife. Magic he hated. An ex-wife he didn't particularly like. So, why did his heart lurch into his throat? Why were his knees shaking, and his tongue stuck to the roof of his mouth? Time unraveled, and he was twenty-two again, picking her up for their first date.

Her magic had seduced him.

Her smile had tipped him into the abyss of love.

Her laughter had trapped his heart.

Her deceit had destroyed him.

And here he stood, an idiot begging her to do it again.

Dazzler stood at the top of the stairs, a white-knuckle grip on the tray in her hands. The bone china cups rattled a little, and hot cocoa sloshed into their floral-painted saucers.

From the living room below, Todd's family radiated waves of hostility.

She gulped, swallowing the lump in her throat. This was worse than when she'd made salted cookies for everyone on her seventeenth birthday.

As if sensing her fear, the staircase threatened to skewer those below with the balusters. The Victorian house trembled, preparing to throw open its doors so a gust of fall wind could sweep the offending visitors away. She shook the riled beehive of thoughts from her head. The strangers meant her no harm.

This was Todd's family trying to protect him.

From her.

Or at least who they thought she was. The irony tasted bitter. She'd looked forward to meeting them forever, and now she appeared as her cousin Willa. Her skin tingled under the glamour. The scent of earthy spice swirled around her and melded with the aroma of human-based magic.

"I hope everyone likes cocoa."

Statues and silence greeted her words.

She sought Todd's gaze. His shock disappeared under a wave of anger. Figgy pudding! Had she misread the situation? He had said they would consider Candance's ideas, which included the thin layer of glamour. Willa's semblance was the only one that had stuck. Her magic had picked a bad time to misbehave. Not that it mattered now.

Taking a deep breath, she descended the oak staircase. The walnut furniture vibrated as if to rush to her defense. The cotton-and-silk upholstery volunteered to get into the mix by hog-tying and gagging the intruders. She exhaled slowly.

Magic crystals danced in the air, calming everything. Glistening like fireflies, the crystals penetrated the bubble of love surrounding the family.

Todd shifted. His parents lurched after him. Did they plan to grab him and shove him behind them? That would be fun to watch.

Dazzler's smile crinkled the corners of her eyes.

Todd rushed forward, his grin stretched tightly over his white teeth. "Let me carry this for you." His voice dropped. "I thought I said no magic."

"I'm sorry. When you mentioned Candance's idea..." she whispered, then spoke louder for their audience to hear. "Thank you."

His fingers brushed hers. A little zing shot up her arm, and she released the tray quickly. He caught it without spilling a drop, then leaned in close, fogging her world with his scent.

"You look just like her. Except for your smile."

Her insides tumbled. She thought she looked exactly like Willa. She flattened cool palms against her heated cheeks.

"That's an improvement." He winked.

She boxed up the warm feeling cascading through her. Todd had loved his wife; Dazzler was a poor substitute.

Shaking off the feeling of inadequacy, she surveyed the crowd. She could do this.

"I can't tell you how I've longed to meet you again." Her attention cut to the younger women. "Or for the first time."

The oldest man snorted.

"You must be Todd's father, Burl." She grabbed the reindeer mug of cocoa from the tray Todd held and offered it to the man. His stocky frame and white hair reminded her of Santa. His frown reminded her of Mr. Claus when he was angry. "I made this for you. To go with the cookies."

She held her breath, waiting for him to refuse the peace offering. To reject her as so many elves did.

After a moment, Burl Dugan lifted the cup and sniffed it. His bushy white brows lifted a little. "Why is it so dark?"

"Dark chocolate. Straight, none of the frou-frou stuff." She inwardly cheered. The cocoa magic worked.

She sidestepped to stop before a woman at the back end of her middle years. Laugh lines aged her peach complexion and stood at odds with the angry hashmarks streaking her forehead.

"And you must be Martha." Dazzler selected a rose bone china cup. Cream and vanilla sweetener lightened the contents. "I don't know that this will be as sweet as your sugar cookies, but I think it pairs well with your award-winning gingersnaps."

Martha blushed "Oh, well, I...I think cocoa pairs well with just about everything. And my cookies wouldn't have won if Charity and Patience had entered last year's contest."

Resisting the urge to hug the older woman, Dazzler simply smiled. Suspicion buffeted her. Todd would probably blame her magic for their softening toward her, but frankly, it was the cocoa. She'd yet to meet anyone who could be mad with a creamy cup steaming in front of them.

Too bad Todd only drank coffee. Standing beside her, he vibrated with irritation.

She turned her attention to the man with the paint-stained cuffs. Todd's brother, the artist, Cade. She selected a plain mug. Base notes of cinnamon and nutmeg swirled in the steam.

"This blend is a little unusual, but if your lovely wife and children don't inspire you, this might."

Cade's eyes narrowed, but he accepted the drink.

"What do you say, deer-droppings-for-brains?" Todd growled behind her.

"Thank you." Cade blew on the steam. The mist formed a cottage complete with chimney before dissipating.

Dazzler checked the expression on the family members' faces. No one seemed to have noticed his puff of magic. Could the family have a distant elven ancestor? She bit her tongue to keep from mentioning it. Todd wouldn't be happy at the suggestion.

The woman next to Cade adjusted the sleeping baby on her shoulder and offered her hand. "I'm Egypt. And I prefer tea."

"I know." Dazzler shook the calloused hand. Magic tingled across their connected palms and caused the heart-shaped birthmark inside her wrist to tingle. Even the wives must have a magical ancestor in their family trees somewhere. She selected a teacup filled with clear amber liquid. "It's decaf—cranberry rooibos with just a hint of star anise, and one raw sugar cube."

Egypt took the cup and ignored the saucer. "Lonnie just prescribed that for my sensitive stomach."

"Lonnie is a wise Earth elemental." Dazzler reached for a ceramic mug. Mint and a zing of orange flavored the cocoa. It would not have been her first choice, but it seemed to fit the witch. "I think you'll find this blend works better to soothe the baby than the herbal tea you have been brewing."

Lonnie raised her chin and ignored the mug. "My teas have always worked well before."

The man in the sheriff's uniform threw his arm around his wife's shoulders. "My wife is a very accomplished witch. The head of her coven, in fact."

"Don't crumble your cookies, Nick." Todd stepped closer to Dazzler. "No one's saying your wife isn't the best present complete with a bow and bell."

Dazzler bit her lip. The hostility peaked around her. She hadn't meant to insult the woman or to aggravate the entire family. At least their hostile silence gave her a chance to explain.

"I don't doubt your abilities." The woman radiated waves of rich energy; there was just a spike in it causing the hair on Dazzler's arms to stand up. "It's just that your children are water elementals, not earth. It's causing conflict, and this brew will allow your energies to work in harmony instead of conflict."

Brow furrowed in thought, Lonnie stroked her swollen belly again. "My children are water?" Her forehead smoothed, and she accepted the mug. "My children are water? But then... Oh, that would explain..."

Her daughter skipped over, sniffing the air. "May I have some cocoa, Mama?"

"Uh-huh." Lonnie studied her daughter as if seeing her for the first time.

Dazzler knelt before the little girl. Surrounded by this much residual, she should be able to perform a little magic safely. She turned her palm to the ceiling then swirled her index finger above it. The soft scent of peppermint blended with the earthy tones radiating from Lonnie. "Can you hold this for me while I get your cup?"

The little girl scooped the storm into her hand. "Eebee-doo. I love you." Within seconds, the snow condensed into a tiny snowman that danced then performed a headstand. "Magic, Daddy, just like Mommy."

"I see." Nick poked the snowman. It melted before disappearing in a twinkle of glitter.

Dazzler removed a tepid cup of mint-flavored cocoa from the tray and another with pumpkin spice. "Can you give this to your cousin? I think he's a little shy about meeting me."

"Okay." The little girl snatched up the cups then skipped back to the corner. The beverages formed heart and star shapes above the rims, but not a drop spilled.

Dazzler turned back to the tray. "Your coffee is in the number-one dad mug."

"Nice." Todd winked at her.

His compliment warmed her toes. Maybe he wasn't too mad about her using magic. Of course, if it was for remembering he didn't drink cocoa or gaining his family's approval, she'd be just as happy. She picked up her cup of cocoa, then the last mug— dark chocolate with a bite of cherry.

Nick had rolled up the sleeves of his uniform. His sheriff's star glittered with more fire than many enjoyed in a hearth. He accepted the mug with a grunt. "As you said, you haven't met any of us since Candance was born. So, how do you know who we are and our tastes?"

Tarnished tinsel! Dazzler had given away her true identity. To buy time, she sipped her cocoa.

Todd set the tray on the floor and using his boot, scooted it under the coffee table laden with cookies. "I told her."

Nick pinned her with a stare through the steam over his mug. "You told us you only had secondhand contact with your ex. You didn't even see her to exchange your daughter but went through that she-elf Disaster."

"Dazzler." Todd set his mug down with a thud. "Her name is Dazzler."

"From the stories Candance has been telling, Disaster fits her 'aunt' better." Nick used air quotes when referring to their relationship.

Dazzler swayed on her feet. Her vision misted. She wouldn't be welcomed as herself, either. Why had she ever thought they would? Few others had, even before meeting her.

"Dazzler is close to her cousin, and is like a second mother to Candance. I'm sure between the two of them, they've kept Willa informed of everything in Holly." Todd set his hand on the small of her back.

His strength filtered through her. Dazzler nodded. Despite the warm cocoa, the constriction in her throat didn't ease.

"Boys. Boys!" Martha Dugan clapped her hands. "We have a lot of decorating to do before the sun sets. Do not make me box your ears because of your squabbling. Not a one of you is so old I won't treat you like a naughty child if you misbehave."

"Yes, ma'am," Nick and Todd chorused.

Todd waved a fist when his mother turned to set her cup on the end table. Nick ran a finger across his throat.

Dazzler stared at her cocoa. They couldn't really be threatening violence, could they? Her drink didn't answer.

Burl Dugan shook his head at his sons' antics. "Now, I say we set up the tree in front of the window."

"We can set it up, but we're not decorating it until Candance comes home." Todd's fingers tensed on Dazzler's back.

"Where *is* my niece?" Nick pinned Dazzler with a look.

"Stuffed in a closet." Todd stepped between her and his brother. "Where do you think? She's with her—"

"Friend Michael." Discord itched up her back. This was her fault. She was ruining the holiday for them. She retrieved the tray from under the coffee table, placed her mug on it, then Martha's discarded one. After she collected the mugs, she'd return to her room. "They're playing the latest X-box game."

"Uh-huh." Nick plopped his mug on the tray. Half the cocoa remained. He arched a brow at his wife. "Why don't the guys start on the outside while the women get to work in here?"

"No." Todd shoved his face into his brother's. "We all work together like one big happy family, or you guys leave my house."

A muscle worked in Nick's jaw. Cade cracked his knuckles.

Dazzler's skin tingled with magic. An iridescent film coated her body, ready to stretch out and protect Todd, if needed. Sharp peppermint notes cut through the earthy scent of human conflict.

"Perhaps I should go."

Todd fisted the back of her sweater. "You're staying. You're invited. These guys are just—"

Martha patted Todd's shoulder. "Of course, dear, it is your house. Let's collect the tree from the porch and get started."

"My house. My rules." Todd bared his teeth at his brothers.

Muttering, Nick and Cade stomped outside. Dazzler collected the dirty cups while the others rearranged the furniture to accommodate the tree. Todd stuck close to her side. Was he protecting her, or didn't he trust her not to slip up again?

The setting sun pulled a rose-colored blanket over the horizon. Stars glistened between the gaps in the clouds overhead. Strings of icicle lights outlined the yellow Victorian house.

Working with solar-powered spotlights planted in the yard, the wives strung white twinkle lights across the palm-frond roof of the manger. Cade adjusted the stands of the wooden cutouts of camels and donkeys. Burl hosed down two wisemen propped against the porch. Standing beyond the muddy spray, Todd flashed her a thumbs-up.

Dazzler eyed the nativity. By her count, one wiseman was missing.

Still in his sheriff's uniform, Nick positioned one of the donkeys near the manger. Lonnie shook her head and pointed to a pool of light a foot away. Shaking his head, he relocated the cutout before glancing at Dazzler.

"Does it make that big of a difference?"

She bit her lip to keep from smiling. They'd been doing that more often lately, including her in their banter. She liked it. Sometimes, she could almost pretend she belonged here.

"It *is* in the spotlight."

Nick snorted.

Cade rolled his eyes. "Why do you bother to ask? You know the wives always stick together."

Egypt elbowed her husband for his slip. Martha Dugan sieved air through her front teeth at the mention of wives.

Right. Dazzler wasn't a wife, nor was she Willa. "Why don't I find that third king?"

Mouths clamped shut to stop any protest.

She mentally pinned the corners of her lips up in a smile. Thankfully, her magic was holding up. Her glamour hadn't slipped once. She must be on the right track to fixing her problem.

Todd tossed the wet rag in his hands at the dripping cutouts. The towel cleared off the mud as it slid onto the grass. He glared at his family. "I'll help you."

Burl Dugan opened his mouth. His teeth clicked together before he bent to pick up the rag. "Be careful, son."

"Of what, Dad?" Todd shot back, fists planted on his hips. "Splinters? Spiders?"

Martha Dugan raised a hand as if to dispel the rising anger between father and son. "Now, Todd, dear."

Figgy pudding! She was causing strife in the family. Again. "Let me find the king. If I need help, I'll ask."

Todd whipped toward her.

"Please," she whispered.

Jaw thrust forward, he nodded once. "Fine. I'll take care of things here."

Turning, she hustled toward the back gate. A chirp and clack greeted her.

The squirrel Pip sat atop the fence, holding an acorn in his front paws. The animal aimed Cheddar's eye at her, then the back yard.

Visitors had arrived. Magic visitors, from Cheddar's warning, ones looking for her.

Dazzler glanced over her shoulder. The Dugan family had stopped assembling the nativity to circle around Todd and his father, faced off in front of the two wisemen. Fingers pointed. Complexions turned florid.

How could she celebrate her magic behaving when Todd's world was unraveling? She sighed, stepped into the sunset-drenched back yard. With a shake, she shed Willa's appearance in a sparkle of glitter. Cheddar had been right. She was making things worse, not better, for Todd. Time to present herself to the magical visitors and return to the North Pole to face the Board.

A cool fall breeze carried the bite of peppermint. Two figures stood near the shed. With heads bent together, the lanky couple leaned over a snow globe. Recognition tumbled through her.

Her parents were here.

Crimson poinsettias crowned her mother's braided white hair. Matching embroidery adorned her ivory tunic. A Santa hatpin on her lapel proclaimed her association with Santa's inner circle.

"Dazzler must be close," she said.

Wearing a matching lapel pin, Dazzler's father, beside her, fed seed to the cardinal roosting in the evergreen wreath circling his head. Silk pinecones added a touch of brown to his green tunic.

"Why don't you try to find that human whose company she prefers? Despite our efforts, she won't be far away from him."

"What do you think I'm doing?" Aurora Twinkle-Spitfire grumbled. "Making enchanted candy canes?"

Combing the rest of the white from her hair, Dazzler strode across the frosted grass carpeting the back yard. Green patches marked her footsteps. "Mom. Dad. I'm surprised you found me."

Had she really been so easy to track? Rising on tiptoes, she scanned the rest of the area for Willa. Nothing.

The squirrel carried the acorns to a high branch before shrugging. Her cousin wasn't close, so how had her parents managed to track her?

Her father, Tobin, sucked blood from his finger. His blue eyes crinkled. "You're our youngling. We can always find you, sugar plum."

"Besides, where else would you go?" Aurora dissolved the tracking globe into a flurry of snow that drifted slowly to the ground. "It's not like you have many friends to choose from, and you are fascinated by humans. Particularly that male Todd."

She held open her arms. Dazzler embraced her mother and kissed her on the cheek. Her father hugged her a bit longer than necessary before releasing her to pull two gingerbread cookies from his pocket. He offered her one before biting off the antlers of the other.

"Where is that strange snowman you insist on keeping with you? In this heat, I fully expected to find a stream of water leading right to you."

"Cheddar switched to a scarecrow so he could blend in better with the season." Dazzler tucked her dark hair behind her ear and shifted so they would be hidden behind the shed. Leaves rustled on the branches of the oak tree, but her friend didn't re-form. Instead, Cheddar's acorn eyes and the squirrel settled down to watch the reunion.

Her parents exchanged a look. Dazzler knew that look. She had disappointed them. Again. She shifted on her feet and waited for her mother to speak. In most elven households, the mother was the disciplinarian.

"I must insist you come home, dear." Mom crooked a knuckle under Dazzler's chin and lifted it so she could look her in the eye. "Spitfires do not run away from trouble. We meet it head-on."

"I didn't run away." Leaning back, Dazzler pulled out of her mother's hold but didn't break eye contact. "I'm not due to testify until after Christmas. Not that what I say will matter. Disaster strikes again."

Her mother winced. "Don't call yourself that. It's a dreadful nickname your cousin gave you. You shouldn't answer to it."

"I don't, but that's what others call me." A chill coiled down Dazzler's spine. She rubbed warmth into her arms. "Of course, I haven't messed up. Not once in the three months since I've been in the forgotten-letter department."

"That's my girl." Her dad ruffled her hair. "We Spitfires have never found any job too menial or low to accept. It's good that someone is finally addressing all those letters, and to think Mr. Claus created the department just for you."

More likely it was damage control in the smoothly-run North Pole. Dazzler broke her cookie in half and stuffed it in her mouth before she responded.

"You need to be with your family during these trying times." Her mother switched topics. "We will show everyone that the Spitfires can hold their heads up high despite having another Review Board hearing."

And there it was. Dazzler was an embarrassment to the family name. The cookie turned to ash in her mouth. She swallowed hard to wash down the pap. She could really use a cup of cocoa right now. Maybe she'd even throw in a few marshmallows. Boy, she could imagine the shock as the news spread.

"I'll be cleared of any wrongdoing in the ornament caper."

Her father cleared his throat. "I know you will, sugar plum. Human children are very quick. Old St. Nick has nearly been spied by them more than once."

"But the Magic Review Board isn't just looking into the ornament case." Her mother scraped a hand down her ageless features. Her pointed ears twitched, a sign of nervousness. "They are reviewing all your off-Pole activities."

Stars twinkled in Dazzler's vision. She inhaled quickly and chased them away. She'd heard rumors of the expanded investigation but to have it actually confirmed...

"I...I see."

Her mother squeezed her hand. "They're even talking about removing your magic. That it is too powerful for one elf to wield."

Her father threw his arm around Dazzler's shoulders and tucked her head under his chin. "But we have a plan, sugar plum. One where you can take your rightful place at the heart of North Pole society."

Dazzler blinked and shrugged out of her father's embrace. Her dad might be speaking, but those were her mom's words. And her mother's plans never jibed with Dazzler's. Besides, her magic was behaving. Santa's advice had been spot-on. Not that she'd tell them. It was too soon in her investigation, and she didn't want to jinx things.

Mom jiggled with excitement. "Sterling Frost has agreed to a union. You know he's always had a soft spot for you. Well, he plans to make it official on St. Nick's Day. It will be the event of the season. And the expansion he plans for the two of you to do will erase any stumbles you've had so far."

Dazzler frowned. Marry Sterling? He'd ruined Todd's marriage. Sure, he'd always been kind to her, but she'd never seen any warmth in his icy heart.

"Sterling doesn't love me."

Her father stared at his pointed shoes.

Ignoring Dazzler's words, her mother waxed on. "The Spitfire name will be on the new tech building. He's even placed your office next to his on the top floor. Of course, I don't know your exact duties, but anything is better than a forgotten job in a dark corner sorting letters no one cares about."

"I care about the letters, Mother." Dazzler shifted to stand in front of her mother. Anger radiated in waves from her skin. A dandelion burst from the ground around her, spending its entire life in a heartbeat. "So do the children who write them."

Her mother's mouth snapped shut.

"Now, sugar plum," her father soothed.

"I am spending the holiday here in Holly." Dazzler stomped her foot. The dead grass turned green for yards in every direction. "Todd and Candance have invited me. And they are family, too."

"But not your family," Dad whispered. "You're just borrowing them from your cousin—against her will, I might add."

Willa didn't want Dazzler to see Candance and Todd? Had she ever said such a thing? Dazzler tried to remember. Her head ached for her trouble.

Mom waved her fingers in front of Dazzler. "If you had just done as you were told, the humans would be happy in their world and you would have a family in ours."

Dazzler raised her chin. "Todd and Candance *are* family to me."

"Wake up, child. Candance has her mother to teach her how to use magic properly. She doesn't need you. And her father is only using you to win a bet. It's time for you to stop playing house and grow up." Snowflakes swirled like angry ice hornets around Aurora. "How quickly do you think he'll rescind his invitation once you've been stripped of magic and are no longer of any use to him? This fast."

She snapped her fingers, disappearing and taking Tobin with her.

Winter's grip rolled across the green grass, forcing the budding life back to sleep. Dazzler peeked into the metal shed. A dusting of frost scraped paint from the wiseman's purple robes then melted into a puddle of slush at his feet.

Her mother was wrong. She wasn't playing house. Todd and Candance were family. They liked her without magic. Todd insisted on it.

But would he help her keep it?

She'd worry about that later, right after she touched up the paint on the cutout.

CHAPTER 6

Todd hung the last of the lights on the brass hooks under the eaves. He had missed the old icicles. He had missed Christmas. Sure, every year he'd strung the red, yellow, green, and blue blinking lights along the slopes and angles. Every year, his family had plopped a Christmas tree on his porch and told him to put it up or else. Every year, Cade and Nick had shown up to encourage him to set out the nativity.

At least, this year none of them had black eyes, bruised ribs, and bloody knuckles.

Although his brothers had promised retribution.

Let them. Todd chuckled. He could handle them. Of course, if it was four against one, he might have to use two hands.

He sealed the last plug against the weather. The metal ladder creaked under his weight. Not bad. But he'd wait until Dazzler passed judgment. Living in the North Pole made her an expert on this kind of thing.

Behind him a hinge creaked. Had someone come through the gate? He prayed it wasn't his parents with their concerned glances and booby-trap questions. If the visitors were his brothers things wouldn't be much better. Dazzler didn't seem to appreciate the finer nuances of his relationship with them.

But she would. Given time. Just as they'd come to like her despite their determination to remain jerks. Cade had caught himself laughing at her jokes about the reindeer being snitches. Lonnie had spent hours talking herbs and natural remedies. Egypt had changed his lawn into a chaotic landscape of bushes and trees with drawings in the margins of the newspaper. Even Nick had smiled a time or two, and it hadn't cracked his face once.

Granted, he *had* offered to rearrange Nick's nose if he didn't lay off Dazzler.

Not that his family could have known her real identity. And there was the rub. She'd used magic.

He hated magic.

Still, this time it had worked in his favor. And yet, he knew, out there, somewhere, a shoe waited to drop.

A boot scraped against the stone walkway leading to his porch.

"You can stop your fussing." Todd scooped two acorns from the rain gutters and tucked them into his pocket. He'd give them to the squirrel later. "Not even Mrs. Claus has a house this decked out for Christmas."

"I've been to Mrs. Claus's house. I can tell you that you don't have nearly the decorations she does."

That oily superior tone could only belong to one creature. Frost.

Todd mentally swore a blue streak. Sometimes deer droppings and other Christmas-themed substitutions just didn't cut it.

Ice formed snowflakes across the window panes and sent shards to his heart. Where was Dazzler? Still in the backyard searching for the last wiseman?

He had to get rid of Frost before she returned.

"Never having been to the North Pole, I still wouldn't take your word for it. You're a thief. I don't doubt you're a liar as well." Taking a deep breath, Todd descended the ladder. His footfalls echoed hollowly on the steel rungs. He leapt off before reaching the bottom two, and dug his bootheels into the ground.

"I am many things." Frost jerked his pointed chin. His white-blond hair rose in jagged peaks atop his leonine face. Blue tinted his pale skin, enhanced by his ocean blue tunic and trousers.

"And you're here." Todd could happily have lived a century without encountering his ex's lover.

"I always visit here. I just tend to wait until people least expect me." Frost smirked.

Todd's fingers curled into fists. Would the elf's jaw shatter like ice if he punched it? "I guess if no one wanted me around, I'd have to sneak from town to town, too."

White ice tinged the grass under Frost's pointed shoes. "Are we finished with the pleasantries already?"

"I'd say we're finished. Period." Todd jerked the ladder away from the roof. Metal rattled as he collapsed it. Turning on his heel, he faced the back gate. By Kringle, he couldn't stalk away in victory. Dazzler was supposed to be in the shed. Even if her glamour worked on Mr. Icicle, Todd wouldn't risk exposing her. Magic complicated everything. He set the ladder against the gate. "Do you need a hand leaving my property, or should I have you arrested for trespassing?"

The mayor was his best friend, and his brother was the sheriff. They owed him. Maybe enough to hide a body.

"Still pining for Willa." Frost gave up the pretense of smiling. "Does Dazzler know she's a poor substitute for your ex?"

Todd's skin burned. He bit his tongue instead of rising to the bait. "As I already stated in front of the whole town, I don't know where Dazzler is."

Although he had a better idea this time around.

Frost waved his hand. Snowflakes swirled near his fingers. "I always know where to find her. Alone, shunned by the others, and covering her pain with a smile."

Todd squared his shoulders. He wanted nothing more than to rip off Frost's hand and shove it where the sun didn't shine —right next to Frost's black heart. Black ice was always the most deadly.

"Do you know I'm Dazzler's only friend at the North Pole?" Frost cocked his head. "Everyone else steers clear of her because of her errant magic."

Todd ground his back molars. Dazzler had plenty of friends. She was kind, caring, and always happy. That's why she smiled so much. He would know if it was otherwise. "This conversation is over."

He jerked the ladder off the gate. The acorns rattled in his pocket. Could Cheddar turn himself into a dog? One big enough to dispose of Mr. Icicle? The chill remained on the back of Todd's neck. Frost was as dense as an iceberg.

"Given that you're positive Dazzler isn't here, I guess you won't mind if I search your house for traces of her magic?"

Todd's fingers bit into the metal ladder rungs. Whipping around, he faced his enemy. "I wouldn't let you into my house if the fate of the world depended on it."

"The fate of a world does depend upon my finding Dazzler." Frost studied his pristine nails. "Or at least that little world she created. You know the one. It's full of dinosaurs and unicorns all those poor sick children long to see before they pass."

Dazzler's realm. Todd thought only she had the key to finding it. How had Frost learned of it? Or had he? Todd wouldn't put it past the elf to bluff.

"Dazzler has permission to help those children. That's more than anyone said about you."

"Without me, there wouldn't be nearly as many trees, bushes, and flowers you humans seem determined to destroy." Frost's eyes narrowed, and ice crackled over the dead lawn. "Elves should have destroyed humans instead of leaving this precious world to your care."

"Spare me the public service announcement." Todd carefully set the ladder against the gate and stalked to Frost. He stopped just within punching distance. Cold bit into his ankles and caused his toes to burn. He wasn't about to back down. "Get off my property, or I'll rent a dog just to bite you."

Frost jerked his chin once. "Tell Dazzler when you see her that if she wishes to keep all her magical creatures alive, she will turn herself in to me."

Pivoting on his heel, Todd headed for the backyard. There wasn't enough gold ribbon in the world to convey that message. He flicked the latch.

"You know, I always find it ironic that she considers you her closest friend." Frost's words misted the air. "And obviously the feeling is mutual. Why else would you risk your town's reputation and the magic of the holiday season to shelter someone who has destroyed your life?"

"You're confusing Dazzler with Willa." Todd clamped his lips together. He shouldn't engage Mr. Icicle in conversation. He wanted the elf gone.

"Dazzler never told you?" Ice crusted the gate as Frost moved closer. "Sweet, innocent Dazzler. At least, everyone considers her sweet and innocent. It's how she's gotten away with abusing her powers for so long."

"Dazzler doesn't abuse her powers." Even if she did use magic against his wishes. He yanked his finger from the icy latch before his flesh stuck to it. Wedging his boot against the gate, he inched it open.

"She's not using them for the greater good but for her own selfish purposes."

Todd snorted. "And I suppose the high-tech expansion orchestrated by you is purely for the greater good?"

"Of course."

The elf could give old Scrooge lessons in selfish behavior. Todd shook his head. He was done with this conversation.

"Just as our marriage will." Frost smirked.

"Now I *know* you're confusing Dazzler with Willa."

"Oh, no. It's Dazzler I'm to wed. Her parents have already blessed the union." Frost skated backward. "After all, elves can't continue to make dolls and balls when the children want tablets and electronics. If we continue to stay in the past, we will be as useless as humans."

Todd would bite off his tongue before he nipped at that bait. "Goodbye, Frost."

"Has Dazzler told you she's the one who rear-ended you that night in Flagstaff?" Frost stroked the rosemary shrub at the base of the porch. "You know the one. The one that made you believe Willa was your soulmate?"

What game was Frost up to now? Didn't matter. Todd wasn't playing. "Of course."

Anything to get rid of the man.

Frost's nostrils flared. "And I suppose she also told you that she pretended to be Willa for the first two dates? The ones where you fell wildly in love with Willa and became determined to marry her at any cost?"

Todd blinked. That couldn't be true. The elf was lying. He had to be desperate. "Goodbye, Frost."

Using his knee, he pushed open the gate and walked through. He kicked it shut behind him. Cold glued his fingers to the metal ladder. Despite his leaving the evil elf behind, Frost's words were a blizzard inside his skull. It couldn't be, could it?

And yet...

Hadn't he felt a sense of familiarity when Dazzler had walked down the stairs disguised as his ex-wife? No. He knew Dazzler. The real Dazzler had been in the smile. He'd fallen in love with Willa after that first kiss. He pushed aside the thoughts. Frost wouldn't get inside his head.

A quick scan of the back yard revealed nothing. Where had Dazzler gone? He bit his tongue to keep from calling out her name. Then a thought hit him. So diabolical, conniving, that he wouldn't put it past either Frost or his ex. The exchange in the front yard could have been a distraction while Willa whisked Dazzler away.

Increasing his pace, Todd crossed to the shed near the back fence. The interior of the aluminum shed was empty of decorations. Only two rakes and two shovels remained. Hanging the ladder on the hooks on the wall, he checked the dust patterns on the concrete slab for signs of a struggle. Nothing.

A frigid breeze brushed the back of his neck. Rolling the tension from his shoulders, he closed the doors. Dazzler must have sensed Frost's presence and hidden. But why take the wiseman? His muscles trembled with the need to run inside the house, but he kept a steady pace to the back porch.

Once inside, he leaned against the door until it closed, then threw the lock. The acrid scent of paint caused his nose to tingle. Dazzler must be painting, but what?

Instead of calling out to her, he closed the curtains above the kitchen sink. The blinds rattled as he shut out the night in the dining room and parlor. He checked each pane as he went. No sign of Frost.

A squirrel scampered across the porch railing and gathered up two acorns.

Right. Frost might have a spy like Dazzler had Cheddar. Todd's heart raced as he wandered into each room. No wiseman. No paint can. No Dazzler.

Where could she have gone?

He paused by the Christmas tree in the bay window before latching the shutters closed. Here, the aroma of pine overrode the chemical stench of paint. By the red pillar candles on the mantle, he caught Dazzler's cinnamon scent.

Dazzler.

She'd turned his home into a magazine spread. On the table, his grandmother's china surrounded a centerpiece of pinecones and poinsettias. Gold ribbon tied garland to the oak banister. Candy cane-striped pillows accentuated the Christmas quilt thrown over the back of the couch, and fancy glass ornaments overflowed a red wire sleigh on the coffee table.

How had she known to decorate it just right?

Near the spruce twinkling with white lights, a box of handmade ornaments sat under the boughs. A bowl of oranges, ribbon, and cloves awaited assembly on the side table, while a handful of Christmas movies lay near the Blu-ray player. Red-and-green paper garland, cookie ornaments with childish handwriting, and beaded ornaments waited for Candance to return from dinner with her mother.

And that boy Michael.

Dazzler would know how to handle that, too.

Was it magic? Had she cast a spell on him?

He was being ridiculous. He shook off his thoughts. He had to find Dazzler.

He stepped onto the bottom riser. A sneeze echoed under his boots.

That sounded as if it had come from his closet. She wouldn't be painting in there, would she?

It made sense. There were no windows, no way for someone to see her. Retracing his steps, he paused by the closet door.

She sneezed again.

He opened the door. "Dazzler?"

"I figured I'd be safe in here while you got rid of Frost. And I don't need magic for this job." She beamed at him. Her face and body might belong to his ex, but that smile was all Dazzler. The purple on the paintbrush in her hand matched the wiseman's robe and the smear on her cheek. "Elves are excellent painters. What do you think?"

He thought he knew of the perfect way to set aside the doubts Frost had raised. Stepping forward, Todd cupped her cheeks in his hands and pressed his mouth to hers.

CHAPTER 7

A spark of electricity arced across Dazzler's teeth. She jerked back in surprise and touched her tingling upper lip. The heart-shaped birthmark on her wrist throbbed. What had just happened?

Todd took a moment before he opened his eyes. A glint flashed in their cobalt depths. "That was unexpected."

"You kissed me." She tried to process the thought. He was her friend. One of the few friends she'd managed to keep since her magic began misbehaving. She couldn't risk their friendship for a kiss, could she? She licked the taste of coffee and creamer from her lips.

His eyes followed the motion. His pupils dilated. "Guess I did."

He leaned in as if to repeat the experience. She shifted to meet him halfway then froze. In his eyes, she saw a blond winter elf. Willa. His ex. He was kissing his ex, not her.

Dazzler's chest tightened. Were her parents right? Was she playing house? "Todd."

"Yeah?" he growled, angling his head just so. His body heat flared along her front.

She had to stop this madness. She had to...

Her eyes fluttered closed. *It's just a kiss. Friends kiss all the time.* She skimmed her palm up his chest. There would be no shock this time. There would just be him and her and—

A door banged. The echo reverberated from the kitchen.

"Dad!" Candance's voice was a bucket of frigid water. "Are you home?"

Cold air filled the space vacated by Todd's heat. Alone. Again. Dazzler opened her eyes. Todd headed to the hallway leading to the kitchen.

She gulped air, and her fingers curled around the paintbrush in her hand. What was she thinking? Kissing a man in a closet? A man who didn't even see her when he closed his eyes. The paint fumes had knocked her off-kilter.

She turned back to the wooden cutout of the wiseman. He beamed in approval. She shook the nonsense from her head. Her mission to fix her magic didn't involve kissing.

"We're in here."

A primitive rasp edged Todd's voice. Dazzler's body tightened at the sound. The paintbrush snapped and fell in pieces to the dropcloth protecting the oak planks. She couldn't convince herself to pick it up.

Her attention bounced around the room. The front door was just across the living room. She needed air. Fresh air. She stepped toward the door, then stopped. Leaving was impossible. Sterling Frost had been outside just moments ago.

She was trapped.

Her gaze flitted back to Todd. He must still love Willa if he was ready to accept Dazzler as a poor substitute. She let her glamour slide off her skin. Magic glowed like falling stars heading for Earth. Would anyone ever love *her* that much?

Angry footfalls stomped on the tile in the kitchen before pounding against the wooden floor in the hall.

"You're not going to believe what Michael did."

Todd's eyes narrowed. Crossing his arms over his chest, he propped a hip against the pocket door. "What did Michael do?"

Dazzler's lips twitched, and the world returned to normal. She knew that fake relaxed stance. The edgy Papa Bear was getting ready to pounce, to rip apart anything that threatened his baby girl.

Candance raked her long brown hair into a ponytail then knotted it in a bun. "Michael decided to hunt for Auntie D with Mom and Unc—Sterling. The traitor."

Todd's shoulders relaxed. Meeting his daughter in the dining room, he wrapped his arm around her shoulder.

"I'm sorry, sweet pea." He kissed her temple.

Candance rolled her eyes but didn't pull away. "Michael is the one who's sorry. A no-good sorry sack of—"

"Candance," Todd warned.

"Coal." She widened her eyes, the picture of innocence, then ruined it with a grin. The picture of her father. "What did you think I was going to say? Swearing isn't acceptable at the North Pole any more than it is at home."

He shook his finger at her. "I bet you learned that lesson the hard way."

Bending, Dazzler picked up the broken paintbrush. A sweep of her finger mended the shaft before she set it carefully in a Mason jar of water. "Did you at least get to play the new video game?"

Todd's mouth dropped open. "I hardly think that's relevant."

"Oh, yeah." Candance bounced on the balls of her feet. Her makeshift bun unknotted, and her hair tumbled around her shoulders. "The graphics were off the charts, but the storyline was the same old aliens invade, save the Earth. Blah, blah, blah." She flapped her hand in dismissal. "Elves will do so much better once the new tech center is up and running."

Dazzler stared at her red Christmas socks. The tech center. The one everyone counted on her to build. She wouldn't mind helping out. But Sterling was involved. Sterling had ruined Todd's marriage.

Sterling only wanted her for her magic.

He thought he could fix her. So, why was she here dreaming of kissing a man who didn't want her to use magic at all?

Clearing his throat, Todd pulled her away from her thoughts. "Do you know where your mother is looking for Dazzler?"

Her ears twitched. Could they have seen her in the backyard, talking to her parents?

"Everywhere." Candace narrowed her eyes. "Why do you have paint on your nose, Auntie D? And why does Dad have it on his cheek."

Dazzler opened and closed her mouth, but no words came out. She couldn't tell the girl she'd kissed her father. What would Candance think?

"I, uh, was painting, and..."

"Your aunt was just touching up the wiseman, and I—" Embarrassment brushed Todd's cheeks as he swiped at the paint, and he shifted on his feet. He didn't meet Dazzler's gaze.

She swept her hand over her face. Her skin warmed as magic cleaned her.

Candance squealed. "Oh, my God! You have the Christmas tree up already." Rubbing her hands together, she skipped into the family room. "I knew Auntie D would make this the best Christmas ever!"

"You give me too much credit." Dazzler smiled. There really was nothing better than a bare tree waiting to be decorated. And the scent of pine... "Your grandparents, aunts, and uncles brought it over. And helped decorate the house."

"Dazzler decorated the mantle and banister. Threw on the Christmas quilts and pillows." Todd strode forward. His step faltered as he drew abreast of Dazzler. He raised his hand but moved past without touching her. "We saved the tree trimming for when you returned. As is tradition."

Dazzler's smile wilted. Would they ask her to leave? She wasn't Todd and Candance's family. Not really. She edged toward the stairs. Maybe she could make cocoa for everyone and watch from the sidelines.

"Dad!" Skirting the sofa, Candance rushed over to the box of ornaments perched on the Queen Anne chair. Dipping her hands inside, she tugged out a handful of crudely made decorations. "I can't believe you saved these. What were you thinking?"

She dangled a bean-shaped piece of brown foam from a ribbon.

"I was thinking you made them, sweet pea." Todd held up a star splashed with yellow paint. "So I kept them."

Dazzler sidled closer. Human children created ornaments, too? She peeked into the box before selecting a glittering ball from the mix.

"I like them." The ornament spun at the bottom of a loop of ribbon. A chubby-cheeked Candance beamed back at her. Dazzler had the same preschool picture on her project board at home. "All parents keep ornaments their children make."

"Yes, but as an elf, I should have done so much better." Candance frowned at the hodgepodge mix of brown, red, and white foam in her hand.

Todd disappeared into the closet under the staircase and removed the cutout. "I think I'd be wise to set this outside."

Candance groaned. "That's not punny, Dad."

"Nope, it's clever." Tucking the third king under his arm, he marched across the living room and threw open the door. The bells on the wreath hanging on it jingled. A frigid breeze whistled inside before he shut out the cold.

Returning the ornament to the box, Dazzler carefully removed the foam decoration from Candance's hands. She turned it left, then right. Did the ragged white things belong on the top or the bottom? And what did the red octagon indicate?

"I like it."

"You're holding it upside down, Auntie D." Candance turned it so the white parts were at the top and the red octagon was in the center.

"Oh, well, there it is." Dazzler stalled for time. What did humans like to decorate with? Snowmen. Stars. Ahh, she had it. "A perfect angel."

"It's a reindeer." Candance plucked it out of Dazzler's fingers and turned it around.

Dazzler blinked then squinted. After a second, her brain translated the abstract art into the appropriate form. Antlers and a red nose just like the Rudolph clan's claim to fame. "I think we should hang this up front."

"No. We can't." Candance snatched it and hid it behind her back. Color flared in her cheeks.

Dazzler tilted her head. "What's wrong?"

"It's horrible." The air around Candance twinkled. Peppermint scented the air, and another strand of white joined the streak in the girl's hair. "I've seen the ornaments the younglings create at the North Pole. The trees dedicated to them. I've seen your ornaments, Auntie D."

Biting her bottom lip, Candance shifted the ornament to her side. The foam condensed into a miniature deer body. The white feathery bits twirled down to an impressive set of glittering antlers. The red octagon shrank to a pinpoint but didn't glow.

"You're just learning how to use your magic, Candance. I'm sure you'll surpass my abilities in no time." Especially since Dazzler's magic never behaved. Almost never.

She checked the door. Shut. Maybe she could try a little experiment. She swirled her finger near the ornament's nose. It lit up, washing crimson light over their hands.

"I did it! I did it!" Candance bounced on the balls of her feet. The reindeer leaped from her hands and flew to the tree before finding a home on a bough halfway up.

"Of course you did. It just takes a little practice." Dazzler clapped in approval.

A board on the porch creaked. Figgy pudding. Todd wouldn't approve of this use of magic.

"Now, why don't we...?"

Ornaments danced in the air like sugar plum fairies. Magic transformed the crudely executed gingerbread men, stars, and balls into glittering elf-crafted perfection. Paper garland flattened and glowed into glass links, enhancing the red, green, yellow, and blue lights. The ornaments circled the tree before finding the perfect place to display themselves.

Dazzler plucked a glass bulb from the air. The holographic image of a young Candance beamed back at her. With a thought, she returned the ornament to a styrofoam bulb covered in glitter with a picture glued to the flattened front. There really was something magical about the simple designs. She straightened the metal hanger and reached for the closest bough.

The door opened. A cold breeze rolled across the floor. Todd leaned against the wood to close it, then threw the lock.

"Well, that—" He blinked at the tree then the empty boxes. His nostrils flared as he swept a hand toward the tree. "What did you do?" He pinned Dazzler with a glare. "I told you no magic. You promised."

Dazzler flinched. She'd known the rules and broken them.

"Dad—" Candance squeaked. The glitter around her faded away.

"No, Candance. I said your Auntie D was allowed to stay on the condition she didn't use magic." Todd glared at her. "She broke her word. She—"

Backing toward the staircase, Dazzler struggled to breathe. How could her magic work so well when it was apparently not wanted here? How could she have risked Todd's friendship for a stupid experiment? Did she have figgy pudding for brains?

"By Kringle—"

"It was me." Candance stomped her foot. "I did it. My magic. Me."

Todd raked a hand through his hair, then sighed and hung his head. "I...I see."

He looked so lost, so afraid his daughter would choose magic over him. Couldn't he see he was the one forcing her to choose? Candance could have both.

Dazzler eased forward. Maybe she could help. Perhaps she could fix this.

She held out the ornament in her shaking hand. "We saved the last one for you to hang."

A muscle flexed in his jaw. Being careful not to touch her, he removed the hook from her finger. "Thank you. This one is my favorite."

"Mine, too. I remember it was taken at her preschool play when you guys still lived in Flagstaff." When Dazzler had still been invited to school functions. She ducked her head, but he avoided her gaze. Perhaps she was partially at fault. Certainly, her ornaments had inspired a little mutiny. "About the magic..."

Todd traced the curve of young Candance's cheek on the picture before hanging the ball on the tree.

"You guys need to stop."

Candance crossed her arms. "Dad!"

"I could smell peppermint from the porch." His fingers steadied the swinging ornament. "With the hunt on for your Auntie D, we don't need that bloodhound Frost hanging around our house."

"Oh." Candance glanced at the untied shoelace on her sneaker. "I didn't think about that."

Dazzler wrapped her arm around the girl's shoulders. "Your dad is just trying to protect me."

"Right. Um." Todd cleared his throat. "Why don't I make us some hot cocoa while you guys clean up?"

"Sounds wonderful." Dazzler kissed Candance's temple then released her and turned toward the empty boxes. How to broach the subject of magic with the girl?

The wood floors creaked under Todd's weight as he headed toward the kitchen. Silence dispelled the lingering magic, wrapped around Dazzler's shoulders, and pulled her down. How could she fix their problems when she couldn't solve her own? She gift-wrapped her doubts. She had to try. Candance and Todd were family.

"Your father is proud of you, you know?"

Candance shrugged.

"I think he's trying really hard to let you know that he loves you just as you are. No magic needed."

"Will your parents love *you* if the board takes your magic?" Candance nested the boxes one inside the other.

Dazzler blinked. Would they? Her dad would definitely. But her mom had dreams. Such big dreams. Shaking her head, she focused on the question at hand.

"Of course."

Candance sealed the top box. "I've messed up a lot since I started at the North Pole. Will they try to take my magic, too?"

"Oh. No! No, of course not." Dazzler flicked her wrist. The boxes skidded across the living room floor. The closet door flew open, caught the boxes and swept them inside. She caught Candance's hand and dragged her to the couch. "Why would you think they'd take your magic?"

Candance dropped onto the cushion and sagged against the back. "Because they want to take yours."

"Oh, sweetie, that's so different." Dazzler chaffed the girl's hand. Fear had turned it to ice.

"How? How is it different?"

Dazzler sighed. How had the conversation turned to be about her? "I…"

The words died in her throat. Candance cocked her head, waiting.

Scraping her index finger and thumb across her eyes, Dazzler collected her thoughts. She'd come here for help. Maybe Candance would offer new insight.

"You've heard the tales of Fern of Leahway?"

"Yeah…" Candance's features scrunched up. "She was the elf who went mad and created the mini-ice age in Europe. It took the Sylvan elves nearly twenty years to hunt her down and banish her to the South Pole where she couldn't do any more harm. But that's a myth."

Dazzler grimaced. "It was real. All of it."

And so much more that the stories didn't tell. But she knew. Every piece of magic gone awry. Every bit of damage inflicted. Every name of those who'd suffered. Santa had made her read the notes from the meeting before sending her on this journey.

"I don't understand." Candance scooted closer and rested her other hand on Dazzler's.

"You know magic comes from the heart, right?" Dazzler swallowed hard, mentally paring the information down to the basics. No one needed to know how much Fern had suffered. "Well, Fern never joined with another."

Candance's fingers tightened around Dazzler's. "There are plenty of single elves at the North Pole. I know five of them."

"Two lost their mates young during the penguin fiasco of Eighty-nine. The other two…" Dazzler swiped her thumb over Candance's fingers, loosening her grip. Her fingers tingled as blood recirculated. "The other two are Winter elves."

"I don't understand."

"I'm thirty-four. I don't have a single silver hair. Not one." The confession slipped past her lips and bruised Dazzler's heart. She'd looked every day since she was sixteen, promised to give up cookies and cocoa for just one. Yet, none appeared. "If I had some silver, even a few strands, my power could be channeled by the others, siphoned off and made safe."

"Made safe. Made safe?" Candance jerked her hands away and pounded her fists on her thighs. "You've never hurt anyone in your life. You've only helped people. Those sick kids in Flagstaff. Heck, you help sick kids everywhere."

A board creaked. China rattled. Todd.

Dazzler's skin prickled. He might as well know of her impending judgment. "The older I get, the more uncontrollable my magic becomes." She glanced at the sparkles gathering around her fingers. Although, had it really? Sure, it acted up, but she'd always actively tried to use it when things skidded on ice. "I can control a lot of magic. I can do a lot of damage. The board is really just thinking of everyone."

Todd slid a Santa mug with a mound of whipped cream toward Candance. "What happens to you if they take your magic?"

Dazzler set her hands on her knees so they wouldn't see them shake. "Well, um..."

Swiping her finger through the whipped cream, Candance scooped it into her mouth while slouching in her seat. "Auntie D could die, that's what. Elves are magic. You can't remove her magic and expect her to live."

Todd wrapped his hand around the reindeer mug on the tray. "Is that true?"

"I don't know." Dazzler stared at her hands. If she *gave* away her magic, she wouldn't be harmed. "Magic can only be given away when the heart wills it. I love my parents and family, the Clauses, and everyone. I suppose it could be enough to release my magic without harm if I did so for them."

Candance snorted. "Right, like that's gonna happen. I..." She straightened. "I've got it. We'll find you someone to love!"

Dazzler blinked then tugged on the point of her ear. Her hearing must be acting up. "You expect me to fall in love between now and Boxing Day?"

Todd frowned as he lifted the mug of cocoa. "Candance, I don't think..."

"Please." Candance flapped a hand in dismissal. "There's all sorts of matching sites on the internet. I'll get my laptop and—"

"No." Todd shoved the mug at Dazzler. Catching it, she slanted him a glance. Could the solution really be so simple? Her mind spun with the notion.

"I don't know."

"Come on." Candance swiped at the whipped cream again. "Everyone knows elves recognize their destined mates as soon as they see them. This will be easy. You won't even have to waste time on bad dates."

Todd shook his head. "What if she becomes infatuated with some guy? She'd lose valuable time due to a crush."

Dazzler blew on the steam from her cocoa. Two marshmallows floated on the dark surface. Marshmallows never solved anything, but she had nothing to lose. Nothing. She fished them out and popped them into her mouth. The sugar hit her stomach and sent warmth through her.

"Elves don't get crushes."

Todd's mouth thinned for a moment. "You have to."

"Once we fall in love, we're in love. Forever." Dazzler drained her cocoa and slammed down her mug. Hopefully, the cocoa will mitigate the effects of the marshmallows. She needed a clear head. "Let's do this."

Candance squealed, leaped to her feet, and jogged for the stairs. "My computer is in my room."

Dazzler followed at a slower pace, since the room had started swaying. Tarnished tinsel! She hadn't expected the marshmallow to affect her so quickly. When she hit the landing, she glanced back.

Todd studied the coffee in his mug and muttered, "She can't really still love me. She can't."

Dazzler's heart sank. Oh, fudge. Were Todd and Willa about to reunite?

CHAPTER 8

Todd stared at the coffee maker. Dark tears plopped into an ebony puddle and the hiss of steam fogged the air. He inhaled deeply. Too bad the caffeine didn't get into his system through his nose.

Stifling a yawn, he rubbed the grit from his eyes. Four in the morning, and the reindeer needed to be fed. He might as well brave the cold. Sleep had eluded him.

A floorboard creaked behind him. His heart raced. Dazzler. Spinning around, he spied his daughter. Relief slipped past his lips in a big exhale.

Candance tugged a sweatshirt over a cocoa-stained T-shirt. Her knees poked out of the worn spots in her jeans, and her nose wrinkled as she yawned.

"Auntie D isn't up?"

"No." Thank heavens. She'd haunted him all night, driving sleep away. He knew that kiss was a mistake. So, why had he spent the night scheming to steal another? This time he'd kiss Dazzler looking like Dazzler, not his ex-wife. No point in egging on magic to mess with his head and make him ache for impossible things. Not that magic worked for him.

Candance propped a hip against the counter. Crossing her arms over her chest, she closed her eyes. She swayed on her feet.

The coffee pot gurgled as it finished brewing, but he didn't take his eyes off his daughter. "What kept you up so late?"

If it had been thoughts of Michael, Todd might have to hitch up the reindeer and take the kid on a long ride. He heard Hawaii was nice this time of year. And that was as far away from the North Pole as he could think of at the moment. He stared at the streak of silver in his daughter's hair. Winter elves didn't like sun and sand.

Candance shook herself and blinked. "We spent hours looking at men on the internet."

Todd straightened. What had he missed in this conversation? "Men?"

Plural? Shouldn't she be interested in boys? By Kringle, when had she grown into a young woman?

"Yeah. I was surprised at the number of men in our county seeking love." She frowned and shuffled forward. Her reindeer slippers slapped the tile floor. Stopping, she took a mug from the cabinet by the sink.

Todd jerked the coffee carafe off its platform and poured the dark brew into his waiting cup. His daughter couldn't seriously be that broken up about Michael she'd turn to the internet. What kind of person looks for a mate on the internet, anyway? None that would date his daughter, that's for sure. At least with Michael he knew the boy's parents, knew where to find the kid if he stepped out of line.

"Shouldn't you be focusing on exploring careers at the North Pole? And focusing on graduating high school."

Yeah, that sounded parental and not like caveman dad.

Candance rolled her bloodshot eyes before shambling to the refrigerator and opening the door. She squinted at the contents before selecting the hazelnut creamer in front of her face.

"Dad. It's not for me. It's for Auntie D. Don't you remember?"

Todd sipped his coffee. He remembered kissing Dazzler when she looked like his ex-wife. He recalled moving in for another just as Candance stormed into the house. He downed a gulp and ignored the burn in his mouth and throat. The bitter brew hit his gut and infused his bloodstream with caffeine.

Candance hitched a hip and slid onto a barstool. Bracing her elbows on the granite counter, she stuck her face in the steam wafting from her mug.

"Auntie D needs to fall in love so she can keep her magic. We were looking for a mate for her."

Deer droppings! He had forgotten that bit. No, not forgotten. Deliberately ignored it. Dazzler had said elves only fell in love once. A love-at-first-sight kind of thing. It couldn't be true. He stared into the depths of his coffee while his mind traveled back nineteen years ago.

It had been the best day of his life.

It had been the worst day of his life.

He'd decorated his apartment in Flagstaff with all the tropes from every sappy movie and chick flick he'd been forced to watch. Rose petals speckled the tan carpet from the door to the folding table set with his hand-me-down Chinette. Candlelight gilded his sagging, torn leather sectional sofa and pitted coffee table.

The diamond ring nearly burned a hole in his pocket.

The doorbell chimed at five minutes until seven. It wasn't like Willa to be early, but she must've sensed something wonderful was about to happen.

He had practically skipped to the door. His cheeks ached from his goofy grin. Love was amazing. Wonderful. Magical. He'd thrown open the door.

It hadn't been Willa.

Dazzler bounced on the balls of her feet on his porch. With her jeans and T-shirt, she could have been just another student at Northern Arizona University. The pointed ears told another tale. She charged forward, pushing him back yet not touching him. Her hand stopped inches from his chest.

Tingles raced across his flesh. His skin heated under his white dress shirt. Willa had said Dazzler wielded a ton of magic. How did one little teenager handle it all? He shook aside the thought. Time to figure out the wonders of magic after he and Willa married. And speaking of marriage, he had to get rid of Willa's kid cousin.

"Willa's not here."

He hoped she took the hint. Todd had only little brothers, who were dumber than dirt. He hoped girls were smarter, and she took the hint.

"Good." The air around Dazzler turned incandescent, twinkling as if swallowed by a giant bubble. Under her feet, the rose petals formed perfect buds complete with stems.

Todd blinked. Magic currents buffeted him. "Look, kid, can't you come back another time?"

Dazzler stomped her foot.

"No. And I'm not a kid. As for this..." She opened her arms. Her magic restored the shabby couch and filled in the grooves in the wooden coffee table.

Holy smokes. When he married Willa, he would never have to buy furniture again. His elven wife could restore everything magically.

His elven wife. Todd rubbed his hands together; he didn't know which idea sounded better—wife or elf. Both were better without a teenage audience.

"Look, I don't mean to be rude—"

"There's something I have to tell you." She took a deep breath. The air around her twinkled, but she didn't continue.

Todd waved his hand at the sparkles. Geez, being around the kid was like living in a snow globe. He checked his watch. Two minutes till seven. If Willa arrived in Willa-time, he had twelve minutes to get rid of Dazzler.

"Speak. Fast. Willa and I would like to be alone."

He patted the lump in his pocket. Yep, he still had the ring.

"It's going to change everything." Dazzler sighed and pushed her dark hair behind her pointed ears. Standing on tiptoes, she looked him in the eye. At barely seventeen, she was half a foot shorter.

He rolled his eyes. Never in his twenty-two years had he seen such a drama queen. Maybe it was a female thing. The kid probably wanted to be Willa's maid of honor or something.

"Make it quick."

Dazzler raised her hands. The flames above the candles formed wreaths and snowflakes. Others burst into trees and flowers. Todd said a quick prayer, glad his future wife didn't wield such power.

"You can't marry Willa." The words rushed out of Dazzler.

Todd froze. Was this some kind of elf-human thing? "What do you mean I can't marry Willa? She loves me."

She had to love him. It was how things worked in his family.

Dazzler's face scrunched up. "*I* love you. It took me a while to realize it, you understand. But now that I'm seventeen..."

She shrugged as if she had aged a hundred years because she'd celebrated a birthday.

Oh, boy. Talk about awkward.

"Look." Todd placed his hands on her shoulders. His palms tingled, and he jerked them back. It was just her magic, not any feeling on his part. "I'm flattered. Really."

"Flattered? Why would you be flattered?" She frowned at him. Static electricity crackled in her hair.

Todd backed up a step. Magic had a dark side. What if she turned him into a Christmas tree or something? "What I mean to say is, I love Willa. I'm going to marry her."

"But you can't. Don't you see? I love you." She repeated her confession as if it explained everything.

Todd sighed. She was just a kid. Willa was a woman. Besides, all of his time had been spent with Willa, Dazzler had been passed out drunk in the passenger seat when Willa had rear-ended his car. Dazzler had been snoring loudly when Willa had asked him out. She'd also been asleep on the couch when he'd picked up Willa for their second date. And had been nowhere around on their third. He'd barely said two words to Dazzler. And she'd spoken little more to him.

"You're not in love with me."

Dazzler burst into tears.

Todd shoved down the pity rising within him. This was being merciful. Get everything out of the way now, and avoid those awkward family reunions once he married her cousin.

"I won't tell anyone about this."

"No, you don't understand." She stomped her foot. The apartment complex behind her went dark. The candlelight dimmed, creating pockets of darkness in his apartment.

Doubts crept into his resolve. His father had said lights would go out when he met his match. Could this kid be it?

The emergency lights kicked on. Willa stood in the glow of light.

He was right. Willa was his mate.

"Is something the matter?" Willa glanced at her cousin, a smile on her lips.

He joined her outside on the balcony. He'd decided. The kid would have to get over her crush.

"Everything is just fine."

Dazzler had disappeared, and Todd's life would never be the same.

The sound of Candance's voice tugged him out of the past.

"Really, I think he's about perfect for her." Candace yawned.

"Who?" Todd winced. He sounded like an owl, which was better than the jerk he'd been in his memories. It was a wonder Dazzler had volunteered to ferry Candance to her mother's and back after the divorce.

"Dr. Fergus." Candance finished the rest of her coffee. "Don't you think he's perfect for her?"

It took a moment for Todd's sleep-deprived brain to link a name to a face. "The kid doctor?"

"Yeah, that's why it's so perfect. They already know each other. They both love children." Candace stared off into space. "Do you think they would let me babysit their kids?"

No. Hell, no. Dr. Fergus had no chin, and his nose was too big. Dazzler deserved someone with at least average features.

"I think you're getting a little ahead of yourself, sweet pea." He drained his cup. Gah, it was more bitter than usual. He rinsed out his mug in the sink. "Besides, they've met many times before. According to Dazzler's rules, she would know if she was in love with him. Love at first sight, remember?"

So, why didn't she remember telling him she loved him? Come to think of it, after his divorce, the first time they met she hadn't mentioned it at all. He'd thought it was mature of her at the time, but now he wondered. He'd bet his last nutcracker magic had something to do with it.

Magic hated him.

And if she really loved him, that could explain why her magic had started acting up.

Dazzler would have to lose it to be with him.

Could he do that to her?

Did he want to? Weren't they better as friends?

But there was that kiss. If he had another one, he might know for sure. He rubbed his temples. Jiminy Christmas, now his head hurt.

"Maybe she doesn't know she loves him." Candance rubbed her eyes. "I mean, Stacy at school had been friends with Liam forever. Until their senior year, she swore they were best friends. Only best friends. Then he started making googly eyes at Abby, and boom, Stacy realizes she's in love with him."

Todd retrieved his Thermos from the sink. Hadn't Dazzler said something very similar? "Maybe that works for teenagers, but Dazzler's a woman grown."

Yet, she didn't remember.

Maybe another kiss would jog her memory. It might be worth a try.

Candance shrugged and yawned. "I should be dressed in five minutes. I'll knock on Auntie D's door. I'm sure she'll want to go with us to feed the reindeer."

"No!" Todd barked. The last thing he needed was the two of them tagging along. He had thinking to do and didn't need the distraction of Dazzler's low-cut sweater or kissable lips. "Go back to bed. I got this."

"But..." Candace protested half-heartedly.

Todd kissed her temple and aimed her in the direction of the stairs. "Rest. There will be plenty of days for you to feed the reindeer before you return up north."

"You don't have to tell me twice." She hotfooted it out of the kitchen. Guess she was worried he'd change his mind.

Shaking his head, he poured the rest of the coffee into the Thermos and screwed on the cap. He could only see three ways out of this mess.

Like in the fairy tales, he could hope a kiss would jog her memory. But loving him could cost her all her magic, since it didn't work around him. Which made this holiday season very important. She would see how great normal holidays could be and start adapting to her life without powers.

He donned his coat, hat, and mittens and headed out the door. Cold air washed the stupid out of him.

Who was he kidding? Life without magic sucked. And what did he have to offer her in return? Did he even love her like that? His blood quickened. Maybe he could love her like that. And friendship wasn't a bad place to start.

Yeah, he was being a great friend to have her settle for someone she didn't love.

Which led him to option B.

He could help Dazzler find someone to love online and succeed. She could keep her magic, and live happily ever after with a chinless, big-nosed doctor.

He mentally threw up at the thought. Tucking his chin against his chest, he turned into the frigid wind and headed toward the stables.

Option C. He would tell her about that teenage confession and release her to find love elsewhere and keep her magic, possibly losing her forever.

Yeah, life sucked without magic. But without Dazzler, he knew it would get worse. Much worse.

CHAPTER 9

Dazzler stared at the pineapple ceiling tiles in her bedroom.
She'd given up counting them at 323. Sleep just wasn't coming. The voices downstairs beckoned.

Candance.

And Todd.

She pulled the blanket to her chin. She really wasn't up to facing Todd just yet. Nor Candance, for that matter.

The girl had been positive Dr. Fergus was the right man for Dazzler. The doctor was a good man, kind and caring. So, why did Todd's image keep popping into her head? She snorted. Rolling over, she punched her pillow. A faint floral scent of laundry soap surrounded her.

Who was she kidding? No one's eyes were the right shade of cobalt blue. Their noses were too straight or crooked. Their jaws too stubborn or weak. When had her standard become Todd Dugan? She flopped onto her back and resumed staring at the ceiling.

She knew the moment. When he'd kissed her. She traced her lips. Her fingers couldn't duplicate the right pressure. Ack! She was doing it again!

The aroma of freshly brewed coffee drifted up the stairs. Her stomach grumbled. She needed hot cocoa. Cocoa understood. As a bonus, she didn't even need to go downstairs. Shoving aside the quilt, she straightened her red-and-white-striped Christmas socks and padded across the wooden floor.

Coward. You'll have to face him sometime.

Only once she had a plan to address that kiss.

Pushing her hair out of her face, she stopped in front of the dresser. and waved her hand. Elf lights twinkled, gilding everything within a few feet. The Theobromator's shiny chrome gleamed in its nest of cocoa boxes. Her fingers hovered over the assortment of exotic flavors before selecting a silver-and-blue box. Unfolding the foil, she held it up to her nose. She smiled at the sweet scent of chocolate and sugar. A plain one this time, nothing exotic, just the deep notes of the chocolate to hit the right spot.

Picking up the half-empty water bottle near an empty mug, she poured the liquid into the heating reservoir. She frowned. Water would work, but...

She held her hand over the cocoa maker.

Todd said no magic.

Surely, a little wouldn't hurt. And she did need to test Candance's hypothesis that finding love was the key. Not that she was in love with Todd, er, Dr. Fergus.

She snapped her fingers. Magic sparkled in the air and showered the water in the reservoir, turning it into cream. So much better. She paused with her hand on the switch. A ginger undernote now lessened the bite of peppermint from her use of magic.

Her heart beat in her throat. Her magic had changed, but what did that mean? Was finding her mate really the key?

And could he be Doctor Fergus?

Or Todd?

The cocoa maker hissed and gurgled. She banished her thoughts to the mist above the infusor. Todd was her friend. Nothing more. Unless...

Hope rioted in her chest then condensed into a lead ball and plummeted to her knees. If Todd was her mate, then why hadn't she known when she first met him? That was how it worked, wasn't it?

The walls shimmered and shifted. Her heart stopped. She dug her nails into the wood dresser. Had Sterling and Willa found her? Would they drag her back to the North Pole, keep her locked up until her hearing? She wouldn't go. She...

She wasn't moving. A bark of laughter hit her teeth before she clamped her lips together to pen it in.

An image of a yellow Victorian overlaid her reflection in the mirror above the dresser. She blinked as she recognized the house. This house. Yet, the angle was wrong. She tilted her head, left, then right. The reason why snapped inside her head.

She was up high.

Like she was sitting on a branch of the oak tree in the back yard.

Rough bark brushed the pads of her hands. Something fuzzy swept over her feet. She saw through Cheddar's eyes. Her spine tingled with excitement. She hadn't performed this bit of magic for years.

There had to be a connection between love and her magic.

She could be fixed! She could keep her magic.

A woman laughed, the notes as sharp as fresh icicles. Willa!

Dazzler's attention pinned to the back porch. Two thin figures stood on a berg of frosted grass. The cold pricked the oak's roots, and the shrubs shuddered. She gritted her teeth. Had they no consideration? If winter came on too fast, it could kill the plants. Her nails bit into her palms, preventing her from reaching out to the heart of the planet and bringing up some needed warmth. She couldn't risk her spell going horribly wrong and exposing her.

Or creating a small volcano in northern Arizona.

Willa glided forward, then stopped under the window in the turret. "I say we enter when Todd leaves, find my cousin, and use a binding spell to take her home."

Dazzler glanced behind her, thinning the shared vision link to check the window. Her lips twitched. She wasn't in the turret. They didn't know she was here. They were only guessing.

Too bad it was a good guess.

With a thought, Dazzler's vision merged with Cheddar's again. The image of the house bounced, tiny bounces indicating the squirrel still carried Cheddar's eyes. They climbed straight up.

Branches shortened. The trunk narrowed. The squirrel stopped above the rooflines. Frost painted the clock tower in the town's square, carpeted the lawns, and sparkled on the roads. The early cold sent shockwaves as roots protested the abrupt arrival of winter.

Dazzler stumbled back as waves of pain buffeted her. Needles prickled her skin. Tears stung her eyes. She wasn't strong enough to tuck everything into their winter's nap at once. Would anything survive to awaken in springtime?

"What if he doesn't leave?" Sterling's voice cut through the early-morning darkness.

"Of course he'll leave. He has to feed those stupid reindeer." Willa's words formed puffs of white in front of her. "Once we put an end to reindeer pulling the Fat Man's sleigh, we'll cut humans out of Christmas."

Sterling slanted her a glance. "You don't want to use our magic for humans and Christmas?"

"That's not what I meant." Willa planted her hands on her slim hips. Her white robe caught the moonlight. "Humans don't need to be involved in the running of the magic realm. You've testified to the review board yourself, trying to impress upon them how even one union between our kind and humans is diluting our magic."

"It does not seem to have affected Dazzler." Sterling walked around the turret and stopped under her window. Grass crunched. "She's the most powerful elf in generations."

The skin between Dazzler's shoulder blades itched. He couldn't see her. It was just her imagination. The cocoa maker gurgled then clicked off. She jumped. Had they heard that?

Willa stomped her foot and poked Sterling's shoulder. "What good has all that magic done her? What good has it done anyone? She can barely use it to dress. Every time she tries to use it for anything bigger, things explode, break, or the production line ends up with food poisoning. We spend days fixing her messes. She's a disaster."

Dazzler bit her lip. Was that really what her cousin thought?

Keeping her sight blended with Cheddar's, she groped for the mug of cocoa.

"Don't worry." Sterling patted Willa's hand. "You'll get your revenge."

Willa jerked out of his grasp. "Don't humor me. You want her powers even more than I do."

Dazzler's fingers stilled on the mug. Warmth seeped into her fingers. Why did Willa want revenge? What had she ever done to her cousin? An ache started inside her wrist.

Sterling shrugged. "We'll both get what we want, but not by breaking in, searching Dugan's house, and dragging out Dazzler forcibly."

"Don't you believe she's in there?" Willa snorted.

"Oh, I know she is." Sterling spun on his heel. A burst of cold shot out of his fingers and zoomed toward Cheddar.

Dazzler held her breath.

Bark exploded nearby. He'd missed.

Then, the squirrel squealed. Her vision jostled as it scampered down the tree. Dazzler's backside burned. Sterling had shot a woodland creature. What a rotten thing to do. How could her parents expect her to form a union with someone so cruel? She would rather lose her powers.

Smirking, Sterling polished his fingers on his snowy tunic. "Marching into Dugan's house and binding her won't do at all."

"It will be a start." Willa crossed her arms over her chest. "She ruined my marriage. She drove a wedge between my daughter and me. I was never allowed to be a proper mother to Candance because 'Auntie D' was always there first."

"Exactly." Sterling studied the shutters on the kitchen window downstairs. "You want to hurt her like she hurt you. Destroy her friendship with Todd. Have *him* turn Dazzler over to us."

"Todd would never turn her in," Willa spat.

"Not yet. But if they weren't friends. If she betrayed him..." Sterling smiled.

Dazzler shuddered. Her grip tightened on the mug. Todd would never turn her in, would he?

Willa angled her body toward Frost. "How do you plan to make that happen? Todd is stubbornly loyal."

"By destroying the one thing that means everything to him." Sterling's eyeteeth gleamed, revealing the predator within.

Willa's hands fisted at her side. "You will not harm my daughter."

Sterling waved his hand in dismissal. "Of course not. I'm talking about the stupid Christmas lights. He's responsible for them. Solely responsible."

Dazzler shook her head. No. No, they wouldn't...would they?

"We will destroy the Christmas light display and point the blame at Dazzler." Willa's lips twitched before stretching into a wide grin. "And when Todd hands my cousin over, her spirit will be broken. She'll have no friends. No safe refuge to shield her."

How could they be so cruel? Dazzler dropped to her knees. Hot cocoa splashed and scalded her hands. She set the mug on the dresser with a scrape of ceramic on wood.

Sterling steepled his fingers and rested his chin on the tips. "Exactly. And I'll be there to pick up the pieces. She'll be so grateful, I'll get my expansion before the review board's hearing. Then you can take her magic."

With a snap of Willa's fingers, they disappeared.

By Kringle, not only would they fail, Dazzler would have them permanently assigned to the Naughty List. Her nails bit into her palms, and her connection with Cheddar snapped. She would stop them. She—

Two soft raps sounded on the window behind her. She jumped up and spun about. The heavy drapes did not stir. Heart thudding in her chest, she set her hand on the dresser. Should she look? Willa and Sterling were supposed to be gone, but it could be a trap.

A frigid draft of peppermint-scented air invaded her bedroom. Leaves fluttered like angels' wings, rising in a cyclone before transforming into a scarecrow.

Cheddar stood at the foot of her bed. Stick fingers molded reindeer lichen into a vest over his barrel chest. The squirrel wiggled out from under Cheddar's Santa Claus hat and handed over the scarecrow's acorn eyes.

"You're never going to believe what I just heard."

"Sterling and Willa are planning to destroy the light festival to get Todd to turn me over." She sagged against the dresser. Saying the words aloud made it all real. She had to warn Todd.

Squaring her shoulders, she eyed the door to the hallway. She needed more than courage; she needed cocoa. She groped for the mug and latched on.

"How did you know?" Cheddar scratched the squirrel behind his ears before offering Pip to her.

"I saw it. I saw the whole thing and heard it through you." Dazzler sipped her cocoa, swallowing the entire contents without stopping. Warmth spiraled through her and infused her limbs. Setting the cup down, she held out her hands.

Tiny feet scampered across her palm. With an indignant chirp, the squirrel pointed to a white patch near his tail. Fur was broken off, exposing reddened skin.

Her fingers warmed as she stroked the bald patch. Fur sprouted then swirled softly around her fingertips. The squirrel's tail vibrated with pleasure; then he hopped off her palm, scrambled up Cheddar's head and hid under the Santa Claus hat.

Cheddar tilted his head to the left. "You haven't been able to merge our vision in ages. How can that be?"

"Candance suggested love was the solution to my problem." Or at least one of them.

Dazzler returned the mug to the dresser. Running her finger along the interior, she whisked it clean. There it was again. A gingery mix to the usual peppermint smell of her magic.

"You love everyone and everything." Cheddar sputtered. "That makes no sense."

Not everyone. Her cousin and Sterling had slipped into the squinty-eye category.

"Not that kind of love. The soulmate kind." Her stomach fluttered. Imagine loving someone no matter how messed up their magic was, no matter if they occasionally substituted salt for the sugar in the cookies. Could she really have it?

The scarecrow's eyes narrowed. "And who is this he-elf? I don't believe I've met him."

Her cheeks heated. "I haven't found him yet. It's just the hope of finding him."

"Oh." Cheddar stared at his boots made of bark. "I guess we can't go home, then."

"Not yet." Now that she knew she was looking for her soulmate, finding him should be easy, right?

The squirrel's tail emerged from under Cheddar's hat and dangled over the scarecrow's eye. He tucked it back, then adjusted the cap over his pinecone ears.

"What is your plan to stop Willa and Sterling from sabotaging the light display?"

Dazzler raised her hand to use magic to change her clothes then stopped. No magic. She didn't want to upset Todd. Not that she believed he'd turn her in. He'd already proven himself by standing beside her when everyone else had left. She pulled a green wool sweater from her assigned drawer and brown slacks from a wooden hanger in the closet.

"I don't think they're going to sabotage anything."

"You just heard them. They're going to make Todd turn you over. You know how important that light display is to him and to the town."

Dazzler quickly dressed, wadded up her nightclothes, and tossed them into the corner. "Yes, yes, that I know. I just don't believe Willa and Sterling just happened to be discussing all of their nefarious plans in front of the oak tree in Todd's yard." Especially when Sterling had harmed an innocent woodland creature. She stepped into her boots and laced them up. "I smell a trap. Given the source of wonder and delight this town generates, I can't see either of them chancing Santa's wrath by interfering."

Cheddar sighed. "How can you take the chance?"

A floorboard squeaked in the hall.

"We'll tell Todd. It wouldn't be unusual for him to check." She strode across the room and jerked open the door. "Todd?"

Candance shuffled down the hall, her reindeer slippers slapping the wooden planks. "Dad's feeding the reindeer." She yawned and stretched. "You could probably catch him if you hurry."

"Thanks." Dazzler rushed for the landing. In a rustle of leaves, Cheddar followed.

"You can't let anyone see you, or Todd won't need to turn you in. Everyone else will."

"I plan to use the no-see-em incantation." Unlike an invisibility spell, people would notice her, but they wouldn't remember once they looked away; as a bonus, she wouldn't be stepped on or bumped into.

"Nice." Cheddar slid down the railing and landed with a thump at the bottom. "That spell always works."

But how to get out of the house? Pausing at the foot of the stairs, Dazzler stared about the unlit room. Shadows always worked. She gathered up the darkness and draped it over her head like a veil. Cheddar joined her. Leaves crinkled against her back.

She opened a side window and crawled over the sill. The scarecrow quickly joined her. The boards on the wraparound porch remained silent, and the frosted grass crumped underfoot when she landed, with Cheddar close behind. The veil obliterated their footprints as they followed Todd's to the reindeer pen.

Soon, they reached the edge of town. Dazzler sniffed the earthy scent of human-based magic. She entered the stand of trees and threw off the no-see-em veil.

"We have to be close."

Her skin tingled as she ducked under a pine bough. She'd breached the ward. Turning back, she threw a handful of elf dust against it. Green sparkles. No other elf had penetrated the ward. She was safe. The hole made by her and Cheddar's entrance quickly closed. Wiping her hands, she surveyed the woods.

The scarecrow straightened his green vest. "How far to Todd?"

"Shouldn't be far." Dazzler headed deeper into the woods. Loud thuds rumbled in the early morning light. Feeding time.

Older reindeer pawed at the frost to lip the exposed grass. One glanced up and sniffed the air. Brown eyes trained on Cheddar. Oversized nostrils flared, and he snorted puffs of white as he trotted over.

Cheddar stiffened. "Uh-oh."

She froze and scanned the woods. Had she missed something? "What?"

Two more reindeer zeroed in on the scarecrow. The trio moved fast among the trunks. Another joined the bunch.

"My vest is made of reindeer lichen. Reindeer love reindeer lichen. And everything else I'm made of." Cheddar sprinted for the clearing; the reindeer herd following him increased in number.

CHAPTER 10

*Cold air bit into Todd's cheeks. Stars glittered on the black-*velvet sky, and the full moon hung like a sugar cookie on the dark canvas. Hunching his shoulders against the cold, he turned on Spruce Drive and headed away from the town. The number of Craftsman bungalows thinned the longer he walked. At a sign warning of reindeer crossing, his skin prickled.

Magic.

In the corner of his eyes he detected movement, but when he turned his head, all he saw was flickering shadows in the woods.

The wards were up.

Outsiders wouldn't see the meadow of frolicking reindeer or the teams lined up in pairs, practicing for their leg of Santa's midnight ride. A voice inside his head cautioned him to look away. Todd blinked. That was new. No doubt his sister-in-law's spell.

He tripped over his boots, nearly dropping his thermos. He caught the silver cylinder then tucked it securely under his arm. His stomach clenched. How could magic affect him? Magic didn't work on him. Not even a little.

Unless it did.

Which meant that Dazzler might not have to give up her magic and—

He squelched the thought. Lonnie's magic worked on him because her family had cursed his over a hundred years ago. Apparently, some magic was grandfathered in. Besides, he could easily overcome her magic.

He turned off the road at two worn spots. Frosted grass crunched beneath his boots. A stand of birch trees rained golden leaves on him; the lichen-spotted trunks stood picket in front of the gate to the reindeer pasture. Spruce, pines, and a few bone-white sycamores rose in place of the barn and out-buildings.

All a mirage. Just a mirage. Holding his breath, he closed his eyes and stepped forward. Magic pulled on his skin, and his motions slowed as if he slogged through warm taffy.

Maybe magic affected him a little.

The thought left along with the sensation. Bells jingled, and he opened his eyes. As expected, once inside the ward, every-thing looked normal. Young bucks and does frolicked in the frosty meadow. Fawns kept close to their mothers and the pro-tection of their large racks of antlers. The older males sorted the young reindeer into teams, keeping them in imaginary traces and beginning their training for pulling Santa's sleigh. A set of eight reindeer, five with full racks, flew in formation above the ground and landed on the patches marked as rooftops.

Todd clapped as they hit their mark.

"Good work. Santa would be proud."

The reindeer preened. Others broke ranks and angled to-ward him. The younger ones immediately perked up, dangling frosted meadow grass glistening from their mouths. Guess they didn't like their dinners frozen. Of course, it wasn't him they were interested in but the anticipation of magic corn. Given they'd started flying high so early, he may have overdone it.

"Allright, guys, you know the drill." His words were puffs of white in front of his face. "First, I feed you, then I clean your stalls."

He could have sworn he heard them giggle with excitement. Shaking the fanciful notion out of his head, he followed the rutted sleigh tracks to the stables. They sprawled across the area on his right. Lodgepole beams, pine logs, and cedar shingles covered a building more suitable to the North Pole. Or some

Scandinavian country. But then, that was pretty much the stables' inspiration.

He pushed open the double doors and walked into the warmth of the barn. The fecund scent of animal mixed with the earthy aroma of baled sedges and grasses. Scaling the wooden ladder, he reached the loft and switched to his work gloves. He clenched and unclenched his fingers, softening the cold leather. He hit the switch. Light blazed across the neat stacks of feed, and a golden aura surrounded the barrels of magic corn lined up against the wall.

An assembly line was folded up accordion-style against the left eave. Silver tracks ended at the gaping maw of his pneumatic feeding cannon. Metal clanked as he straightened and stretched the line, pulling it closer to the feed. He quickly loaded six bales and shoved them closer to the cannon. After stuffing the first one into the barrel and removing the baling wires, he crossed to the corn and removed a scoopful.

He turned back to the cannon then looked down. Holy mackerel! His boots barely touched the loft floor.

"But if magic *does* work on me then where does that leave me?

With a fourth option? One where he didn't lose Dazzler? Dare he hope?

A boot scuffed the ladder. Lonnie Dugan, his brother Nick's wife, stuck her head over the edge of the loft before scrambling all the way up. She checked her oversized belly then glared at him.

"I suppose that depends on the kind of magic you're talking about."

Todd tightened his grip on the scoop of corn. Clamping his lips together, he crossed to the cannon and threw the corn on the hay. Just his luck—he wanted to be alone, and suddenly there was a party at the stables.

"I wasn't expecting you this early."

Lonnie wiped her hands on an orange handkerchief. Her fingers glistened with oily residue that perfumed the air with pungent herbs. "So, you're avoiding me, huh?"

Todd grunted. He liked all his sisters-in-law. It was their playing fast and loose with magic he didn't trust. And Lonnie was a card-carrying witch.

He shut the cap on the cannon and sealed it with a crank of the wheel. Pulling his smartphone from his pocket, he tapped into the control app. Seals were checked. He threw open the window and stuck his face into the cold breeze.

"Does Nick know you're hanging out in lofts in your condition?"

"Don't change the subject," she snapped.

Reindeer assembled in the meadow within the cannon's range. This year's chosen eight stood in the center, protected by the rest of the herd. With a touch of the button, Todd adjusted the trajectory. Gears ground as the barrel aimed for the herd's left flank. The compressor rumbled to life. In a safety check, the vent hissed and fell silent. A bar graph on his screen climbed from white to green as the pressure built. Sensors measured the weight and optimized for delivery.

"I'm used to the Dugan men being nearly comatose in their silence, but you have perfected it to an art not even Nick has managed to achieve."

The button flashed green. Todd tapped it. The barrel cover opened with a magic-dampened thud; grass and corn rained softly down on the herd. He waited as the system performed its safety checks before opening the cap and loading another bale of hay.

He'd be a fool to turn down Lonnie's offer. After all, she was a witch. He could use another opinion on his Dazzler problem. Tapping the bottom of the scoop, he crossed back to the corn.

"Have you ever known someone to give up their magic?"

Lonnie squinted at the eaves for a moment. "Sure."

Todd relaxed. So, it was possible. If he could think of all the benefits of life without magic, he could—

"They weren't successful." Lonnie rocked back in her rubber boots. She opened and closed her mouth before she spoke again. "You're worried about your imaginary friend Dazzler."

"She's not imaginary." Todd chucked the corn inside and slammed the cap.

"No one's ever met her. No one in the family. It's like you're hiding her or something." She tugged the scoop from his hand.

Todd's ears burned. Her words were closer to the truth than she knew. He adjusted the cannon's trajectory and waited until boom time.

Lonnie had no respect for boom time. "Beings born with magic, like elves—they can refuse to use it. Like a muscle they don't use, its strength will diminish, but it doesn't actually go away."

That didn't sound at all like what Frost had described.

Todd pressed the button. The cannon's thud echoed hollowly inside him. "The North Pole Review Board wants to take away Dazzler's magic. Claims they can do so easily without harming her."

Lonnie shook her head. "I don't see how. Magic is as much a part of an elf as her heart or lungs. If she's even half as powerful as your wife, the attempt will kill her."

Kill her.

Kill Dazzler.

Todd hung onto the closed cap, using the cannon to keep himself upright. He had to tell Dazzler the truth to save her. Maybe his confession would make her fall in love with him again.

Maybe *he* could make her fall in love with him again.

To save her.

"You're not immune to magic, you know." Lonnie interrupted his thoughts.

"I got through your wards, didn't I?"

Lonnie rolled her eyes. "They weren't meant to keep anyone in the family out. And the fact that you're sensitive to the wards proves my point."

Jiminy Christmas, she didn't give up. Straightening, he threw open the cap and drew the next bale forward. One more to go and he could escape. "How do you figure?"

"If you were insensitive to magic, you wouldn't have noticed the wards." She waved the scoop of corn under his nose. "And if you were immune to magic, as you claim, you would never have seen the glamour I created."

She smirked as she added the corn.

Todd sealed the cap again and listened as the system processed his orders. One more load, and he could get the straw and muck the stalls. Surely, she wouldn't stay for that.

"I'm concerned about you. Everyone is." Lonnie set her hand over his, stopping him from pulling the last bale forward.

He sighed. After he talked to Dazzler, and while keeping the lights on, he was gonna have a serious talk with his family about meddling in his life.

"Your wife wields strong magic." Lonnie's eyes narrowed, and she brushed her hand near his shoulder. "I can see traces of it attached to you."

He glanced at his shoulder. He didn't see anything. Not that he expected to. "Willa is my *ex*-wife."

"There's no distance in these bonds." She wiped her hands on her jeans. "They're strong, and they're binding you to her."

"I'm sure there's a reason for that." Stepping back, he created enough distance to finish loading the last of the grass bales.

Lonnie hurried to add the corn.

His thoughts filled the silence. Could Dazzler's love have changed them both? Made her magic misbehave and altered him, too? He'd never really dated after his divorce. And the few times a woman had stuck around for longer than a month, she'd invariably complained about his relationship with "Auntie D".

Breakfast with Dazzler would be interesting.

Probably not in a good way.

The cannon went off. The herd converged on the feed covering the ground. A few nipped at the kernels and grass on the backs of their neighbors.

Todd shut the window. Lonnie returned the scoop to the barrel and sealed it.

"Of course, the connection may just be an offshoot of her link to Candance. That one is definitely there, although it feels different. And it's powerful."

Auntie D was more of a mother to his daughter than Willa had ever tried to be.

"She loves Candance." Todd collapsed the assembly line and shoved it out of the way. It was what made Dazzler one of his favorite people. That, and her compassion, and her laughter, and her charm. She was good-looking, too. Not that he usually noticed. Funny how those five years had been an eternity when he was twenty-two, but now their age difference seemed just right.

"I would offer you a talisman, to mitigate her effect..." Lonnie shrugged. "But I'm not anywhere near that strong. I don't even think my entire coven could lessen it."

He preceded his sister-in-law down the ladder, preparing to catch her if she fell. She threw a leg over the edge of the loft and planted a foot on the top rung, then shimmied her belly around the ladder before descending.

"On top of all the magic, I sense deception. It's intentional. And that's not good for anyone. Especially you. She's here under false pretenses."

Lonnie landed on the ground and rubbed her belly.

"Maybe she was just trying to make a good impression." Todd stuffed his hands in his pockets. Dazzler's little charade as Willa caused his head to hurt.

"The fact you're defending her has me concerned. The rest of the family is, too."

And they'd circled back to that again.

Adjusting his work gloves, he headed for the door. "I'm going to bring in more straw."

Lonnie sighed. "Fine, I'll drop the subject, but you should know. I checked out the young reindeer, to make sure there was no harm done after the magical escapades yesterday. Magic corn didn't cause it. It was direct magic. Elven magic. And there was only one elf here yesterday."

Todd paused. There had been two at the time everything went sideways. He'd have to talk to Dazzler. If she loved him, that would solve the problem of the lights, too.

"I appreciate your concern, but I think I've got a handle on things."

Too bad it felt more like he was wrestling a greased reindeer. But he had a plan. Three plans, in fact. One was bound to work.

He shoved open the door. The floodlights glistened on the frosted ground. The herd had finished feeding and shuffled toward the forest on the rim of the pasture, no doubt in search of their favorite birch and willow leaves. Turning up his collar, he aimed for the tin-roofed shed. The stable door didn't slam shut behind him.

"There's just one more thing."

Pivoting, he faced his sister-in-law while walking backward. "Were you Colombo in a previous life?"

"I just wanted to warn you." She hovered on the threshold "The curse my family put on yours. The one that will have you try three times to kill your chosen mate."

Todd stopped. "That's nuts. Where did you hear such a piece of malarkey?"

"Your brothers. Their wives. Your parents." She ticked them off on her fingers.

No one had ever mentioned this twist before. He'd never tried to kill Willa. Nor had he attempted to kill Dazzler, not once during all their vacations. Proof that magic didn't work on him. Or that neither really loved him, or he them. Although Willa *had* pushed him and his car onto train tracks when she'd rear-ended him the night they met.

"All I'm saying is, your ex has pure magic. Your family's curse will boomerang, and it will be you who almost dies."

"I'm not in love with my ex-wife." But if he pursued Dazzler, if she really loved him, would he be risking his life? Still, better he take a chance on a silly curse than the certain death facing Dazzler if the Board decided to take her magic.

"Don't bother coming back. I'll get Nick to muck out the stalls." The stable door slammed shut.

In the meadow, a reindeer raced into the woods. Three fawns peeled away to follow. Soon the whole herd were headed to the woods. Todd shook his head. No doubt one of the more adventurous does had found a fresh patch of reindeer lichen.

A hint of a sunrise glowed on the horizon. Hooves thundered as the herd practiced their gallop. His stomach growled. After he loaded the straw, he'd inspect the stables then head home. His brother was better suited to mucking stalls.

Removing the tarp from the bales, he eyed the set-up. Some yahoo had left a single row of bales, six high. Did they want someone to get crushed? Obviously, matrimony had made his brother stupid. He'd need to find the ATV and trailer then knock down the tower and—

Something slammed into the side. Leaves fluttered near the top. The tower wobbled. The top bale tilted toward him. He backed up a step. Two.

Another thud followed. A reindeer grunted. A fawn honked.
The bale broke free, bringing the others with it.
He turned, but the weight caught his leg, and he went down.

CHAPTER 11

"Todd!" A scream tore from Dazzler's throat as straw bales tumbled over, threatening to bury him. How had this happened?

Cheddar.

Chased by reindeer, the scarecrow had dissolved in a flurry of leaves, twigs, and moss upon impact with the bales, and now they were tipping over. She had to protect Todd.

Raising her arm, she splayed her fingers. Energy surged up through her feet and zinged along her nerves as it rushed up her body and out her fingertips. The debris hovered in the air. Bales circled a point.

Todd grunted.

He was hurt! Her heart stopped, and her mouth dried. With a flick of her wrist, she sent the floating remains of Cheddar's stuffing and reindeer bedding to the side. The threat was cleared. Almost.

One bale pinned Todd's leg to the ground.

He glanced up. His cobalt eyes locked with hers. Would he be angry that she'd used magic? It wasn't like she could deny it. Cloves and ginger scented the air. The frost under her feet had melted, leaving her standing in a puddle of mud and spring-green grass. The heart birthmark on the inside of her wrist tingled. Her mouth opened. No words came out.

Reindeer trotted under the awning protecting the straw. They crowded the space, munching on the leaves and moss.

Planting one boot on the bale, Todd shoved the straw rectangle off his leg. A crimson leaf fluttered onto his thigh. He picked it up, spinning it between his fingers.

"Is Cheddar all right?"

"Oh!" She clapped her hands over her mouth. Would he get mad if she discussed magic?

He held up his hand. "Of course he is. I remember our trip to Tampa when he appeared as a mini sand dragon. Candance squealed as he chased her along the beach, then broke down in tears when a wave washed him away." The skin around his eyes crinkled. "She made him sit on her shoulder for the rest of the week, to protect him from any water."

Dazzler blinked as images buffeted her. Not her memories, but Todd's. Her lips curved, mirroring his smile as his emotions linked to the slideshow. He didn't think of Cheddar as magic, but as a pet, like a cat or a dog. The scarecrow would not be flattered.

"The hotel staff thought he was a sculpture."

"Until he moved." Todd chuckled.

"And the waitress dropped that stack of dirty dishes." Closing the distance, Dazzler dropped to her knees beside him. His happiness in the memories blanketed her. Dandelions bloomed around them.

He tilted his head. "And not a single plate or glass broke on the tile floor. Did you...?"

She jerked her chin once. "It was bad enough no one believed her. I couldn't have her paying for broken dishes, too. She needed every dime to pay for her last semester at school."

"You always made our holidays so much fun." Dropping the leaf, he raised a hand; his fingers stroked through her hair. "Have I ever told you how amazing you are? Helping others, not calling attention to it, just helping out?"

His gaze dropped to her lips.

Her muscles quivered. Bracing one hand on the ground, she leaned toward him.

A new tension coiled through her. Something was happening, something unexpected. Her stomach clenched. There was no reason to be afraid. Todd was here.

He wouldn't let anything happen to her.

"I don't know what I'd do without you." Cupping the back of her head, he urged her closer still.

He really had such amazing eyes. Such a deep blue, warm, not cold like the winter elves at the North Pole. She could lose herself in them.

His warm breath enveloped her.

Her eyes fluttered closed.

An outraged squeak yanked her back to reality. Removing his fingers from her hair, Todd cleared his throat.

Roasted chestnuts! What had almost happened? She rocked back, sitting on her heels. And why was she desolate that it hadn't?

Pip chittered angrily from atop a bale, holding two acorns. With a swish of his tail, he swept leaves off the straw. Cheddar's leaves.

Dazzler opened her hand, palm up. "Cheddar will be fine. There's plenty of leaves in the forest for him to form again."

A reindeer caught a tumbling leaf mid-air and slurped it into her mouth. Two others locked antlers after slurping up the reindeer moss that had comprised Cheddar's vest. The squirrel chittered once more, hopped about, and scampered toward the woods.

Todd cupped his hands around his mouth and shouted after the creature, "He might want to pick something other than willow leaves and moss as stuffing. Who am I kidding? The herd loves pretty much anything a scarecrow is made of."

He glanced her way once. Twice. Then his attention stuck.

Her heart bumped in her chest. Love. That word kept coming up a lot lately. She licked her dry lips.

His gaze caught the motion. "We need to talk."

"Sounds serious."

"It is."

Air whooshed out of her lungs, and her shoulders bowed. A heartbeat later she mentally slapped herself and clenched her jaw. If he wanted her to apologize, he would be waiting a long time. Couldn't he see she'd had to use magic? Or would he have preferred to be squashed under straw bales? And it had been so easy. So flawless.

She tucked away the thought. Later, she'd take it out and examine it. "Well, then, let's speak somewhere warm and dry."

Frost crept across the puddles. The dandelions shifted from yellow petals to white seeds and dispersed. A blink later, the brown stem dissolved into the ground.

She held out her hand, offering him help up. His fingers walked across her palm. Tingles started at her wrist and spread. A kaleidoscope of butterflies took wing in her stomach.

Oh, no. With all this talk of love, she couldn't have her foolish heart fixate on Todd. They were friends. Good friends. How could she risk it for...something more. Something better. She bit her lip.

He shifted his legs then winced.

"You're hurt." Dazzler set her hand on his shoulder, holding him in place. "Let me check your leg."

He raised his hand as if to set it on hers, but let it drop to his side before making contact. "I didn't know you'd added nursing skills to your impressive repertoire. Wanting to impress Dr. Fergus?"

Why was he bringing up Dr. Fergus? From the look on his face, he must have swallowed some of the mud.

"I've bandaged enough of Candance's boo-boos to qualify as a nurse's aide. And that's not to mention that time in Mexico when you burned off your eyebrows while starting the bonfire."

"I didn't know you had already added lighter fluid before I did." He touched his eyebrows, visibly relaxing as he smoothed them. He moved his leg again and hissed through his teeth. "My leg might be a little beyond bandages and aloe vera."

"Stop being a baby and let me look." Walking on her knees, she paused near the tear in his jeans. Blood stained the fabric and exposed skin. Her weight pressed her into the hardening mud. Her nervous system buzzed as tendrils of the Earth's ley lines connected with her. The air sparkled around her hands. She bracketed his lower thigh, careful not to touch, and moved slowly down his leg.

Her ears pulsed with the thud of tiny feet and hooves in the pasture and woods. The heartbeat of every creature resonated within her chest. The link spiraled out, farther and farther. She began to dissolve in the music of nature. Sweat cooled her forehead. She clasped the silver chain binding her soul to her body, but the tide sucked at her resolve.

If she couldn't control her magic, she would be absorbed into the lifeforce of nature.

It wasn't a bad fate.

Maybe...

Todd's boot twitched, touching her wrist. "Is it broken?"

Dazzler slammed back into her body. The melody of life settled into background noise. Sighing, she shook her hands, dispelling the tingles to a manageable level.

"Dazzler?"

"No. No, it's not broken, just cut and bruised." The words tumbled out of her mouth before the images flooded in. Green tendrils of energy sprouted from the frosted mud, curled around his ankle, and slipped under his jeans. Her magic had never worked like this before. She swiped her finger down his leg, cutting the fabric with the precision of a scalpel. The healing energy slipped inside the opening.

"It feels...warm." Todd wiggled his boot.

The bands of energy snapped, and an accompanying sting hit her chest. The connection was working both ways. She set her hand on the toe of his boot. "Stop that."

The leg of his jeans sloughed to the ground. Muscle rippled under the light dusting of hair covering his shin, knee, and thigh. Blood wept along the cuts made by the baling wire. The abused skin swelled, shifted from red to purple.

Todd leaned back. Planting his elbows in the ground, he stared up at her. "I don't remember you being this bossy, Nurse Ratched."

"I don't remember you being this twitchy." Dazzler stuck her tongue out at him. "Now be still."

He arched an eyebrow.

Keeping her hands a couple inches above his injuries, she took a deep breath. The cold winter air stung her lungs then faded. The air warmed; then the perfume of spring surrounded her. Fresh grass. Blossoms. Fecund soil. Purple, red, and yellow flowers of light bloomed over his leg. The gash closed. The bruises yellowed then faded.

Squirming, Todd squinted at his shin. "That tickles."

"It's warm." The heat filled her from the inside and the energy—she could have run a marathon. How was it this hadn't drained her like the other times she'd performed magic?

He levered up. "Are you working magic? On me?"

She nodded. The flowers faded. The tendrils of power retreated. Yet she felt the murmurs deep inside. "You have to admit magic is far better than that alcohol you daubed on my elbow after I fell skating in Venice Beach."

He grunted. "I did blow on it and kissed it to make it all better."

Her breath locked in her lungs, and her cheeks heated. Candance had goaded her father into the kiss. That had stung worse than the alcohol. Focus. She needed to focus.

She skimmed her fingers down his legs, cleaning the blood and stitching the fabric as she moved. The hair on his legs tickled her palms. She peeked at him from under her lashes.

A few pieces of straw stuck out of the vee of his shirt. Was that just as soft? Her fingers spasmed with the need to touch it, test it for herself.

The hem of his jeans ruched into pleats. "Sorry about that."

She quickly smoothed it out.

Todd shook his head. "If that's the worst your magic does, I can't see why the Board would take it away. Or try to take it away."

"It usually doesn't go this well." She rubbed her hands against her pants. The mud dried and flaked off, leaving the fabric clean.

Todd frowned at his leg before rolling to his feet. Mud tumbled off his clothes as the cloth dried. He plucked at his jeans. "Magic doesn't work on me."

She rolled her eyes and raised her hand, demanding his help up. "Magic works on everyone. That's why it's magic."

"Maybe." He grabbed her hand and tugged her to her feet.

She stood in his space, breathed in his exhales. He was pine and sunshine. She was water and summer breezes. They fitted like the elements. How had she not noticed it before?

Her palm molded to his chest while her fingers toyed with a piece of straw caught in his collar. "Of course, you have to help, too."

He curled his fingers under her chin and swept his thumb along her jaw. "You have a spot of mud just here."

She closed her eyes, leaning into his touch. Would he kiss her now? Would everything change?

His lips stirred the air near hers.

She held her breath and waited for contact.

"I can see my concern was for nothing."

The woman's voice shattered the spell. Dazzler's eyes popped open, and she pressed her hands to her cheeks to cool them. The tingle of magic brushed her palms. The woman would see her but not remember unless...

Unless she was the sister-in-law who was the witch.

Todd growled, and his touch was gone. Cold air rushed in to fill the emptiness as he moved away.

"Lonnie. I'd forgotten you were here."

Dazzler's stomach clenched. By Kringle, she'd thought her luck had changed.

Lonnie bounced on the balls of her feet, causing the buckles on her loafers to jingle. Fleece lined the heavy jacket straining against her pregnant stomach, and curly hair poked out from under her orange knit cap. Hugging a satchel to her chest, she ping-ponged her attention from Dazzler to Todd, then back again before thrusting out her hand.

"Auntie D, I presume."

Dazzler gasped. The witch recognized her.

Todd planted himself in front of Dazzler. "If you tell a soul..."

"Then what?" Lonnie feinted right then left. "You'll turn me into a frog? Oh, wait. Only witches do that. And I'm the only witch here."

Dazzler didn't want to cause friction between him and his family. She tugged her sleeve over her birthmark before reaching around him and shaking hands with the witch.

"How did you recognize me?"

"Are you kidding?" Lonnie used their connection to nudge Todd aside. She beamed at Dazzler. "All Candance talks about is Auntie D this, and Auntie D that, and then there are the hours of photos she shows me after every family vacation you three take. Then there's—"

"You can't—" Todd butted in.

"Tell Frost, or your heinous ex." Lonnie waved her free hand, letting the satchel swing near her hip. "No slush, Sherlock. I would rather eat eye of newt than hobnob with those two. But why did you hide who you were from the family last night? You had to know we wouldn't turn in the amazing Auntie D."

Embarrassment heated Dazzler's cheeks. She didn't know about amazing. "I was hiding."

Todd clasped her hand and brushed against her side. "They can't be allowed to find her."

"Of course they can't. Hiding in plain sight. Very clever. Is changing your appearance easier than this no-see-'em spell?" Lonnie beamed at her. Her face brightened. The ground seemed to purr under the witch's feet.

The rumble echoed through Dazzler and vibrated her link with Todd. She stared at their connection. Bells jingled. That was new.

"What no-see-'em spell?" Todd's forehead wrinkled.

Dazzler cleared her throat. What the Dickens? He had better not get upset about her using magic now.

"When I look at Auntie D, I kinda see her." Lonnie squinted and tilted her head. "But when I look away, she disappears, and I forget she was there."

"Making it impossible for anyone to tell Willa or Frost they saw you." Todd scraped a hand down his face. "Very clever."

Dazzler wasn't sure if that was a compliment. "They're both fundamental magic."

"Maybe for an elf." Lonnie opened her arms wide. "It took two days for my entire coven to enchant this woods so the visitors didn't find it and spook the reindeer. You can do the most intricate spells with ease. That's more than clever. That's some powerful magic."

Reindeer clomped over the frosty ground, and sleigh runners swooshed across the grass. Sheriff's badge shining on his chest, Nick Dugan drew a blue-and-white sleigh to a halt.

"Auntie D *better* be powerful. The whole jingle-jangle town has gone dark, and that ex of yours is riling up the townsfolk. If we can't get those lights on faster than Santa goes up a chimney, this Christmas may turn into a Halloween nightmare."

CHAPTER 12

"Oh, no!" Dazzler clutched Todd's arm, her nails digging into his bicep. The mud under her feet solidified into packed dirt, and one of the dozen reindeer milling around them chomped on grass that changed from green to brown as he watched. Propping a hand on the doorjamb, he waited for the world to settle on an even keel. After a burp and a quick swallow, he opened his eyes.

Todd set his hand over hers and felt it trembling. He mentally swore. She should feel safe in Holly, not hunted by her cousin and Frost.

"Don't worry. Lonnie will make sure my brother doesn't blab." He glared at his brother for good measure.

After hooking the reins on the sleigh, Nick held up his hands and climbed out. The sheriff's badge on his shirt winked in the pearly gray dawn.

"I'm not duty bound to turn her in."

Lonnie shifted her satchel of magical herbs to her other hip and slid an arm around her husband's waist.

"What he means to say is that since you're family, he wouldn't turn you in."

Nick winced. "Yeah, that's what I meant."

Dazzler tugged once on Todd's jacket. "But that's not what *I* meant." Hashmarks appeared between her eyebrows before she shook her head, wiping them away. "I mean, I'm grateful you're not turning me in. And...and I didn't think you would."

Lonnie scratched her swollen stomach, and her breath formed white puffs in the crisp morning air. "We both know the pain ratting out someone inflicts."

"Exactly." Nick's fingers balled into a fist, and he glared back at Todd. "Nor do we appreciate being called a tattletale."

Todd snorted. He could take his little brother, might even enjoy knocking the eggnog outta him.

Dazzler sidled between the two. "But don't you see? This is exactly why I came here."

Shifting his focus, Todd concentrated on her. He'd much rather look at her than his ugly brother. Sliding his fingers under hers, he pried them off his sleeve and tucked them between his palms. She really had the softest skin.

He shook the notion from his head and replayed her words. "Why *did* you come here?"

"To warn you." Her fingers spasmed in his hold. "Cheddar overheard Sterling and Willa talking. They plan to cause so much trouble with the lights you'll be forced to turn me in."

Turn Dazzler over to his ex-wife and Frost? He would rather quit celebrating Christmas.

Ducking his head, he locked eyes with her and nearly lost himself in the kaleidoscope of green flecks in the brown depths.

"Not going to happen. Not now. Not ever."

Dazzler bit her bottom lip. "But the lights..."

His lungs seized, trapping the air inside. How could she think so little of their friendship? Of him? Releasing her hands, he cupped her cheeks. Her eyes fluttered closed then opened again, and she leaned into his touch.

"I know how much the lights mean to Holly. To you."

He shook his head. He had to make her see. He had to tell her about her confession all those years ago. But would it help her or hurt her? There was only one way to find out.

He opened his mouth. Nothing. Shutting it, he groped in his mind for the words.

"Hang the lights."

Deer droppings! That wasn't what he'd planned to say at all.

Nick cleared his throat. "In the limited time Frost and that she-elf have been in town, they haven't endeared themselves to the locals."

Lonnie turned up the collar of her jacket against the cold. "I don't think anyone would hand the *Grinch* over to them."

"Really?" Dazzler blinked then smiled. Her skin glowed, and her eyes literally sparkled. The air around her twinkled.

Todd's knees nearly buckled. When had she become so beautiful? Maybe he had to have a heart-to-heart talk with himself. His feelings at the moment walked the "just friends" line like a newborn reindeer calf. Falling wasn't the issue, but that abrupt splat at the end just might kill him.

Humans and elves didn't mix. He'd already learned that lesson once.

He staggered toward his brother's sleigh. "Come on. Let's see if we can find out what's wrong with the lights."

"Together?" Dazzler trailed after him as if testing the ground to see if it would bear her weight. Reindeer munched on the flowers and spring grass trailing behind her.

"Together." Todd stepped to the side, pausing by the back bench seat. "I'm pretty sure your magic can undo anything they try."

"You want me to use magic?" She paused with her hand on the gilded rail. Hope blazed across her delicate features before she banked the fire.

"Of course." Todd mentally smacked himself. He'd been an idiot to forbid her from using it. Just because magic didn't work on him didn't mean she should deny herself or anyone else.

After all, magic wasn't just something she did; she *was* magic.

"They know you're here anyway. Why not let them see it?" He held out his hand to help her into the sleigh.

Clapping, she bounded into the back then ran her fingers along the red velvet upholstery.

"The first sleigh ride of the season. The only thing that would make this better is to share our trip with Candance while sipping a big mug of cocoa."

"Maybe tonight." If she was still speaking to him.

Nick finished tucking the quilt around his wife then shoved a pile of fleece-lined blankets into Todd's gut.

"Do you think this is wise?"

Reindeer ambled closer. Antlers bobbed as they lipped at the grass. Todd quickly transferred the blankets to the back seat then eyed his brother. One kick, and he would sweep the legs out from under Nick, and he would land on his backside in the mud.

"What? I'll call Cade to finish here. Unless you'd rather the little artist didn't get dirt under his nails."

Nick scratched the side of his nose with his middle finger. "Just because we won't turn Dazzler in doesn't mean she's out of danger."

Deer droppings! Todd stilled. He should have thought of that.

Dazzler patted the empty spot on the seat. "You can drop me off at the house. I'll make cocoa and breakfast while I wait."

His stomach grumbled. Breakfast sounded good, but not if it meant leaving her alone. What if Frost discovered her and whisked her away? Not on his watch.

But he had to get those lights on. "Let me call Cade."

The sleigh's runners dug into the mud when he climbed aboard and flopped down. The seat's springs squeaked. He tugged out his cellphone,

With a snap, Dazzler unfurled the blankets and covered his lap. She scooted against his side and tucked them both in. Her eyes sparkled, and she vibrated with joy. A cranberry cardinal landed on the rail behind her. She rubbed its throat before feeding it a seed she conjured from thin air. With a whistle of thanks, the bird flew away. She tucked her arm through Todd's and laid her head on his shoulder. Sleigh rides were growing on him. Her body heat warmed his side, and he sloughed off part of the blankets.

Climbing into the front, Nick glanced over his shoulder then rolled his eyes at his brother. Lonnie cleared her throat and shook her head once.

What was all that about? Todd squinted at the backs of their heads, hoping to interpret their unspoken language.

Nick tapped the reins against the reindeers' rumps, and the sleigh lurched forward. Mud splashed the frosted ground as it bumped over a rut.

"Oh, my! Is it supposed to be this rough?" Dazzler blinked.

Todd patted her hand. "There's not really enough snow for the sleigh, so Nick's using the training wheels."

The wheels attached to the runners could grind over asphalt—tourists wanted a sleigh ride, snow or not, and the reindeer were bred to pull sleighs. Only the suspension complained.

He thumbed on his cellphone. One missed call. His stomach clenched. His mother. God only knew what she wanted, but this early in the morning, it couldn't be good. He switched to his contacts and selected Cade's number. His brother answered on the second ring.

"What the Hello Kitty is wrong with you?"

Todd held the phone away as his brother inhaled for a rant. He didn't have time for the prima donna's tantrum. Risking his eardrums, he returned the cell to his ear and spoke into the pause.

"The reindeer stalls need to be mucked, and I've got lights to fix."

"I'm not talking about that, and you know it," Cade growled.

Right, and Santa was giving up cookies this Christmas. Mr. Artiste was too good to take care of the family herd. Todd tucked his free arm around Dazzler's shoulders as they turned onto the road.

"Then, what, little brother, are you talking about?" He'd give him enough licorice rope to hang himself.

In the front seat, Nick glared over his shoulder and mouthed, *You're an idiot.*

His wife set her hand against his cheek and turned his head so he faced front. "Let them sort it out."

"Like you don't know," Cade grumbled over the phone. "Already figured I would be up at this ungodly hour to do your dirty work."

In the background, an infant cooed and gurgled. A woman chuckled.

Todd squelched the spurt of jealousy. He and his ex had never had that quiet intimacy. Toward the end, he didn't even think she liked him.

"Oh, look." Dazzler pointed to the petal-pink sky. A meteor blazed a path of light across the horizon. "Make a wish."

She closed her eyes, and her lips moved. Todd tightened his hold and caught a whiff of her floral shampoo.

"Enlighten me, brother."

"I just got off the phone with Mom. She had an early-morning visitor. Seems your ex showed up for coffee. Coffee, mind you." Cade stressed the drink. "Seems the wicked elf of the North Pole doesn't like cocoa. Not even a little."

Todd mentally smacked himself. Last night, Dazzler had discussed the benefits of cocoa as she served his family. He should have known magic would backfire on him. He glanced down. Dazzler's eyes were closed, and her head lolled against his shoulder. A soft snore slipped past her full lips.

He should take a picture of her, complete with sound. She always claimed she never snored, even when both Candance and he lost sleep because of the noise.

"Hey, deer droppings for brains," Cade snapped into the phone. "Are you even listening anymore?"

Todd winced and moved the phone a couple inches away from his ear. "I can hear you. The whole town can hear you."

"Then warn Dazzler. Willa's taken up residence in Mom's front parlor to keep watch on your house."

The sleigh approached the turnoff to town. The reindeer shifted left to make the turn. Todd kicked the bench seat under his brother.

Nick turned around. "What?"

"We can't go home. Willa's at Mom's, staking out my place."

Nick grunted and adjusted the sleigh's trajectory. "Frost?"

Before Todd asked, Cade answered. "I don't know where that elven popsicle is, but I'm sure he's watching, too. Probably from the back yard."

Great. That was just great.

"Don't forget to muck out the stalls." Todd stabbed the end button.

"On to Plan B?" Nick guided the sleigh past the turn. The town formed gray blocks on the right.

"Yeah."

Todd shifted on the seat. Dazzler turned so her breath warmed his neck, and her fingers hooked around the button of his jacket.

Lonnie covered a yawn. "What *is* Plan B?"

"Haven't figured it out yet." But he would. He had to. His daughter wanted Auntie D with them this holiday season. And so did he. Besides, Dazzler was counting on him to keep her safe.

"Don't think I'm going to drive around until you figure out a plan." Nick threw his arm around his wife and kissed her forehead as they skirted the town.

Lonnie hmmed. "We could drop her off at our house."

"No!" Todd barked. His brother lived one town over. Four miles away. Not going to happen.

Dazzler mumbled in her sleep. He combed his fingers through her hair, and she sighed.

"Then, where are we going to stash her?"

"Just drive."

Nick and Lonnie's house was too far away. Todd's ex was at his mother's. Where could he take Dazzler?

Leaning his head against the gilded railing, he stared up. The sway of the sleigh tempted him to sleep. Dazzler curled closer. He could get used to this. His eyes grew heavy. Dawn's pink rays sparkled like diamonds on the power lines running along the streets.

He straightened. Frost crusted the trees and coated the grass along the road.

Maybe he was overthinking this.

Nick steered the two-reindeer team to the side of the street, preparing to turn down the road hugging the south side of town.

"I need a destination, dirt for brains."

Todd ignored him and eased Dazzler against the bench. Rising, he peered into the dawn light. A kitchen window blazed brightly through the trees. He checked his right. The town was still dark.

But someone had power. "Keep going straight."

"Straight? Have you lost your last chestnut?" Nick straightened the team. "The only thing down there is Henderson's house, and there's no way he would help you. He moved to have you run out of town when the lights went out yesterday, remember?"

Todd tore his attention off the icicles strung along the power lines. Ole Henderson wanted him out of town? He shook the thought from his head. Later. He'd deal with the old man later.

"Is something wrong?" Dazzler pressed her hand against his back. After a yawn, she smiled. Magic danced around her like fireflies.

His future unfolded in front of him. Waking up beside this woman every morning. Laughing with her when hard times stretched into endless minutes, while their life sped by in short decades. The vision caused him to nearly double over. He gripped the front seat.

"Todd?" Rising, Dazzler draped her arm around his shoulders and guided him to their seat. Her warmth surrounded him, kindled a fire deep inside his belly. Maybe...

Nick stopped the sleigh. "Is everything all right back there?"

"I know what caused the power outage." Todd pointed to the icicles. The answer was simple. Nature. He should be glad. Instead, it proved magic didn't work for him. No family curse. The lights would never go out in Holly when he found his true love.

So, what did that mean for his and Dazzler's future? Did they even have a future? She was magic. Pure magic. And he was nothing. Maybe that's why they could work. Opposites attracted, right? And he would get to enjoy her magic secondhand. That wouldn't be so bad, would it?

It was practically a family tradition

Nick had married a witch. Another brother lived in the magic town with the gods of Valentine's Day breathing down his neck. A third loved a woman who'd lived as a ghost for a century while the gods of time schemed to control her future.

Marrying an elf would be easy. And this time, they were starting off as friends. His plan could work.

Dazzler's hand rested on his thigh as she leaned forward. "I see lights up ahead."

Best of all, he would help her. If she loved him, she'd get to keep her magic.

"The power lines must've snapped from the weight of the ice." Nick handed Lonnie the reins and unzipped his jacket. "I'll call the power company."

Dazzler cracked her knuckles and wiggled her fingers. Magic caused her broad cheekbones and pointed ears to glow.

"No need for that. I can fix this."

Nick and Lonnie exchanged a glance. Doubt creased Lonnie's features.

"Are you sure?"

Todd ground his teeth. Damn his ex and her lies about Dazzler. She wasn't a disaster. She was amazing.

Her lips turned down, and she hunched against him. "Perhaps not."

Todd nudged her with his shoulder. "You can do this. I know you can. Please. It'll be faster."

Peeking at him from under her lashes, she bit her bottom lip. "I—I'll try."

Lacing his fingers between hers, he squeezed gently. "You'll do it."

Old man Henderson stomped the ground and swung his arms as he paced the side of the road. His path was a furrow of dirty slush. Red patches quilted his chin, cheeks, and nose.

"'Bout time you showed up."

Nick eased the sleigh to a stop across the street from the fallen power lines. The black cables writhed along the frosty ground. Sparks sputtered in their wake.

Todd helped Dazzler out. Old man Henderson squinted at her then harrumphed.

"Guess we need one o' them elves to fix this mess."

Todd shifted in front of her, protecting her from the old man's view. "It's just a downed power line."

The old man pointed a gnarled digit at him, then at the white ground. "Only magic snow doesn't melt with that much heat. You up for the task, missy?"

There was that. "She is."

Nick and Lonnie joined Mr. Henderson. Dazzler stared from the lines on the ground to the ones still attached to the poles. She shifted closer, milking her fingers as she went.

Todd fisted the back of her jacket and pulled her back. Magic or not, no creature could withstand that much juice running through their body.

"Not too close."

Stepping free, she raised her hands. The air twinkled. The cables lifted off the ground, swaying like charmed cobras. The air crackled with power.

The hair on Todd's arms stood up.

The lines rose another foot. Two feet. Three. Sweat beaded her upper lip. Ice snowflaked from her heels and spread across the blacktop. Flurries danced around her dark form.

The cables danced higher. Ten feet. Eleven. Her breathing turned shallow. Her mouth opened. They dropped to ten feet.

"You got this. You can do it." He would lend her his strength. His fingertips brushed her back.

Her magic fizzled. The air hissed like a pipe letting out steam. The lines dropped and sprayed the ground in a shower of sparks.

CHAPTER 13

Dazzler bit back a cry. The cables dropped from her magical grip and whipped the road, sending a fountain of sparks across the frosty street. Her magic was supposed to be fixed, but it was worse than ever.

"It's all right." Todd backed away from her. His gaze took in the street, the surrounding woods, Ole Henderson, and the damaged power lines.

Anywhere but on her.

Her stomach clenched. She'd let him down. She knew how much having the lights on meant to him. Why, oh, why had she involved him in her troubles? She had to fix this.

Pushing up the sleeves of her sweater, she raised her hands. "Let me try again."

Her toes curled in her boots. Weight filled her feet, traveled up her ankles, and tugged on her shins. Her muscles trembled to keep her arms up.

Standing near the sleigh, Lonnie, Nick, and Ole Henderson inhaled sharply.

Ice crackled. Pain speared her right knee. Her right leg threatened to buckle.

"Stop." Todd scuttled forward. "Rest. You're tired. You've been up all night."

He dropped to the ground in front of her.

Her breath made puffs of white around her. When she glanced down, ice encased her feet, ankles, and calves. Cold prickled her flesh. Willa's magic had never affected her before. This must be the work of Sterling Frost.

"Give me a minute." Todd tore at the jagged ice above her knee. It melted at his touch, and water poured through his hands. He paused for a moment then skimmed his fingers down her shin. The ice turned to slush and ran in rivulets before he reached it.

Warmth flooded Dazzler, chasing away the chill. Todd had to have some magic at his disposal to dispel Sterling's spell so quickly. Maybe that's why her magic had worked on him so easily before.

"Neat trick." Nodding his white head at the puddle at her feet, Ole Henderson blew on his clasped hands before tucking them inside his pockets. "But that ain't gonna get the lights on."

Nick rolled his eyes. "Not to mention you two don't want to be standing in that puddle when the water reaches those power lines."

Lonnie dug her elbow into her husband's side. "What he means to say is that he'll call the power company."

Ole Henderson shook his head. "You better have them lights on pronto quick. I don't want the whole town at my house for coffee and a hot shower."

"The bakery has a generator." Todd pushed to his feet. He brushed Dazzler's back before stuffing his hands in his pockets. "I'm sure everyone will go there before bothering you."

Mr. Henderson sniffed. "The Hutchinses were smart, ordering that generator when they learned *you* were gonna be in charge of the lights." The old man shook his head. "Knew it was a mistake the minute someone brought it up."

"That kind of meanness gets someone on Santa's Naughty List." Dazzler stomped out of the puddle and stopped in front of him. "I know Todd will make this the best holiday season Holly's ever seen."

"Not if he doesn't wake up and smell the coffee." Mr. Henderson spun on his heel and stalked away.

Dazzler opened her mouth then shut it. She'd have to talk to him later. No one should take the threat of being on the Naughty List lightly.

Nick cleared his throat. He raised his eyebrows at Todd and jerked his head toward her. She held her breath. Was he encouraging his brother to turn her in?

Todd's face scrunched up. *What?* he mouthed.

"Nothing." Lonnie stepped between the brothers. "Don't you have a call to make?"

"Sure." After fishing his cell out of his pocket, Nick stabbed the screen. His wife stood on tiptoes and kissed his cheek.

"I'll take them to town."

Todd raked his fingers through his hair. He helped Dazzler into the back of the sleigh, tucked the blankets around her legs, then climbed into the front seat. "How about a cuppa coffee until we can figure out a way to smuggle you back home?"

Home? Dazzler stiffened. Was he talking about his home, or hers at the North Pole?

Dazzler sighed as the sleigh wheels bumped over the cobblestones. Garland swayed across the empty streets, casting long serpentine silhouettes in the early-morning light. Dark Christmas bulbs outlined the buildings, and the windows of the houses remained blanketed in shadows. Clenching her hands together, she tucked them between her thighs to keep warm. She should never have come here to fix her magic. At least, then she'd still have her friendship with Todd when the North Pole Review Board took it away.

Now, he didn't care who saw her. She was going back to the North Pole.

He glanced over his shoulder as the sleigh slowed. "We'll let you out here."

"Thank you." She shivered and shook out the blanket before folding it. Taking a deep breath, she screwed up her courage. It wouldn't be so bad. She'd still have her friendship with Candance, and Cheddar would never leave her.

Lonnie looped the reins around the rail then inspected the reindeer. She didn't even look at Dazzler.

Dazzler set her hand on the metal railing. Cold bit into her palm.

Todd covered his hand with hers.

"Dazzler." He squeezed. "The Hutchinses will keep you safe from Willa and Frost. In fact, they might even have a few ideas about how to smuggle you back to the house. Then we'll just have my mother to deal with."

Dazzler blinked. "You want me to stay?"

"It wouldn't be the holidays without you."

He tugged on her hand. She stumbled out of the sleigh but stopped short of colliding with him. He held her hand tight, then cupped her cheek with his free one, turning her face to his.

She refused to lose herself in his eyes.

His thumb swept across her skin. "We'll figure this out."

"Yes." Her breath hitched. He wasn't sending her away. Joy chased away the chill, and her lips tipped into a smile. She glanced down. Yep, her boots still touched the sidewalk. She knew true friendship could withstand anything. "Yes, we will."

Angry voices rumbled from the town's square. Men shouted about the electricity. Women murmured about the darkened displays. Someone predicted the ruin of Thanksgiving a day away.

"It'll be all right." Todd looped his arm around her shoulder, guiding her toward the red-brick bakery.

Dazzler sucked on her bottom lip. She hoped so.

"Please be calm and patient." Mayor Browning's baritone rumbled. "We knew this might happen."

The high-pitched squeak of the former schoolteacher sliced through the crisp air. "We also discussed ejecting Todd Dugan from town."

Kick him out of his home? She couldn't allow that to happen. She'd use her magic to...Ah, who was she kidding? Her magic was unreliable.

She scanned his face. He winked.

"I think Frost and Willa will be asked to leave once the townsfolk hear about the damage to the power lines."

"That makes sense." Her shoulders bowed. But would her cousin and Sterling actually leave? Or would they use their magic to ensure the town tossed her out as well?

"Stop worrying." Releasing her, Todd reached for the handle of the bakery's door. "We'll figure out something once we have food in our bellies."

Painted green vines, scarlet and gold leaves, and orange gourds covered the glass door panel and surrounded the *Closed* sign. A jack o'lantern held a wooden sign declaring pumpkin spice season. In the corner of the pane, a decal of a fluffy white cloud blew a stream of smoke from pursed lips, indicating the approach of peppermint season.

She held her breath. Would the door be locked? Would they be trapped outside, at the mercy of the angry crowd?

"Everything Babette and her husband Fred make is divine, but I recommend the pumpkin scones." He focused on her mouth for a second, then shook himself. "And some warm cocoa to wash it down."

"Cocoa sounds wonderful." She'd drink anything, even coffee.

He tugged open the door.

A bell tinkled overhead. Warm air washed over her. Walking inside, she identified the forms of tables, chairs, and a long glass counter in the darkened room. A single fluorescent light shone on the half-filled metal racks lining the back wall.

Dazzler's nose twitched at the yeasty scent of fresh bread, of pungent cinnamon and sweet vanilla. Her stomach growled.

From the darkened hallway leading deeper into the store, a man's voice boomed, "We're not open yet."

Dazzler turned to leave. Todd shook his head.

"It's Todd. Todd Dugan. I need your help."

Her skin prickled in the silence. Would the bakers refuse him?

"I'll handle it, dear," a woman answered. "Be right there, Todd."

Rubber soles squeaked on the tile seconds before a white rectangle of light cut into the hallway. A voluptuous figure darkened the doorway. She brushed the wall, and three lights flickered on. The corridor blazed, but the store remained in darkness.

"Well, Todd Dugan, I was wondering if we'd see you today." Flour dusted the Rubenesque woman's cheek, and she held a glass carafe in each hand. The dark brew sloshed in the sparkling glass. She paused before a silver industrial-sized coffee urn percolating on the counter, and the carafes scraped metal as she returned them to their warming spot on small hotplates near the sink.

"You see me every day." Todd's fingers skimmed the small of Dazzler's back before they landed on her hip. "Especially if you're still making Babette's famous fall scones."

Babette blushed, and her smile brightened as she gazed at Todd. "Of course, I am. It's not December yet. Unfortunately, you're a bit early. Fifteen minutes early, to be exact. There's nothing wrong with the reindeer herd, is there?"

"No. Cade's offered to feed them this morning." Todd grinned.

Dazzler eased closer to him. She would never understand his delight at teasing his siblings. She'd always wanted a brother or sister. Willa had been the closest she'd ever come.

Babette's attention slipped to her. For a moment, the woman's forehead wrinkled, and she squinted. Dazzler shifted. Obviously, the avoidance spell she'd cast was affecting the baker.

"Harrumph." A petite woman stepped out from behind Babette. Her cap of gray curls trembled, and her pigeon chest swelled under her cranberry tracksuit. "You're not the sharpest crayon in the box to bring your houseguest here. Now that the power's out, everyone in town will be banging on the door for coffee and a pastry." She glanced over the rim of her glasses at Dazzler before pushing them up her nose and trying again.

Dazzler forced a smile. Why didn't Todd introduce her? Didn't he expect the women to forget about her?

"Nick is waiting for the utility company—ice took out the power lines." The words rolled off Todd's tongue as if he'd been practicing them. He paused, then sighed. "Patience Wimmer and Babette Hutchins, meet Dazzler Spitfire. Dazzler, Babette is the best baker in Arizona and Patience the best innkeeper."

Babette's smile dimpled her full cheeks. She wiped her hand on the leaf-patterned apron covering her white uniform then shoved it over the counter. "Dazzler Spitfire. Do all elves have such amazing names?"

Dazzler's skin heated. "My ancestors generated fire. A handy trait when Santa moved our people to the North Pole."

"I'll bet." Patience propped a velour-covered hip against the counter. "Since you're not all pale and wintry, can you still create a fire?"

Waving her hands, Dazzler watched magic glitter around her fingertips. Todd caught one hand, and the sparks faded.

"I don't think we need a fire indoors."

Someone rapped on the window. Dazzler jumped. Humbug! She'd forgotten the townspeople.

Cupping the glass, Lonnie peered in through a yellow painted leaf. She made a drinking motion with her hand then tapped her wrist.

Todd rocked back on his heels. "Can I get two cups of coffee to go. Black. No sugar."

"Of course." Babette shook two paper cups from the sleeve under the counter. They plopped hollowly near the urn. "Do you want your usual to go?"

"Actually, I think we would prefer cocoa." He nodded to Dazzler. "One to go, and one to stay."

Dazzler shook her head. "*I* want cocoa. Please. Todd needs a coffee. Cream and no sugar."

Babette and Patience exchanged a look. The baker sealed the first two cups with white lids and pushed them toward him.

"Take these to your sister-in-law. Oh, and..." She jerked a napkin from the black-and-silver aluminum holder, grabbed two cherry danish from the cooling rack, and handed them to him. "Give this to her, too. She can give one to her husband or eat both of them herself. I'm sure that babe she's carrying will enjoy it."

Balancing the pastry on the lid of one mug, he glanced at Dazzler. "I'll be right back."

She nodded, then yawned.

"Oh, you poor dear." Babette grabbed another cup and filled it from the pot behind her. "Did thoughts of those two elves hunting you keep you up last night?"

"No..." Dazzler's teeth clicked together. She would rather go without eggnog all year than tell about her online search for love.

Patience squeezed in behind the counter. Liver-spotted hands wrapped an apron around her waist then looped the strings twice before tying it off. Autumn leaves in oranges, reds, and yellows decorated the brown fabric. Rising on tiptoe, she retrieved ceramic mugs from the shelf near the coffee pots. "I know the perfect recipe for cocoa."

"She does, too." The folds of Babette's face creased, nearly swallowing her button eyes. She added another mug near Dazzler's. "We're certainly in for a treat."

Patience removed a jug of half-and-half from the fridge. Carefully unscrewing the cap, she sniffed the contents.

Babette glared at her. "Everything in my bakery is fresh."

"Naturally." Patience inclined her head. "Now, Dazzler, Candance sent me an email and asked about a room for your special friend."

She blinked. "My special friend?"

The bell above the door tinkled. Cold air blew around her ankles. By Kringle, she'd forgotten about Dr. Fergus.

"You know—the doctor you think you could be in love with." Patience smiled and sprinkled cinnamon in the bottom of the mugs.

"No! You...You..." Babette sputtered.

"Don't hold the doctor's room just yet." Todd set his hand on Dazzler's back. "Can we use your office, Babette?"

A thin man with a few strands of hair strapped to his pink scalp entered from the hallway. Hearts decorated the oven mitts covering his hands, and steam danced over the tarts cooling in the pan he held.

"Better use the kitchen. Babs has the office stock-full of Christmas bargains. Not even I'm allowed in."

"Thanks."

Todd guided Dazzler down the hall. Patience followed with the half-and-half in hand.

"I'm glad you see reason, Todd. There's no call in looking at outsiders for a match for your elf friend. People in villages like ours are used to magic. And after all, you must have plenty of friends you can set her up with."

Todd's hand tightened on the back of Dazzler's jacket. "Not gonna happen," she heard him mutter.

Her hands fisted at her sides. She knew the love thing was a long shot, but...maybe he had a better idea.

She stepped through a wall of warmth into the kitchen. A pair of brick ovens stood against one wall. Two old-fashioned cast iron stoves bracketed a stainless-steel sink overflowing with silvery bowls and utensils. Muffins, cookies, and sweet breads cooled on racks in the center of the room. Casting a yellow light, two proofing ovens emitted a yeasty smell. Flour dusted a square marble island near an oversized work surface. Beyond a small archway, bags of flour, sacks of sugar, and plastic containers filled metal racks.

A pan clanged. The gas burner lit with a whooshing sound. Patience hummed as she poured milk into a cast iron pan then shaved dark chocolate into it.

"Don't mind me."

Growling, Todd guided Dazzler to the storeroom. "About this love business..."

She set her palm against his chest. The buttons on his coat scratched her skin. "Love is the source of an elf's power. It's a good plan."

Her only one to save her magic.

He opened his mouth. A bell tinkled. He glanced around the cramped room. "Great. No door."

"Where is he?" Mayor Browning barked. "Dugan is always here at this time."

Todd closed his eyes. His lips moved as he counted. "I'll be back."

She followed him halfway across the kitchen then stopped. The mayor might not be alone.

Patience stopped humming. "You two..." The older woman's eyes rounded, and she pointed to Dazzler's leg. "The bakery has a squirrel infestation. I'll have to tell Babette to call an exterminator."

Dazzler's attention dropped to the floor. Pip held two acorns in his hands. Cheddar. Did he have news of Sterling and Willa?

"I'll take care of it." She reached for the creature.

The acorns rose on a swirl of sparkling magic. Empty sacks twirled into balls then lengthened into arms and legs. Others fattened into a torso and head. Mittenlike hands fitted the acorns into sockets for eyes. The stitching design on the bag wiggled then parted. A puff of flour left Cheddar's mouth.

"Sterling Frost is outside."

Waiting for the townspeople to turn her in.

She glanced at the back door. Could she make a run for it?

A spoon clattered to the floor. Patience covered her mouth with her hand. "Oh, my!"

Cheddar shuffled to the innkeeper's side, accompanied by the swish of fabric. Bending, he picked up the spoon and held it out to her.

Patience didn't move. "What...are you?"

"A scarecrow." Cheddar set the spoon on the stove near the pan. His mitten brushed the burner flames. He stared at the curling smoke then blew on it. Red flared and ate at the fabric. Tongues of fire burst from his hand.

CHAPTER 14

*Todd stood with his back to the bakery hallway. Mayor Brown-*ing crowded into his space, his finger drilling the air near Todd's shoulder.

"You know the townsfolk won't put up with Christmas being ruined. You better do something about those lights."

Ignoring the dark town square visible through the bakery's fall-themed windows, Todd fixed his attention on the mayor. Any glance down the hall would betray Dazzler's presence to his best friend. He didn't want Browning's nose in the matter, or him looking at Dazzler. Not until Todd fixed things. Too bad he couldn't figure out what he had done wrong. Or why she would think he would send her back to the North Pole.

Browning snapped his fingers in front of Todd's face. "Are you even listening to me?"

Todd shoved his thoughts aside. One thing at a time.

"You're so far in my face my mouth nearly moves when you're speaking." He retreated a step, creating space. Decking his friend wasn't exactly in the Christmas spirit. "If you want to make sure the lights stay on, kick Frost and my ex-wife outta town. The power lines snapped because of ice. You know we don't get ice this early. It can only come from one source."

Winter elves.

Browning crossed his arms over his chest. "I only have your word that ice is the cause. The whole town knows about the Dugan curse."

Todd rolled his shoulders in his jacket. Old friends sucked when they pushed those buttons. He prodded Browning's shoulder. "Since when isn't my word enough?"

Behind him, Dazzler gasped.

Todd stiffened. His heart thudded in his ears. He couldn't have heard it, and yet he did. How was that possible? More important, had anyone else? He had to check on her, go to her.

Browning's eyes narrowed. He pushed Todd's hand away. "Listen, Todd—"

Todd's cell phone rang. AC/DC's "Thunderstruck" indicated Nick was calling. Perfect. His tin-star brother always did have perfect timing.

Thumbing on his phone, he pushed it into Browning's fancy buttoned-up coat.

"If you don't believe me, listen to my brother. He *is* the sheriff."

Browning fumbled with the phone, nearly dropping it. Spinning on his heel, Todd headed down the hallway. The scrape of hard-rubber heels sounded behind him.

The mayor better not be following. He would hate to have to punch out his friend's lights to protect Dazzler. He caught the baker's eye. Babette shoved a loaded rack across the hallway behind him.

"Mayor, let me get you a cup of coffee."

"And a danish. Fresh from the oven." Beefy Frederick Hutchins lumbered after her into the mayor's path, holding the specified warm cherry danish in his oven mitts.

Tendrils of black smoke wafted into the hall. Todd increased his pace to a jog. Dazzler. He had to reach her. His soles squeaked on the terrazzo as he turned into the kitchen.

Flames danced around the arm of a petite elven-sized figure. "Dazzler," he croaked.

The figure turned. Acorn eyes stared at the blazing arm. "I'm on fire."

"Cheddar?" Todd's brain took a moment to process the scene. The scarecrow was on fire, not Dazzler. That was a good thing, right?

"Cheddar, do stop moving." Dazzler raised her hand. For a moment, the air crackled with magic. A blue glow surrounded the scarecrow's torch-arm, then coated it like a gel. A heartbeat later, the gel exploded in a flurry of butterflies. The swarm circled Cheddar then Todd before disappearing into a cloud of smoke as the scarecrow's arm blazed up again..

Dazzler stamped her foot. "Why is my magic acting up?"

Todd's gut clenched. His lack of magical ability couldn't be affecting her, could it? Nonsense. She was an elf. Magic-born. Nothing he did could affect her.

But he wasn't completely useless. Shrugging off his coat, he wrapped it around Cheddar's flaming arm.

The scarecrow disintegrated on contact.

Todd followed the collection of rags to the ground, swatting and smacking the stray flames. The flour sacks dissolved into white moths that disappeared into smoke. He wiped his forehead.

"What happened?"

Dazzler stepped over him and turned off the burner. "Thank you. I hope Mrs. Wimmer isn't hurt. She was making me cocoa when Cheddar startled her."

Levering up, Todd glanced at the orthopedic shoe near his head. Innkeeper Patience Wimmer lay sprawled across the tile floor, a wooden spoon not far from her hand. He crawled over to check her pulse.

Patience pinned him with a blue-eyed stare before shooing him away. "I'll be fine. Tend to your lady friend."

"I'm unharmed." Pushing up her sleeves, Dazzler held out a hand to help him to his feet. He slid his palm across hers. Such small hands, and yet so capable.

Patience pointed to Dazzler's wrist. "Oh, dear, I think you've burned yourself." She poked Todd's back. "You'd better see to that, young man."

Keeping Dazzler's hand in his, he rotated it slightly to look at the injury. Red formed a heart shape on her pale skin. "It does look like a burn."

She shook her head. "It's nothing. Really."

She jerked on her hand, but he held tight then pulled her closer.

"Let's put some aloe on it."

"It doesn't need aloe." She stood so close. Her eyes locked with his.

The earthy scent of cinnamon teased his senses. His attention dropped to her lips. Soft and supple. He wanted another kiss. And he knew how to get it.

"If you don't want aloe then I'll just have to kiss it and make it feel better."

"Kiss it?" Her chest rose and fell in short waves. "That's what you do with children. I'm not a child."

"No, you're not." And neither were his feelings for her. Pinning her with his gaze, he pressed his lips against the red mark. It was cool to the touch.

Her lips parted. Her pupils dilated. "Oh. Oh, my."

Something fluttered against his lips. He shifted her wrist. The burn mark wiggled and squirmed. One edge of the heart shape lifted up then split into two. The left side joined it. Soon the burn sprang free into a pink butterfly. It circled his head, gaining speed, then dove into Dazzler's chest and disappeared in a burst of sparkles.

She gasped. Her fingers settled over the butterfly's landing spot. They started to glow a soft blue. The color invaded her brown eyes in piercing shards.

"I never expected...I...I..."

"Dazzler?" He cradled her in his arms. Did elves faint? What if something was really wrong with her? Could he call a human doctor?

A woman shouted for him from the bakery floor. He ignored her. The air warmed like a summer day. The scent of roses perfumed the space between them.

Dazzler's eyes fluttered then opened.

In their reflection, he saw himself as her friend. Another blink, and he was a man, just like any other. But the third was something else, something...primal and possessive. No woman had ever looked at him like that before.

She pressed against him, breasts to chest. He held her arm by the wrist, but it was she who trapped him.

The smile started in her eyes then dropped to her mouth. "I love you." A soft laugh slipped between her parted lips. "Not Dr. Fergus. Not anyone else. Just you. I love you."

Her words were magic. He transformed, turned into some-one else—better, stronger, more vulnerable. When would she remember how he'd turned her down, how he'd treated her? Would she hate him then? His legs threatened to buckle. He stumbled back a few steps.

She followed and looped her hands around his neck, a part-ner in this shadow dance. "Don't get me wrong. I've always been fond of you. But you married Willa, and I...I must've bottled it up so as not to stand between you and happiness."

His tongue stuck to the roof of his dry mouth. "I broke your heart."

"Your rejection hurt." She twirled him to the left and backed him into a refrigerator. Her body pressed against his, curves against planes, soft flesh against hard muscle. She bracketed his head with her hands. "But I know how you can make it up to me."

One idea was definitely growing on him, but it involved a soft bed, not a stainless-steel fridge. And both of them naked. He'd even undress first. She'd be a close second. He stroked her hair, allowed the silky locks to slip between his fingers, and inhaled the scent of summer rains wafting from her skin.

"How can I make it up to you?"

Her eyes twinkled. She rose on her toes, sliding her body against his.

His response twitched in his jeans. Friction. He loved it, every blessed inch of it.

She skimmed her mouth over his, soft as a butterfly caress. His body jerked at the teasing. That wouldn't do. Not at all. He gripped her hair, tilting her head just so, and deepened the kiss. His tongue explored her lips, willed her to open them for him.

With a sigh, she did.

He drank her in until there was no him, no her, just them. One. Why had he waited so long for this?

She pulled back for air. Stars twinkled around them.

Someone cleared her throat, soft at first then louder. Todd returned to the kitchen. Jiminy Christmas, how could he have forgotten she was in danger?

He gripped Dazzler's hips, switching their positions so he stood in front of her, blocking her from view.

Candance beamed at him from the doorway. "Mom is waiting in the square, along with everyone else. Uncle Sterling is with her."

Todd grunted. His daughter approved. He doubted his ex would. Frost certainly wouldn't. He smiled.

"If we can keep them preoccupied, Dazzler can go home." He glanced at her over his shoulder. "My home."

There'd be no misunderstanding this time.

Dazzler clapped her hands like an excited child. "Yes. Yes, I'll go home. I can have my cocoa there."

"Cocoa?" Candance shuffled into the kitchen. "I could use some cocoa."

"I'll make it." Dazzler pressed her hands together. Her palms warmed with magic; then a ring pressed into her skin. She widened the gap, yet kept the fingers touching. A cup formed. When her fingertips no longer touched, the rim curled. She handed the cup to Candance then shifted her attention to Todd. "Would you like something, too?"

"I can wait." Todd kissed her cheek, lingering a moment longer than necessary. "Until later."

He hoped she knew he wasn't talking about cocoa.

"Auntie D makes the best cocoa in the North Pole." Candance hurried down the hall in front of him.

Dazzler was the best thing about the North Pole. And she loved him. He hoped it stayed that way. He could face anything with her beside him. Although a bear claw would help. He grabbed a pastry on his way out the door.

Dazzler floated to the door. Love. She was in love. And with Todd Dugan, no less. It all made sense to her now. The two glorious dates they'd enjoyed while she'd pretended to be Willa. The sparks when their hands touched as they both reached for the popcorn at the theater. And that magical kiss goodnight before she'd glided into the apartment where her cousin had slept off her last marshmallow binge.

Why had she blocked it?

Her memories dropped a curtain, stopping further viewing. She shook herself. They would come to her. She just had to be patient.

She touched her lips. The pressure of her fingertips was so different from Todd's mouth on hers. She licked her lips, tasting the frost from outside and him. Heat spiraled through her, and she smiled.

Todd must love her back.

She stopped where the terrazzo grout line edged the hallway. She couldn't go forward without risking being spotted. The quarter-sphere-shaped mirror nestled between the ceiling and wall allowed her to see down the throat of the hall. No one hovered near the offices and restrooms on her left, but people loitered by the door of the bakery—the solid square of the mayor's shoulders, the crooked frame of the town's ancient librarian, and the muscular build of the man who'd wanted her ejected from town when the lights had first gone out.

Dazzler held her breath as Todd and Candance reached them. Memorized the angular line of his jaw, the play of muscles under his flannel shirt, and his sure stride. It was all so familiar, yet she saw it with new eyes. Would he look back? Just to have one last glimpse of her?

Todd speared through the crowd and jerked open the door. The brass bell tinkled. He strode through without glancing back.

She released a shaky breath. Of course, he couldn't look back. He would give away her presence. He was protecting her.

Someone moaned behind her.

Oh, dear. Mrs. Wimmer. She'd forgotten the innkeeper had passed out when Cheddar went up in flames. Spinning on her heel, she rushed across the kitchen.

A muffled squeak accompanied the wiggling bulge under the flour bags and Todd's jacket. The squirrel poked out his head, whiskers twitching. After one more squeak, Pip scampered out holding two slightly charred acorns. He swished his tail then chittered in outrage.

Cheddar's eyes blinked up at her.

Dazzler planted one of her palms on her hip then held out the other to the squirrel. "Don't look at me like that. I knew Cheddar would be well. He *is* magic, after all."

The squirrel huffed then scurried through the kitchen and attached storeroom for the back door. His tail fluffed in outrage. He paused by the metal door and glanced back at her.

"Allright, I'll let you out." She raised her hand. The air twinkled with magic. The hair on her arm stood up. The deadbolt turned. The door popped open. A crisp breeze swept a handful of red leaves inside. "It should be safe for you, provided Cheddar doesn't revert to scarecrow form."

She eyed the innkeeper. "How are you feeling?"

Patience covered her open mouth with a liver-spotted hand. "A living scarecrow. In all my years, I've never seen such a thing. Is it all right?"

"He's fine. Todd saved him. Not that fire can harm him. He's magic." Dazzler held the jacket to her nose. Despite the acrid smoke, she detected pine and sunshine. Todd's scent.

Patience held out a hand and cleared her throat. Dazzler's cheeks heated. Her parents would not be pleased with the lack of respect she'd shown her elders. Folding the coat over her bent arm, she helped the innkeeper to her feet.

Patience smoothed her cranberry tracksuit over her hips while eying the coat. "I'm afraid that coat is ruined."

"I don't know." Running her fingers through the charred fleece, Dazzler liberated bits of ash. Gray soot stained the floor. "I'm sure it's nothing a little magic can't fix."

And since she was in love, her magic would work again.

Patience shuffled to the sink. The heels of her sneakers streaked the ash. "I've never known anyone to be so happy over a ruined coat. Hate the owner, do you?"

"Oh, no! I love him." Dazzler flattened her palm against the blackened lining. Her toes tingled as she pulled magic from the earth. Leaves sprouted from a wedding cake order tacked against a bulletin board. Roots grew from the unground coffee bean on the counter. The ash swirled and danced before lifting off the floor. It fluffed out, like kernels of popcorn before knitting itself into the worn and damaged parts of the jacket. The air thickened with the scent of cinnamon and cloves.

"That looks like Todd Dugan's jacket." Patience pursed her lips, deepening the wrinkles. "I thought you were in love with that doctor fellow who's staying at my place."

"Oh, no. I love Todd Dugan." Dazzler tried out the words. They tasted sweet. Wonderful, even. Everything was wonderful. The range in the kitchen. The gleaming countertops. The frosted glass of the fridge. The whole world.

"'Bout time." Metal scraped metal as Patience removed a pot from the back burner. "Milk is scorched." She splashed the mixture into the deep stainless sink. "I'll have to start again if you still want cocoa."

"Thank you kindly for your offer, but my magic works fine now. Allow me to make *you* a cup for your trouble." Dazzler quickly spun another cup from thin air.

Patience clapped her hands. "Marvelous. Wonderful."

Dazzler turned her hands so the cup balanced on her palm. Dark chocolate bubbled up from the bottom. Steam swirled at the top then condensed into a thick dollop of whipped cream.

"Oooh, I know witches can work magic, but elven magic is very different from their kind." Patience set the pan in the sink and eased the cup from Dazzler's grip. Closing her eyes, she inhaled deeply. "My sister will be so jealous."

Dazzler flexed her fingers, easing the pins and needles from her flesh. The air sparkled. "Shall I make her a cup, too?"

"Don't you dare." Patience snapped then cleared her throat. "I mean, I don't want to tire you out."

"It's not a problem." The spell had been effortless. Proof that she really loved Todd. Not that she doubted it. She just didn't remember being so achy after a casting.

Patience sipped the mug. Her eyes bulged. She sealed her lips against a cough then spit her mouthful into the sink. The air stank of coffee.

Coffee?

Dazzler had made cocoa. Her magic was still acting up. There was something she was missing. "I'm sorry. I—"

"Don't worry, dear." Patience patted her hand. "No one thought this adventure would be easy."

The bell on the bakery's front door jingled. A frigid breeze rushed down the hall and curled into the kitchen.

Goosebumps skittered across Dazzler's wrist. Only one elf could affect her that way. Her attention flew to the back door.

"Welcome, Mr. Frost." Babette's voice boomed down the hall. "We're just about to wheel the coffee and pastries outside, but I see no harm in offering you one now."

"I don't like hot beverages." Sterling Frost words fell like shards of glass. "I know Dazzler is here. And I want her."

Dashing across the kitchen, she threw Todd's coat around her shoulders. She had to leave. Sterling wanted to return her to the North Pole, to keep her under house arrest until the Review Board hearing. She couldn't do that. Not yet. Her magic was still acting up.

Patience set the cup on the counter and retrieved the pan from the sink. After testing the weight, she settled it on her shoulder like a baseballer up at bat.

"I'll hold him off."

CHAPTER 15

Cold wind smacked Todd in the face as he exited the bakery behind Candance. *Frost.* He didn't see the winter elf so much as sense him.

Across the street, Mayor Browning held court at the corner. Nearly swallowed by her parka, the town librarian pointed an arthritic digit at the motionless display of Santa's workshop in the town square. The former high school linebacker flapped muscular arms at the stationary train. The breeze carried away their words. Darkened Christmas displays softly reflected the early sunlight.

Candance popped the lid from the cup of cocoa Dazzler had created. "Good thing lynching would put everyone on the Naughty List."

"The lights will be back on soon." Todd stuffed the last of the bear claw into his mouth, swiped the crumbs off his face with a paper napkin, then tossed it into the gift-wrapped trash can before crossing the street.

Browning shook Todd's phone at the crowd. "Sheriff Dugan just called. The power company has arrived to fix the lines. The power should be restored soon."

The lights in the town square flickered on. Inside the workshop dioramas, tiny elven hammers plinked against wooden toys. An animated Mrs. Claus removed cookies from her oven while Santa rocked in his chair and reviewed the Nice List in his hands. Multicolored lights outlined the brick buildings surrounding the square while glowing candy canes channeled people to the Grecian courthouse and nearby gingerbread gazebo.

The crowd scattered to check the displays their families had set up. Todd shook his head. How many times did he have to tell them magic didn't work on him? Neither did the curse.

Browning's heel tapped impatiently as he waited. After flicking imaginary lint from her snowy robes, Willa stared at Todd. Her gaze narrowed then slipped off him to stick to Candance and soften.

"Willa." Todd jerked his head in a single nod of acknowledgment then turned to the mayor. "Told you Frost had killed the power."

Browning shoved the phone at him. "I'm going home. Try to keep the lights on until I've eaten breakfast." A muscle flexed in the mayor's jaw, but he left without saying another word.

"Sterling Frost dusted Holly with a light coating to give the town a Christmassy feel." Willa crossed her arms. "Nothing more. Certainly not enough ice to cause an outage. I'm sure this is the result of Dazzler's magic. If you turn her over to me—"

"No." Todd shoved the words through his clenched teeth. "Not now. Not ever."

Candance blew on her drink. "Auntie D is family, Mom. We can't turn family in to the North Pole Review Board."

"Oh, for Christmas sake. You're an elf." Willa raised her hand. A swirl of flurries swarmed Candance's drink. The steam above the dark brown liquid disappeared.

"She's also human." Todd glared at his ex. He would not allow his daughter to be ashamed of her parentage. "Why don't you go chill with Frost?"

Willa's mouth dropped open.

"Coffee. I've got nice hot coffee," Babette Hutchins shouted over the squeak of an ungreased wheel. Two silver urns sat on a metal cart. Cups, spoons, cream, and sugar surrounded them.

"Fresh danish and strudel." Fred maneuvered his cart behind his wife's and clacked the metal tongs with his thick fingers.

The remaining townspeople abandoned their displays to rush the bakers.

"I know my daughter is half-human." Willa hissed. "That's not something I can forget."

Candance stared at her cocoa while nimble fingers picked at the paper sleeve. No doubt she wanted to climb in and avoid her fighting parents.

Todd took a deep breath and let it out slowly. Then another. And another. He had to keep his cool.

Leaning closer, Willa wrinkled her nose. "You smell like smoke. Don't tell me Disaster tried to set you on fire."

Candance rolled her eyes. "Her name is Dazzler, Mom."

"There was a small fire in Babette's kitchen, but Dazzler had nothing to do with it." The stupid scarecrow must have forgotten he was combustible.

Todd thumbed through his phone. No message displayed on the screenshot of Candance, Dazzler, and him at the beach last summer. Dazzler looked overdressed in the cover-up he'd bought her. He shifted to put his phone in his coat pocket. His fingers raked his side. No coat. What the Dickens? Oh, yeah— he'd used it to put Cheddar's arm out.

Willa frowned as she watched him. "I know my disastrous cousin's name. You remind me often enough with Auntie D this and Auntie D that."

Todd noticed her glaring at his phone. Could Willa be jealous of Dazzler?

Candance's jaw thrust forward, and she eyed them from behind her fringe of bangs. "I'm going to get some cherry strudel before it's gone."

After one last glare, she fled. The heels of her boots clacked on the asphalt.

Willa raised her hand to cut Todd off before he could speak. "I know what you're going to say."

He tucked his cell into his jeans pocket. Mindreading had never been his ex's strong suit. "What's that?"

"Dazzler's remembered she's in love with you." Ice sprouted from Willa's white heels and radiated outward. "And now you feel obligated to protect her until she snaps out of it."

He rocked back. Had his ex ever said *she* loved him? He couldn't recall a single instance. But Dazzler...she'd told him more than once.

He kind of liked it.

He definitely enjoyed the kissing part.

There was bound to be more that came after. And he wanted it. He wanted *her*.

Willa shifted closer but side-eyed the bakery. "Look, D's getting desperate to keep her powers. She'll try anything, even manipulate her only friend to help her."

Todd stiffened. What was the woman up to now? "I'm sure Dazzler has other friends."

"No." Willa snorted. "She's all alone except for that stupid companion of hers, and he only sticks around because she created him."

Sometimes, he didn't know how he could have ever loved someone so cruel. "I get it. You want Dazzler away from Candance and me. The only way that's gonna happen is if you conjure up a genie, because she's been there for us more than you. And she's been a second mother to our daughter."

The temperature dropped.The ice thickened and crackled under his wife's shoes. He turned his back on her and stomped away. Maybe he could beat Dazzler home.

A frigid wind blasted his back. Snow floated to the ground. In a twinkle of light, Willa materialized in front of him.

"Dazzler is dangerous. She cannot control her magic."

He tried to sidestep her. She mirrored his movements, blocking his path.

"I don't want you or Candance getting hurt."

"Dazzler would never hurt us." Todd set his hands on her shoulders and eased her gently to the side. "She loves us."

Warmth unfurled in his gut. She loved him. And he...

Willa clasped his hand; her nails bit into his skin. "Listen. Please."

He set aside his thoughts. "Five minutes."

"I believe you." She smoothed her snowy hair.

"You believe me?" There was a trap here somewhere.

"Magic doesn't work on you. It never worked on you." She clenched and unclenched her hands before tucking them into the pockets of her cape.

Todd stilled. Finally, someone believed him. So, why did he feel worse?

"I never blamed you because my magic never worked right after we were married." She sighed, her eyes shimmered.

It sure felt like she had.

"What are you saying?"

"I'm saying my cousin believes loving you will fix her magic problems." Willa stared at the sidewalk, stirring the slush with the toe of her shoe. "But your immunity to magic will only make things worse. She'll keep trying, and things will escalate."

"Dazzler would never hurt me." But would loving him hurt *her*?

"Not intentionally." Willa swiped at her cheek. "I know you care for her. I mean, you and Candance spent summers, and school breaks, and long weekends with her for years. You have more pictures of the three of you than you ever had of me."

Todd clamped his lips together. Technology made taking pictures easier than when they were first married.

"Whatever is...broken inside you that can repel magic so strongly will only make my cousin's magic dysfunction worse." Willa sighed.

Broken? He wasn't broken. Besides, magic worked *around* him. "You didn't have any problem magically appearing in front of me."

"That's because I have this." She tugged at the gold chain around her neck. Hanging from the links, an ebony sphere was set into an iron snowflake. Sunlight hit the orb and disappeared.

Todd backed up. His skin prickled, and a lead weight sank deep in his gut. "What is that?"

"A talisman." Ducking her head, she removed the chain. The pendant swung from her fingers. "It'll make sure Dazzler's magic doesn't hurt you or Candance. And..."

She held it out to him.

He didn't reach for the bauble, didn't want anything to do with it.

"And you won't hurt Dazzler." Willa tilted her head. "Look, the Magical Review Board is serious business. If they vote to take her magic, you know it will kill her. The only way she has a chance is to perfect her magic. She can't do that with your problem interfering. I don't want her death on my hands. Do you?"

Todd yanked the pendant out of her hand. "How does it work?"

"Just keep it nearby, and it will neutralize your...whatever so Dazzler can work her magic without interference." She curled his fingers around the talisman, forcing him to hold it.

The cold sphere burned his palm.

"I'll feel much better knowing you have it." She smiled and adjusted his collar. "With your permission, I'll hang a small one near your house and another on your sleigh."

He stuffed the talisman in his pocket. "No need. If I'm the problem, then it should neutralize whatever is broken within me."

Her smiled stiffened. "You can't be too sure, but I understand."

He blinked. His ex was gone, but a fresh layer of ice coated the cobblestones.

Candance bounded over. Cherry pie filling smeared her cheek. "Where'd Mom go?"

"Don't know." And as long as she stayed away from his house, he couldn't care less. He swiped at the red streak, cleaning his daughter's cheek. He should go home. Dazzler was headed there. And he needed to make sure she arrived safely.

Candance dodged his second attempt at cleanup. "Dad."

"You have food on your cheek. Or are you saving that for later?"

Dipping her head, she wiped her face on her coat collar. "Is it gone?"

"Yeah." He hated how grown up she was.

"Good." Raising her cup to her nose, she popped the cover and inhaled deeply. "I hope Auntie D teaches me how to make her cocoa."

She gulped the drink. Her cheeks flushed. Her nose scrunched. Hustling to the grass, she spat out her mouthful.

"What? What's wrong?" He checked her forehead. No fever.

Candance dumped the contents of her cup. Chunks of white dotted the brown grass. Over the scent of cocoa came a wave of curdled milk.

“Auntie D messed up cocoa. Elves never mess up cocoa. Most can make it from the age of two. Dad...” Fear shone in her eyes. “Maybe Auntie D really does need help with her magic.”

Todd brushed the talisman in his pocket. Maybe what she needed was protection from him.

CHAPTER 16

Gravel crunched under Dazzler's feet as she raced down the alley. A calico cat licking its paws near a metal dumpster watched her sprint by. On her left, voices swelled from the row of businesses. She passed a bundled stack of cardboard boxes. A recycle bin. A cranberry-red bicycle. At the end of the alley, Victorian street lamps blinked on. A cheer rose from the town square.

She paused at the end of the block to catch her breath and take stock of her surroundings. No sign of Sterling or Willa.

She fast-walked into the neighborhood. Near the curb of a gray-trimmed bungalow catty-corner from her, a black garbage bag lay split open. Red, orange, and brown leaves swirled into a human shape. Cheddar.

A squirrel darted around her. Puffy tail swishing, Pip placed two acorns into the scarecrow's hands. Cheddar worked his eyes into place then smoothed the black garbage bag into a leather-like jacket, boots, and trousers. Nimble fingers worked a crumpled paper bag into a slouched cap, and snapped a coffee cup lid in half to fix them as his ears.

The squirrel chittered before sniffing the air then dashing away from the main road toward an alley.

"Pip says the way is clear." Cheddar stared at the plastic fork serving as his index finger. "Willa is in the park, and Frost is still in the bakery, but we should take the alley to avoid being seen."

Dazzler dug her fingers into her side, working to ease the pain. "Good."

She followed him to the alley, reaching the entrance just as the squirrel climbed the wooden fence. The skin between her shoulder blades itched. She scanned the neighborhood. No one stirred, but the feeling of being watched didn't fade. Too bad she couldn't open a portal here and walk directly into Todd's house. Of course, with the way her magic was working, she might just end up in the stray letter office at the North Pole.

Why wasn't her magic fixed? She'd found her mate.

Cheddar tilted his head. A light breeze whisked away his left ear. "You look different."

She pressed her palms to her cheeks. Was it that apparent? And if he could tell, then why couldn't her magic?

"I love Todd."

Dipping down, the scarecrow picked up a rock, dusted it off, then worked it into place as a replacement ear. It plopped onto the worn tire tracks in the alley.

"Of course you love Todd. He's your best friend."

Pip leaped from the fence to a sapling. Bare limbs shook as he climbed down and scampered across the open back yard of the next house. Back-porch lights switched off as kitchen lights flickered on. Central heating units hummed to life. Birds chirped in their nests. A few swooped as if to determine whether they should move south for the winter.

A door slammed.

"No. I mean I'm *in* love with Todd." She turned up the collar on her jacket and slouched like Candance. She detected movement from the corner of her eye. A woman in a bathrobe hustled out and picked up the newspaper near the curb. She waved at a couple hustling farther down the sidewalk.

Cheddar flexed his fingers before removing the plastic fork and chucking it into a nearby can. He shuffled one boot through a pile of nearby leaves before selecting a twig. Pursing his lips, he worked it into place.

"That's better."

Pip chirped at them before bounding up a chain link fence. A crow rummaged in dry husks of corn stalks strewn on the ground. Sparrows picked through the stringy remains of a smashed pumpkin.

Poor things. They must be starving.

Dazzler's fingers twitched. The air twinkled; then light zinged toward the birds. Within seconds, pumpkin seeds scattered the ground and an ear of shucked corn lay in front of them. They whistled for joy. She fist-pumped. Yes, her magic *was* coming back.

Pip leaped onto a wooden slat then scaled the last fence. Cheddar worked a mashed pine cone in his head.

"How did you figure out you were in love with Todd?"

She skipped ahead, keeping her eye on Todd's yellow Victorian. "I didn't figure it out. He thought the heart-shaped birthmark on my wrist was a burn and kissed it."

Pushing up her sleeve, she flashed the pale skin inside her wrist. Not even a freckle remained. She raised it to her lips. Her skin tingled, but it wasn't the same. Todd had his own magic. She smiled.

The sweet scent of peppermint thickened the air. Elves had been here. Had Willa and Sterling brought in reinforcements? Dazzler stumbled. Cheddar steadied her with his hand on her arm then paused before the end of the neighbor's wooden fence.

"Pip will check it out."

Balancing carefully along the top of the fence, the squirrel chirped twice, then turned about and flashed his fluffy tail. A dog door swished. Visible through the gaps in the slats, a black shape raced across the yard. The small yappy dog whined softly. Slinking low, it darted across the brown grass and sniffed the air then yipped twice.

A moment passed. Two. Three.

In the yard on the right, an oversized mountain of a dog lumbered out of a playhouse. He stopped at his fence then rose on his hind legs. His nose twitched. The motion rippled down his thick coat. He barked twice, shook his head, then trotted to his favorite tree and hiked a leg.

The yappy dog yipped again. Two more dogs barked, and a cat meowed.

Pip turned to Cheddar and chittered before leaping onto Todd's fence. He tested his weight against a branch from the oak tree in Todd's back yard. The scarecrow fished an acorn from inside his vest and tossed it to the squirrel.

"Whoever was here is now gone."

"Thank you." She moved her hand like she was casting dice. Instead of acorns, snow flurries sprayed the squirrel. Pip squeaked in outrage. The branch swayed under his weight as he raced away from her.

Figgy pudding! Her magic was being temperamental. "Sorry. I'll make sure you have a gigantic store of acorns for the winter."

"I wouldn't do that." Cheddar rose on tiptoes and unlatched the gate. It swung open into Todd's back yard. "Pip is watching his figure. He's courting a certain female two blocks away, and he wants to make sure she likes him before she sees his stash."

"Of course." Thankfully, she didn't have that problem. Todd already loved her. He couldn't kiss her like that if he didn't. "Do you think my magic is just rusty?"

Cheddar eyed the hammock on the porch before stopping near the base of the oak tree. "Maybe *you* don't really love *him*. Maybe you're hiding more memories with magic."

"Don't be ridiculous. Of course I love Todd." Cheddar had clearly used inferior stuffing to form his head. "I may have been sixteen, but I knew love then, and I know it now. Every elf does."

"And Todd loved your cousin Willa. Married her even."

Dazzler crossed her arms over her chest. "Humans can love more than once. It's in their nature."

As for Willa… Dazzler chased a fragment of memory into a blank space.

"Why did you choose to forget?" Cheddar shrank. The pile of leaves at his feet grew.

"Do I have another mark on me?" If she had written some memories on her skin, there might be others. She had to recover the others. Then her magic would work perfectly. She just knew it.

"I think the answer to that question is obvious." He dissolved into a pile of leaves, then bundled himself into the black garbage bag.

Of course, it was. There must be another mark.

She jogged across the dead grass and climbed the porch steps. Once she found that mark, she'd have Todd kiss it. Her attention lingered on the hammock. After she pulled herself together, she intended to spend a lot of time there. A chill ran down her spine. She hoped Todd liked to snuggle.

The screen door opened without a sound. She reached for the inner door's handle. Locked. She let out a puff of breath and a spark of magic. The handle crumbled.

"Gumdrops."

Sterling and Willa would see an unlocked door as an invitation to come inside. As for Todd...

She had to find that mark, or her magic was never going to work right.

With a small push, the door swung open, and she stepped over the threshold. She'd have to find a way to lock the door. A screwdriver. She needed a screwdriver. Todd said anything could be fixed with a screwdriver.

She checked the drawers and cabinets. Nothing. Drat.

Grabbing the broom and dustpan, she returned to the porch. The door handle glittered and sparkled on the latchplate. It was fixed. She shut and locked the door. After returning the broom into the laundry area off the kitchen, she climbed the servant's back staircase to the second floor.

She had to find the next mark.

And get Todd to kiss it.

Her skin warmed. That would be the fun part.

She passed her room and entered the bathroom. Borrowing one of Candance's clips, she gathered her hair in a sloppy bun on top of her head then leaned on the marble top of the double sink, inspecting her neck in the oval mirror. No mark there.

She pulled off her sweater, then her t-shirt and flung them in the corner by the clawfoot tub. Her bra skittered to a stop near the shower stall. She raised her right arm, then the left, and inspected them in the mirror. Not even a suspicious freckle or mole.

Where could it be?

Opening the medicine cabinet, she angled the mirrored door to see her back. She squinted at her reflection. Was there something in the shadow near the small of her back?

She shucked her pants and underwear, kicking them to a spot near the toilet.

No. Maybe. She twisted and turned to get a better look. Just a shadow. Pinching the edge of her socks with her toes, she peeled them off. No mark there, either. She growled. Why was this so hard?

The front door opened and closed. Heavy footsteps made the wooden floor in the foyer creak. Her nails bent as she gripped the medicine cabinet mirror. Was it Sterling? Or Willa? They mustn't find her. Dazzler eyed the linen cabinet. Should she hide, or create a portal?

"Dazzler." Todd's shout echoed up the stairwell and reverberated down the hallway.

Perfect. He could help her look and kiss the mark once he found it.

"In here." She closed the cabinet.

Footsteps caused a board on the landing to groan. The runner in the hall muffled them, but she sensed his approach. Her heart beat faster. She loved him. Oh, how she loved him.

"I just wanted to say—" He drew up short in the doorway. His mouth hung open a little, and he blinked.

"I need your help." She held her arms away from her naked body. "Can you look me over?"

His Adam's apple moved in his throat. "I don't think I could stop." His gaze slid over her.

Her body tightened. Her belly quivered as his attention swept down her neck and shoulders. Her breasts tightened, nipples cinching into hard points. He was touching her without touching her. Her tongue stuck to the roof of her mouth. She forced it to move.

"Do you see another mark? There has to be another one. A reason why I can't remember everything."

"Uh-huh."

Her toes curled into the bathroom mat. Moisture collected in her most intimate place. She crossed her arms, pushing her breasts up. He zeroed in on the tight peaks.

"Are you even looking?" Her voice was breathy, as if she'd been running.

"Yeah, I'm looking." He eased into the bathroom. The space filled with the scent of him—sunshine, coffee, and a crisp fall breeze.

Her thoughts scattered. Reformed. She wanted him to find that mark and kiss it. She wanted him to kiss *her*. She wanted him. Her nails bit into her palms to keep herself from reaching for him. How could he want her if her magic didn't work? She spun around, presenting him with her back.

"And do you see anything?"

"Yeah, I see a lot." He stepped closer, stopping inches from her.

Why was he so far away?

"You do?" She looked over her shoulder.

He nodded. His attention was fixed on her.

Her knees wobbled. She placed a hand on the counter to steady herself. "Will you kiss me?"

He arched an eyebrow. He traced a knuckle down her spine, stopping short of the swell of her bottom.

"Are you sure about this?"

Her lungs sawed for air. She licked her dry lips then nodded. "What shape is it?"

"Beautiful."

He unfurled his hands to flatten his palms against her skin and smoothed the curve of her hips. His lips found her shoulder, then nibbled up her neck. Leaning back, she closed the distance between them. The rough texture of his flannel shirt amplified the softness of his kisses. Moaning, she tilted her head as he sucked on her earlobe then traced the shell to its pointed tip.

"Tell me you love me." He checked her reflection in the mirror. Flushed cheeks, heavy-lidded gaze. Her body responded, but he needed more. He needed her. All of her.

Her sooty lashes parted enough for him to see her brown eyes. "I love you."

He removed the clip from her hair while he watched the play of light in their chestnut depths before spinning her around to face him.

"Always?"

She'd said elves loved only once. Maybe it would be long enough to fix what was broken inside him. She was the only one who could.

"Always." She ran her hands up his chest then undid the top buttons of his shirt. She kissed his throat. "Forever."

He swept her into his arms and carried her down the hallway. "I'll do whatever it takes, be whatever you need me to be, so you can become the elf *you* were meant to be."

"I know." She kissed his jaw. "You love me, too."

He slanted his mouth across hers, drank in the sweetness of her mouth. His body coiled tight. Coming up for air, he turned sideways to fit through his bedroom doorway then kicked the door shut. He lowered her to his king-sized mattress.

Their king-sized mattress.

Her promise of forever stitched together the cracks in his heart. He would never have to say goodbye to her again. Tearing off his clothes, he stretched out beside her. His best friend was about to become something more. He would take it slow, see to her pleasure.

She cupped him in her hands, played with his length. Her strokes became bolder.

He stopped thinking and fell into his senses. The earthy scent of her. The musk of their passion. The spike of fear overwhelmed by the raging tide of her desire.

She ran her nails over his hip and tugged him toward her. "Will you make love to me?"

He rolled on top of her, their bodies fitting together as if made for each other. Pure magic.

"Always."

CHAPTER 17

"Good afternoon, beautiful." Todd's endearment rumbled against Dazzler's ear, and his fingers stroked from her hip down her thigh to her knee.

She snuggled under the blankets and rubbed her cheek against the soft hair on his chest. She could wake up this way every morning and not tire of it.

"What time is it?"

His stomach gurgled. "Time to get up and eat."

She covered her mouth but couldn't suppress the giggle. He swatted her backside through the blanket.

"It's not funny. I've worked up quite an appetite."

Her stomach answered the call of his. Their energy and appetites had always been in sync during their holidays together, just like her parents and all the other elven couples she'd grown up around. Why hadn't she seen the signs before?

Hitching her leg over his, she rolled on top of him then planted her hands beside his ears. Her fingers sunk deep in the down pillow cradling his head.

"You're not the only one. Do you want me to make us something to eat?"

"I don't know. Does your offer entail a visit to the kitchen, or magic?" He smoothed the blanket off her shoulders. His attention slid down her throat and stopped on her breasts. They stood at attention, aching for his touch.

She leaned closer, urging him to kiss them, stroke them, and take them in his mouth. "Magic would be faster."

"And we wouldn't have to leave the bed." He nuzzled her neck while his hands crept around to cup her breasts.

Her eyes fluttered closed; pleasure subsumed her thoughts. Her body tightened. Would he suckle her ear or her nipples next?

He blew a raspberry on her neck.

The vibration scattered the haze of desire. She drew up straight, pulling away from him.

"What was that for?"

He flopped on the pillow. Resting the back of his hand against his forehead, he sighed heavily.

"I picked an elf who can't multitask."

She glared at him, then crossed her arms so they lifted her breasts. His attention shifted to them.

"If you're going to be such a drama queen, I might just tie you to the railroad tracks while a train approaches and I twirl a handlebar mustache."

His lips twitched. "No mustache. I have sensitive skin."

She stared at the ceiling to see if her heart fluttered near the pressed-tin pineapples of the old Victorian. Making love had deepened their friendship, not ruined it.

"But if you're interested in bondage..."

Her tongue stuck to the roof of her mouth. Bondage. Heat washed over her skin. She'd never...The very idea...

"Relax." Sitting up, he wrapped his arms around her and kissed her jaw. "I don't have ropes under the bed."

She exhaled; her shoulders bowed in relief.

"They're in the reindeer barn with my whips and chains." He laughed.

She pushed him back on the mattress. "I'd forgotten how crazy you get when you're hungry."

He laced his fingers together and clasped them behind his head. "What are you gonna do about it?"

"Make lunch." She closed her eyes, shutting out the distraction of him. What should she make? Burger and fries? Her brain zigged to bacon. Todd loved club sandwiches. Perfect. Her skin prickled. The air warmed with the scent of salty bacon and vine-ripened tomatoes. She pictured the plates. The golden brown bread. The—

A frigid peppermint breeze whisked it away. She opened her eyes. Dust motes caught the afternoon sun. No magic residual. No magic at all.

"What's the matter?" He gripped her hips. "You're frowning."

"I can't. I tried but..." Goosebumps pebbled her skin. She shivered from the cold. Rolling off him, she curled into a ball and pulled the blankets to her chin. Her magic was falling away. What would happen to them if it disappeared?

There would be no them. No nothing. At least for her.

"Hey, now." Todd drew her against his side, kissed the top of her head. "I can make food, you know. I'm even willing to make food for you."

A single chuckle escaped her mouth. She caught it in the edge of the blanket in her fist. She loved him. But love hadn't fixed her. There must be something more. Like those memories she'd trapped on her wrist.

Scooting back, she looked at him. "We need to find that other mark."

"I'm willing to look again." He waggled his eyebrows suggestively.

"You've looked four times already." Fatigue pulled on her. She sank deeper into the mattress and yawned.

"I'm not giving up. I know how important it is to you. To us."

"If I can't control my magic..."

He crooked a knuckle under her chin and turned her face to his. "You will. I know you will."

He sounded so sure. And previous experience had shown he was usually right. It was an annoying habit.

Uncurling, she nestled against him and tucked her legs between his. Her body warmed. Everything would be all right with him by her side.

"I'm missing some memories."

"Tell me what you remember." He finger-combed her hair out of her face. "We'll go from there."

She opened and closed her mouth. "I don't know where to start."

"How about where you pretended to be Willa?"

She blinked.

"You knew?" *She* hadn't known, not until he'd kissed the mark on her wrist. Was that why he'd been so cold to her after his divorce? She'd thought he'd been mad at all elves. She had only gone to the custody exchange because Santa had insisted she was the one elf happy enough to undo the damage Willa had done. "When did you...?"

She peered into his cobalt eyes, looking for a hint of anger at her deception. Nothing. He wasn't mad.

"Yesterday. Frost told me." Todd shrugged. "I didn't believe it at first, but then it made sense. The Willa I fell in love with disappeared after the first two dates."

Sterling Frost knew. Willa knew. Her parents. Who else did, and why had no one told *her*? They all claimed they wanted to help her keep her magic, yet none of them had told her about Todd.

"What else did Sterling tell you?"

"He offered that tidbit as proof you couldn't be trusted. Probably wanted me to believe you were using me to keep your magic." Todd's attention shifted to stare beyond her shoulder.

Bile soured her mouth. And he'd believed it, just a little. "I love you."

"I know." His gaze skipped back to her. "You told me the night I proposed to Willa. Your magic worked just fine then."

"Wait a minute. You knew that I loved you, and you didn't tell me?" She raised up on an elbow and poked his chest.

"You were just a kid." He caught her finger and kissed it. "And it wasn't exactly my finest moment."

The memory slammed against her. His apartment in Flagstaff. Candlelight. Rose petals. The setting was perfect for her confession. But he'd turned her down. Flat. Her skin heated at the memory. It hadn't been *her* finest moment, either.

"When I met you in the etherlands to take Candance with me and deliver her to her mother for spring, I was relieved you didn't mention it. Thought it was real mature of you." He tucked her head under his chin.

"Well, that's all right, then." She patted his chest. Although if he had mentioned it, they might have had more than vacations this last sixteen years.

"Maybe it's like amnesia. The memories will come if you don't push them."

She swallowed the lump in her throat. He believed in her. She wouldn't let him down, but she did owe him an explanation.

"I know why I disguised myself as Willa. Do you want to hear it?"

"Sure."

"Willa was in a bad spot." Dazzler stared into the void of her memory, then backed off. Maybe it would come to her later. "I'm not sure why, but she'd been thinking the answer to her problems resided in the bottom of a bag of marshmallows. Her parents were concerned. I was concerned. Since we were as close as sisters then, they thought I might be able to help her."

"I can't believe marshmallows get elves drunk."

She chose to ignore him. Fermented grapes and hops made humans drunk. How silly was that?

"I'd tracked her to a bar near the university campus. It was afternoon. The sun sparkled on the pristine snow. I saw you first. Sitting in the back, wearing green flannel and a ball cap." She rested her chin on her closed fist to stare at him. Her body hummed, just like it had that first time. "You didn't notice me."

She searched his face. Did he remember how special it was, too?

His hold tightened. "Sorry."

She let out the breath she'd been holding. Her coloring made her forgettable in the human world.

"Why would you notice me? I was sixteen. A kid."

Willa was the one everyone noticed. The beautiful one. The one who... Dazzler chased that thought to a dead end.

Todd kissed her forehead. "What happened next?"

"I noticed you watching her." She scraped the words off her tongue. No time to be jealous now.

"I was making sure no one roofied her. I could tell she was drunk. Half the guys in the bar could tell. What I couldn't understand was why she wasn't sobering up with all the hot cocoa she'd drunk."

"I managed to get her into the car with the help of a psyche major, but then I realized I would have to drive us back to her apartment." She should have stuck with what she knew—magic portals. But too many people had noticed Willa. Too many people might look for them. As it was, four guys had followed them outside. Todd had spoken with them, and they'd gone about their business.

"You don't know how to drive a car." His lips quirked.

She pinched him. He knew that now, had even tried to teach her twice on their vacations. Tried and failed. Driving was hard; magic portals were easy. Or had been.

"We don't have cars at the North Pole. But I figured it couldn't be much different than guiding a sleigh."

Todd grunted. "How many sleighs have you driven?"

She shrugged. "One, but that's beside the point." Her magic had repaired the damage she'd done to the sleigh. "It took me a while to work the seatbelts, then I weaved a spell. It must've taken longer than I thought because you were in front of us."

His lips pursed. "And you rear-ended me."

"Not on purpose. You stopped in the middle of the road for no reason." She had no notion people did such things.

"There was a train coming. The barriers were down; the lights were flashing."

He made it sound so obvious. Red twinkling lights and candy-cane poles didn't mean danger at the North Pole. And she'd never seen a train until that day.

"My car crashed through the barrier and stalled on the tracks. I thought I was a goner."

She slid up his body to kiss his jaw. "I did push you to safety and repaired the thing. Plus the damage to your car."

"You did." His eyes locked on hers. "When I got out to inspect the damage, I couldn't believe my eyes. Nearly thought I'd imagined the whole thing."

"And I realized it was you." Dazzler nibbled on her lower lip. "Since you'd been attracted to Willa, I adopted her looks hoping you wouldn't report us if I flirted just a little."

"A little? You asked me out. Said you tapped my bumper to get my attention." His forehead wrinkled. "But you, Dazzler, were sleeping on the passenger seat."

"If I disguised myself as Willa, then Willa had to be me." Dazzler traced her name on his chest. "You were the best-looking thing I had ever seen."

"Past tense?"

She tugged on his chest hair. "Still are."

He grinned. "Good."

"Those two dates were wonderful. Magical." She stared into the past. How could she have forgotten the long walk in the park, the quick stop at a food truck for tacos, or the museum visit, and the debate between modern art and post-modern art over cocoa and muffins? Why would she want to? She pushed against the darkness. It pushed back. She had to find that mark. "You nearly kissed me when you brought me home from the movies."

"I would have, too, if you hadn't yawned."

"It was after two in the morning." She'd gone to sleep with dreams of kisses and forever and had woken up to a nightmare. "Willa woke me the next day. She was nearly incandescent with rage."

Todd flushed. "I may have had something to do with that."

"I don't see how."

"I had met Willa, the real Willa, at the student union. This time I wasn't going to let the opportunity to kiss her slip by, so I grabbed her and planted one on her." He rubbed his jaw. "She smacked me, and I accused her of playing games. She didn't say anything to that, just stormed off."

And rained all over Dazzler's sunny day. "I told her everything. I'm not sure what I expected. Instead of understanding, she called my parents. They were there faster than I could blink, and I was back at the North Pole before I had dressed. Then, my folks had the Review Board lock down my portals. I couldn't return to you."

"She apologized. Said she'd been caught up in finals, that when I'd kissed her, she thought I was a guy she'd just ended things with, and I believed her." He shrugged. "I thought we had something special—her and I. But it was you and I."

"I'm sorry. I didn't know she was seeing anyone until she came back for Christmas. She was happier than I remember seeing her in a long time. And she didn't have a marshmallow hangover." She'd been happy for her cousin. Really. "I was glad until I realized it was you that she wanted. I couldn't let her have you. I knew we had a destiny, and I ripped open a new portal just to see you again. To explain."

"So, you came that day and told me that you loved me." Todd squeezed his eyes closed. "Do you remember how I..."

"Told me that you loved Willa and not me." Dazzler's chest tightened as if someone was squashing her heart. She could have done without that memory.

"Is that where your memory stops?"

"Nearly. I remember Willa dragged me down the stairs where my parents waited. I think we argued, but I don't remember what we said." Dazzler rubbed her temples. Her head ached. "I was stuffed through a portal. The next thing I remember was your wedding. It made me sad, but Cheddar helped me through it. It's odd, isn't it?"

"There's only one thing for it." Todd pulled her on top of him so her knees straddled his hips. "I'm going to have to do another very thorough search."

He pushed down the blankets, baring her to his sight.

"I want you to be happy."

"You make me happy." He threaded his fingers through her hair, tilted her head just so. Rising, he stopped millimeters from her lips. "You have for a long time."

She closed the distance between them. Her lips slanted across hers then met his tongue.

The front door slammed.

She squeaked and rolled off him. She pulled the blankets up to her chin.

"Candance is home. She'll find us together. Do you think she'll be mad?"

"Relax." Todd pulled her close.

Dazzler stiffened in his arms. Easy for him to say. He was the girl's father.

He pinned her to the bed then pushed the hair out of her eyes. "She saw us kissing at the bakery. If she was mad, believe me, she would have let me know in the square."

"She's okay with us?" Dazzler sagged into the mattress. By Kringle, she didn't know what she'd do if Candance didn't approve.

"Are you okay with her and us? In fairytales, stepmothers have a bad reputation."

She pinched his arm. "I'm an elf not a fairy."

He brushed his lips over hers. "In that case, how about we make it official and take Candance out to lunch."

"I'd like that."

"Todd." His mother's voice echoed in the stairwell.

Sighing, he flopped onto the bed. The mattress squeaked. "My mother has the worst timing."

"Stop moving. She might think we're..." Figgy pudding. Candance was one thing, but his mom?

"I wish." He smirked then reached for her. "And since you make wishes come true..."

"That's genies, not elves." Dazzler's cheeks flamed, and she smacked his hands away. "Do you think she'll be mad at me for pretending to be Willa the other night?"

"I'll say it was my idea, provided we can pick up where we left off tonight." He waggled his eyebrows.

She grinned. Her heart fluttered in her mouth. "Of course."

The step at the base of the stairs creaked. "Todd? Are you home?"

"Be down in a minute." After a quick kiss, he rolled out of bed. Muscle and sinew rippled as he stretched. Her tongue stuck to the roof of her mouth at the sight of his naked body.

He winked then shook out his jeans. "Get dressed, but hold that thought."

Pushing out of bed, she rubbed her arms against the chill. She scanned his bedroom for her clothes. Where could they be?

She covered her mouth. The bathroom. She'd left them in the bathroom. No way would she walk naked down the hall with his mother in the house. Hustling to his side of the bed, she scooped up Todd's shirt. Her hand closed around soft flannel.

A spark shocked her hand. She dropped the shirt with the yelp.

Todd's head snapped up. "Are you all right?"

"Static electricity." She shook her fingers then reached again for the shirt. The room swayed. She braced a hand on the footboard of his sleigh bed.

"Your blood sugar must be low." His arm wrapped around her waist, steadying her. "Of course, it serves you right trying to steal my shirt."

She leaned against him, breathed in the musky scent. "My clothes are in the bathroom."

"Ahhh." His cobalt eyes twinkled. "I remember. Still, you should ask. I might let you wear the one I bought in Kauai."

"You already gave it to me."

He squinted at her.

"On the beach." She flattened a palm against his chest and pushed him away. After eying the flannel shirt, she dismissed it. Arizona's dry climate always resulted in a build-up of static electricity. "You said I was getting sunburned in my bikini so you stuffed me in it then put so much sunblock on the rest of me I was Casper-white."

She took a step toward his chest of drawers against the wall. Her stomach bucked, and she stopped until it settled. Definitely needed some food.

"I loaned that shirt to you. It wasn't a gift." He reached for his discarded shirt. His throat bobbed as he swallowed hard. His skin paled under his tan.

"Maybe we should eat sooner rather than later."

"Something light." She opened the top drawer. Neatly folded boxers and nested pairs of socks filled the shallow interior. Goosebumps prickled her skin. Could an illness be the reason her magic was acting up? She selected a pair of wool socks and unrolled them over her bare feet. "Maybe soup and sandwiches."

"Maybe you should get dressed so you stop distracting me." He tossed her a pair of sweatpants with a drawstring waist and then an oversize sweatshirt. The fleece swallowed her smaller frame and surrounded her in warmth and the scent of him. She eyed her reflection in the mirror. She liked it.

Todd held out his hand. "Ready?"

She took a deep breath then let it out slowly. Her palm slid over his calloused one. He interlocked their fingers.

"Don't worry. She'll love you. Just like everyone else who knows you."

Their socked feet slid along the hallway runner. Todd winked at her before touching the metal frame of the photo commemorating their first vacation. Five-year-old Candance showed off her missing front tooth while Disney characters bracketed her and Todd. A spark of light shot between his fingertip and the metal frame.

"Remember to ground yourself often."

He shifted in front of her, leading down the steep, narrow back staircase but kept their hands linked. Humming sounded from the kitchen. Martha Dugan stood on a ladderback chair leaning over the farmer's sink. She licked a suction cup, interrupting the Christmas carol, and stuck it to the window above the sink. The afternoon sunlight blazed on the delicate webbing of the snowflake and highlighted the dark crystal at its heart.

Releasing her, he rushed forward to steady his mother. "Mom, what are you doing?"

"Adding a little festive cheer to the kitchen." Martha stilled the swinging decoration, then climbed off the chair.

Dazzler surveyed the kitchen. Hollyberry-red towels draped the handle of the stainless oven. Gold bows fixed evergreen boughs edging the ceiling. Poinsettias stood sentinel in silver pots by the back door. A crèche filled an emerald placemat on the granite kitchen island. Most homes at the North Pole had fewer decorations.

"I think we decorated enough last night, Mom." Todd lifted the chair in one hand then returned to Dazzler's side. "Mom, this is—"

"Candance's Auntie D." The older woman's attention was a physical blow when it landed on Dazzler. "I believe we met last night, although you looked different."

She resisted the urge to retreat. She'd used magic to fool his mom. "I disguised myself as my cousin Willa. I thought—"

"*We* thought," he interjected.

"We thought we would protect you from any uncomfortable questions."

Martha squinted at her, turned her head, then tilted it left and right.

Crumbled coal. Dazzler had forgotten the avoidance spell. She shook off the magic that would make others look away from her. The prism snowflake glowed then cast black dots on the walls. A wave of nausea roiled through her, and she leaned against the counter for support.

Todd helped her to a barstool on the side of the island. "If you're going to be mad at anyone, Mom, it should be me."

Dazzler wanted to deny it, but she dare not open her mouth.

"Mad?" Martha pressed her fingertips into her plump chest. "Why would I be mad? I *was* a little uncomfortable this morning when the real Willa showed up and I mentioned last night."

"I'm sorry." Bracing an elbow on the counter, Dazzler rested her cheek against her palm. Her skin felt clammy.

"Apology accepted." Martha wrapped a lock of steel-gray hair around the bun at the base of her neck. "Now, I've put the Parker House rolls in your refrigerator to rise for Thanksgiving dinner, but we still need to bring the pies over."

Mother and son exchanged a look. Dazzler's skin prickled with the silent communication.

"Shall I help?"

"You just sit there, child. You don't look well." Martha arched one eyebrow.

Dazzler stifled a smile. Todd used that same expression when he expected someone to comply with his wishes.

He sighed. "I'll fetch the pies after I start warming up the soup."

Martha flicked her bright-yellow apron at him. "Don't bother. I set out a big bowl of chicken and dumplings. You can help yourself when you pick up the pies."

Todd traced Dazzler's spine with his knuckles. "Are you going to be all right?"

She forced a smile. "I'll visit with your mom."

He kissed her temple. "I'll be right back."

"I'll be waiting."

The oak planks creaked as he crossed the hall into the dining room. A moment passed. Two. Martha scrubbed the countertop with the corner of her apron.

The grandfather clock ticked.

Dazzler gripped her hands in her lap. The front door opened. A cold breeze blew into the room. She held her breath, expecting Sterling Frost to materialize.

The door shut. The room temperature rose, but a chill persisted.

Martha crossed her arm. Her lips pursed as if she'd just drunk sour milk. "I want to be very clear. I love my son and would do anything to protect him."

"I love him, too."

"Do you? Or is this just another attempt to save your magic?"

Dazzler flinched. She could see how the other woman might think that. Todd had thought that.

"I've loved him since I was sixteen." She'd bite off her tongue before she told the whole sordid tale to his mom. Todd knew. It was enough.

Martha harrumphed. "You hid it well."

"He wasn't always so keen on elves or magic." Dazzler picked at her cuticle.

"Can't blame him there. Not after the she-elf hurt him."

Dazzler glued her attention to her hands. She shared the blame as well. "I'd never hurt Todd."

"Not intentionally, maybe." Martha glanced over her shoulder. "But with your magic acting up, aren't you putting him in danger?"

"No! I would never—"

Martha held up her hand, stopping Dazzler mid-sentence. "It's obvious from last night you don't have a problem deceiving people."

Dazzler's cheeks burned. "I am sorry about that."

"Look me in the eye and tell me you're not enchanting my son with some spell so you can keep your magic."

She looked up, focused her entire attention on Todd's mother. This one was easy. "I love him."

"Are you sure? Eighteen years is a long time to carry a torch." Martha leaned forward. "How do you know you haven't hidden your love for my son so long it died?"

She shook her head. It couldn't be true. It just couldn't. But wouldn't it explain those missing memories?

"Elves only fall in love once," she whispered.

"That's what your cousin Willa said." Martha poked the countertop to make her point. "Then she told Todd she didn't love him anymore. Maybe most elves only love once, but maybe your cousin isn't one of them. And since you're related by blood, you might share that same bad blood. You might have loved Todd once, but not anymore."

If what Martha said was possible, then Dazzler might have the reason why her magic was broken.

And why it would never be fixed.

CHAPTER 18

Todd's steps echoed as he crossed the porch and raced down the stairs of his house. He eyed his parents' Victorian across the street, the house where he'd grown up. What surprises awaited him there? His mother was being civil. Trouble brewed when his mother was civil. And he had to leave her alone with Dazzler.

A chill spiraled down his body. He shouldn't leave Dazzler alone with his mom, not when she was vulnerable.

Yet, what choice did he have? Dazzler needed help. And he could get it for her.

Rushing across the asphalt, he scanned for signs of ice. None. Too bad it didn't mean his ex and Frost had hightailed it back to the North Pole.

Gravel crunched as he walked up the drive.

"Afternoon, Todd." Mrs. Crumbie, the neighbor, called from her wraparound porch. The old woman glanced at him over her readers as the knitting needles in her hands clicked.

"Mrs. Crumbie." He slowed. Passing the time with her might give him a chance to find out what waited in his parents' house. The windows barely kept the cold out; he should be able to hear his loud family. He glanced at the panes from the corner of his eyes. Nothing stirred. No noise filtered through. But they had to be in there. Waiting. "How are things today?"

"Fine. Just fine. Now that the lights are back on." A long scarf curled like a serpent near her clunky shoes. The knitting needles stopped. "You planning on keeping it that way?"

He swallowed a groan. The town was obsessed with the lights. How many times did he have to tell everyone magic didn't work on him?

"Yes, ma'am."

She looked down. A small smile flattened out the wrinkles around her lips. "That's nice. Although I have to say, I didn't think it would take you this long."

Todd waited a minute. Two. She said nothing more. Great. The town gossip's well had run dry. And this little conversation had gotten him nowhere.

Ducking his head to avoid the Christmas lights, he entered his parents' garden through the wrought iron archway. He rounded the corner, nearly running into the sleigh parked parallel to the back porch. Two reindeer in their traces glanced at him. Dark eyes gleamed under a rack of furry antlers before they nibbled the small patch of grass last night's frost hadn't killed. Lonnie must be visiting. She was just the witch he needed to talk to.

He climbed the steps two at a time. He brushed the hard knot in his shirt pocket. Static electricity stung his fingers. Despite Dazzler's assurances, no way would he trust his ex's talisman unless another magic wielder verified it.

The screen door to the mudroom creaked, but the carved wooden door opened silently. After wiping his boots on the mat, he entered the kitchen.

"Good afternoon."

"Huh." Lonnie slouched at the kitchen table. Elbows planted on the scarred Formica surface, she held her head between her hands. Green tinged her pale skin. She hadn't looked like that when she'd left the bakery.

Then again, she was married to Nick, and his presence always made Todd a little sick, too. He shifted his weight from foot to foot. Maybe now wasn't the best time to bother her.

Nick hurried into the kitchen and draped a throw over his wife's shoulders. Lonnie shrugged it off and glared at her husband.

"Is she all right?" Todd asked him.

"No." Nick crossed his arms. The sheriff's badge on his chest caught the kitchen light.

"Hello? I'm right here." She wrapped her hands around the steaming mug in front of her. "I'm just a little nauseous. It happens when I change my morning routine." She sipped her tea.

"Where's the terror spawn?" Todd stuffed his hands in his pockets. If his folks were willing to watch his niece, then Lonnie would be free to help Dazzler. Provided he got rid of her pain- in-the-rear husband.

Nick jerked his head toward the silent living room beyond the hallway. "She and Dad are taking a nap."

Todd resisted the urge to check. It was too late in the day for an afternoon nap. Besides, his dad snored, and silent kids couldn't be trusted. Still, not his problem if his niece was destroying the parlor. In fact, it might work in his favor if cleaning the mess distracted his mother from Dazzler.

Speaking of his elf...

He shifted the two pumpkin pies on the counter onto a cookie sheet to carry back to his house.

"Lonnie, can I ask a favor?"

She finished her tea. "Is this about Dazzler?"

"Yeah." Todd searched for the words. He helped other people, not the other way around. Leaving the pies, he pulled out a chair, turned it around, and straddled it. But this was for Dazzler.

Nick leaned forward. A glint sparked his eyes, and a smile twisted his lips. One set of knuckles were planted on the table while his free hand rubbed his wife's back. "Don't tell me you've blown it with her already. I mean, the elf *has* put up with you for nearly two decades. Of course, just seeing your ugly mug in the morning could have scared her off."

Todd's hands clenched into fists. His brother was about as bright as a busted light bulb. Dazzler's life was at stake here. "Listen up, knucklehead—"

A thud sounded down the hallway. A childish giggle followed.

Lonnie patted her husband's hand. "I think that's your cue. Keep an eye on your daughter before she draws more dragons on the wall."

Nick's lips thinned. "Call me if you need me. And don't you dare go anywhere with my mentally-stunted brother. He has to earn his happily-ever-after, all by his stupid self."

Backing out of the kitchen, Nick pointed at his eyes with his index and pinky then at Todd. Todd scratched his nose with his middle finger. He'd earned everything he had. He just hoped it was enough to keep Dazzler happy.

Lonnie waited a heartbeat, two. At three, she pushed out of her seat, scratched her swollen stomach, then waddled to the sink and set her mug inside. "Walk me to the sleigh."

He glanced toward the living room. Surely, she could perform magic right from here, couldn't she? "Are you sure you should be leaving?"

"Why is your grandfather covered in sticky notes?" Nick's shout reverberated into the kitchen. A child squealed. "Get back here, you tiny terror!"

The thud of boots on the stairs accompanied Nick's voice. Todd grinned. Karma was only a pain if you were. And Nick was a big pain.

Lonnie chuckled. "I have to finish treating the reindeer. Trust me. It's far easier than dealing with whatever mess my daughter has created."

Todd opened the door then the screen, wedging his body between them so they stayed open. She could very well be his favorite sister-in-law after this.

Drawing level to him, she swayed on her feet then swallowed hard. She shook her head before shuffling across the back porch.

"So, what's wrong with Dazzler?"

"She's fine. Not sick of me." Yet. Cupping Lonnie's elbow, he helped her down the steps. "She loves me. Elves only fall in love once, you know. I'm it for her."

No way would he ask how he got to be so lucky. The universe might change her mind. Or those hidden memories might alter Dazzler's view. Maybe he shouldn't ask for help.

Lonnie eyed him then pursed her lips. "And?"

"Her magic is acting up."

"Isn't that why she's here?" Lonnie heaved herself onto the bench seat, grimaced, then wiggled left then right before draping a blanket around her legs. "Her magic is misbehaving, right?"

"You don't understand." He handed her the reins. "Dazzler's magic isn't working at all." It had mostly worked, until she'd told him she loved him. Until he fell into her arms and decided to stay. Forever. Could it be…?

He shut down the thought.

Lonnie rolled her eyes. "And you think it's because you're immune to magic, right?"

"She's never had problems around me before." Todd examined his memories. Dazzler's nose had scrunched up when she'd tried to conjure them breakfast in bed. The hair on his arms had stood on end. The air around her had twinkled.

But no food had appeared.

"She didn't even magic her clothes on. Just put them on like you or I do. Not like an elf does." She'd always spun around, clapped once, then changed from pajamas to clothes in a shower of sparkles. He'd always enjoyed the show, of course. Now he looked forward to seeing how she undressed.

Lonnie coughed into her mitten before wiping the smile from her face. "I think I get the idea. What do you want me to do?"

Todd bit the inside of his cheek. Magic hated him. But would that extend to Dazzler just because she loved him? She didn't deserve that. She was kind and sweet and always smiling. She deserved better from magic.

From him.

"Maybe you could give her some pointers?"

Lonnie shook her head. "I had to learn magic. Your girlfriend was born magic. And from what your daughter says, Auntie D was working magic from the cradle. What can I teach her?"

Anything. Everything. Loving him couldn't have ruined Dazzler, could it?

"Please."

"I'll try."

"Thank you." Lonnie would show Dazzler how to work her magic. She had to. Because if she couldn't, if he had really broken Dazzler, he had only one option. One neither of them might survive.

With a brittle smile masking the lower half of her face, Dazzler escorted Todd's mother to the front door.

"Thank you so much for inviting me to Thanksgiving dinner."

"Of course, dear." The older woman removed her coat from the hook on the wall and stuffed her arms into it. "After all, you're practically family."

She nodded her white curls toward the gallery of photo collages on the wall under the staircase.

Dazzler eyed the script under each artfully arranged snapshot. Candance's writing changed over time from oversized letters in crayon under gap-toothed photos with the girl and her dad to flowing characters in glittery ink with the three of them crammed into the selfie. Once she hit her teenage years, Candance had taken more photos of her father and Dazzler together, complaining that landscape photos were too boring.

Dazzler scanned the images of her and Todd at Yosemite and the Grand Canyon, of Todd thrusting a cover-all at them at the beach to prevent them from burning, and with his arm around Dazzler on the beach watching the sunset on Martinique.

Practically family. They'd be a real family if she loved Todd. She searched her memory, returning to the moments and warmth captured in Candance's art. She *had* to love Todd.

His mother cleared her throat. Dazzler snapped her attention back to the older woman. It wouldn't do to irritate her, not when she loved Todd.

Martha Dugan stood on the threshold of the open door. Dark clouds gathered on the horizon, and a cold breeze stirred her curls. "Those photos don't do you justice. I'm glad we can now enjoy your presence for the holidays and beyond. My son is a lucky man."

Did that mean she approved? Dazzler blinked.

Mrs. Dugan hustled down the steps and across the yard.

Shutting the door, Dazzler leaned against it. Todd's family accepted her. Really accepted her. Her socks skimmed the wood floor as she floated into the kitchen. The granite counters gleamed. She raised her hands. She'd whip up a banquet, seven courses and...

The snowflake ornament Todd's mother had hung winked in the fading light. A wave of nausea washed over her.

No. Todd was bringing back soup.

Which left her to…

Which left her alone with her thoughts and the gaping holes inside them.

A gust shivered through the tree outside the window above the kitchen sink. The oak's last red leaves spiraled toward the brown grass and the black garbage bag at the base. Pip, the squirrel, peered at her over his bushy tail.

Cheddar!

The scarecrow might know. He had been with her for as long as she could remember. She stomped into her shoes. Leaving the laces untied, she headed out the door.

"Cheddar!"

The bag shifted before opening like a flower bud lifting its face to the afternoon sun. Leaves rolled into spheres and gourd-shapes before forming the scarecrow. He smoothed the plastic over his body, changing it into a leather jacket, jeans, and boots before she'd made it down the stoop.

"Good afternoon."

Milking her fingers, she met him halfway across the yard. He had to know. He had to be the key.

Cheddar adjusted the angle of one pinecone ear. "You look different."

"I love Todd?"

The scarecrow tilted his head. "That sounds more like a question."

Pip scampered down the trunk of the oak tree, scurried across the yard, and sniffed Cheddar's boots.

"I love Todd." The words tasted sweet on her tongue. They had to be true. "But I have holes in my memory. Do you…?"

She couldn't finish the sentence. It felt too much like betrayal.

"You want your memories back." Cheddar avoided her gaze and shuffled toward the porch. The chains squeaked as he sat on the hammock and rocked, staring off into the distance.

He had her memories. He…he couldn't look at her. What was she hiding from herself? By Kringle, it must be bad.

She stumbled up the steps before collapsing onto the hammock next to him. She licked her dry lips. "What is it?"

Pip scrambled up Cheddar's leg and perched on his knee. Dazzler scratched the squirrel under the chin then willed an acorn to form. The air twinkled then dimmed. No acorn. She shook the weight of empty magic from her fingers. Could she be out of magic? How could that be? She loved Todd, and love was the source of all magic.

"I have gotten so used to being here I've almost convinced myself I'm real." Cheddar fished inside his black leather vest and pulled out an acorn for Pip.

She laced her fingers through his stick ones. The twigs were rough against her skin. "You *are* real."

"I am just as real as your birthmark." He turned her hand, exposing the pale skin inside her wrist.

Her chest tightened. She struggled to breathe. This was it. She would know everything. She would fix herself. She could become whole, an elf worthy of Todd's love. Everything was within her reach. She clapped her hands softly. She'd done it!

"What do I have to do?"

CHAPTER 19

Dazzler wiggled on the hammock. The chains rattled in its green metal frame. Excitement coursed through her, chasing away the chill. She dug her nails into the waterproof fabric to keep from pitching forward. This was it. Her memories were within reach, within Cheddar. She must have had cookie crumbs for brains not to realize the scarecrow was the only being she'd trust enough to hold them.

And give them back.

Shifting her thigh onto the hammock, she turned and faced him. "What do I have to do?"

He stared at his twig fingers, as if mesmerized by their curling and uncurling. "Just hold me."

Of course she would have made it easy. Simple. Aside from Todd's embrace, she could think of no better place to be when the memories hit her. She opened her arms wide.

With a ragged sigh, the scarecrow leaned against her, his body stiff.

She wrapped her arms around his broad shoulders, rubbing the cold leather jacket until he softened in her embrace. Inhaling, she filled her lungs with the ripe scent of fall then exhaled softly. Again and again and again. She didn't feel any different. Had she missed a step somewhere?

"When will I know it's working?"

A memory plinked against her brain like a raindrop—the skinned knee she'd earned ice-skating. Another fell, then another and another in a soft rain—being bitten by the bouquet of snapdragons she'd created for her mother, the bump on her head from tobogganing down Sugarplum Mountain.

Odd. Why had she hidden such small things from herself?

"You'll have all your memories when I disappear." Cheddar's twig fingers cupped her shoulder blades.

"When you disappear?" Surely, she hadn't heard right. Straightening, she leaned back.

Moisture collected in the corners of his acorn eyes. "I am made up of your memories. Once they are gone, I will be, too."

"No. No!" She squirmed, trying to break free. The cost was too high. "You're my friend. I would never—"

"I became your friend that day. You had others before me. Although not very good friends. And now you have Todd, and Candance, their family, and the whole town of Holly." He tightened his hold. His shoulders shrank, the leather jacket now hung limply on his frame.

A heavy, dark mass swirled up from her gut and settled like a mantle on her shoulders. She'd had friends once. But then Pepper had laughed when her magic misbehaved. And Pepper had cheered when other names replaced Dazzler's at the top of the magic-weavers' list. One by one, her friends had left the lunch table and joined Pepper's group. Tears stung her eyes. She'd wanted one friend to tell her it would be okay, who would understand.

Just one.

Instead, she'd sat on the hard bench. For months. Alone at a table once crowded with twelve of her besties.

While Pepper held court across the room.

And her cousin Willa never returned her calls.

Cheddar stroked her hair, pushed the locks out of her eyes. Leaves escaped his collar and disappeared in a puff of glitter. "The harder ones won't return to you all at once." His face thinned, turning gaunt then emaciated. Acorn eyes sank until they rested on the shelves of his cheekbones. "You said it might make your head explode."

"Or my heart." More memories trickled in—the birthday celebrations to which no one invited her; the failing marks in school; the wards that kept her out of school parties. Each one linked to the others, like scarves in a magician's trick.

She collapsed against him and hung on tight. His leather jacket turned to plastic, then dried out and flaked away. "How long will you be gone?"

"Forever." His voice cracked. One pinecone ear slid down the side of his head then disappeared in a twinkle of lights.

"Forever?" Her lungs sawed for oxygen. How would she manage without him? "There has to be another way."

"It has to be this way. You'll understand." Twig arms banded her.

Her cheeks burned from the hot tears. A frigid breeze scoured them away. Her scalp tightened. Magic prickled her skin.

"It'll be all right."

His whisper dissolved in the breeze. The branches comprising his skeleton snapped and crumbled.

She pitched forward. Her world tilted and dipped as the hammock swayed. She wrapped her arms around her chest, holding in the emptiness. The air glittered like a snow globe around her. Her hair stood on end, crackling with the excess magic. She felt the tug of pain, the quicksand of loss and sadness.

Memories overlaid Todd's back yard, hurtling her back to her bedroom in her parents' house. The scrolls on her desk, the broken colored pencils and toy designs on drawing paper as she tried to track the cause of her spells' failure, and a gauzy green nightmare floating in her closet.

Her maid-of-honor dress for Willa's and Todd's wedding...

She squeezed her eyes closed, but the memory would not be banished. *A door shut. Footsteps in the hall. Willa's icy laughter.* She'd burrowed under her blankets, flipped her pillow to find a dry spot. Ash stirred in the empty pots in her windows. Shadows danced near the rafters.

A knock on her door.

"Go away." The words left her throat raw.

Willa floated in on a carpet of happy silver twinkles. "Don't mope, D." Her voice remained free of the sickly-sweet stench of marshmallows. "Pepper's agreed to stand up for me at my wedding."

She waved her hand, and the maid-of-honor dress disappeared in a swirl of peppermint.

"Good." But how could Dazzler be happy for her cousin? Willa was marrying Dazzler's one true love. She didn't care what her parents thought. She hadn't picked a human to spite them, nor was this some elfling crush. It was love. The kind that lasted a lifetime. Rolling over, she punched her pillow.

"Don't be like that, D." Willa skipped around the bed and crouched on the floor to be at eye level. "Aren't you the one who said magic obeys a deeper purpose than our will? That great good can come from seeming mistakes."

"I was wrong." So wrong. Dazzler scrubbed her dry cheeks. Her tears had run out an hour ago, but the pain...the pain hammered at her.

"Stop being so selfish." Willa's serene features twisted into an ugly mask. "Todd Dugan is in love with me, not you. I deserve this chance at happiness, and you owe it to me. You know you do, or you wouldn't have pretended to be me in the first place. By Kringle, D, small wonder no one likes you. If you're not the best, then no one else deserves to be, either."

The memory snapped. Dazzler fell into her heartbeats, concentrated on the persistent drum of life. The pain faded to a dull ache.

The gate clattered. Someone had entered Todd's back yard. Dazzler pushed against the hammock and sat up. Sniffling, she wiped the tears from her cheeks then rubbed her eyes. The oak tree came into focus. Pip sat on a branch, staring at her. The air warmed with the earthen spice of a witch's magic.

Lonnie.

She stopped at the bottom of the stoop. A sour undertone tinged the witch's normally earthy smell. She scratched her stomach.

"You look about as bad as I feel. There must be something going around."

The snowflake ornament in the kitchen window cast rainbows around the yard. The squirrel squeaked then darted down the trunk and scrambled through a hole under the fence.

Dazzler's empty stomach clenched. She swallowed bile. "Definitely something going around."

"I could use some help treating the reindeer, and I hear you elves are experts."

Dazzler glanced at the hammock's fluffy pillow. She could choose to curl into a ball until the pain passed, but that hadn't worked so well last time. Maybe this time she would stay busy and deal with the pain. After all, she had Todd now; and with her memories back, her magic was undoubtedly restored. And speaking of Todd, he was supposed to bring them lunch from his mother's house.

"Todd—"

"Knows." Lonnie rubbed her back. "He thought maybe you could use a quiet, out-of-the-way place to practice your magic. Be among family."

Family. Todd was sharing his family with her, and they were welcoming her. She wasn't alone.

She bit her lip as she rose and crossed the back porch. "Let's go."

Dazzler wiped her sweaty palms on her pants as they pulled into the pasture. Reindeer grazed on the browning grass as the afternoon sun flirted with the horizon. Inhaling deeply, she felt the herd's heartbeat and the magical echoes of the corn that would help them fly. She closed her eyes as more memories played inside her head.

Stupid memories. Things that no longer mattered. She'd plucked any unpleasantness from her thoughts, hollowing out space where she only allowed good things. And it had shattered her. Santa hadn't been exaggerating when he said to pull herself together. Everything, good and bad, helped to balance her abilities. Her skin tightened at the surge of power.

A spike of peppermint speared her. She gasped at the pain in her chest. The magic receded, settling to manageable portions.

Lonnie slanted her a glance as she guided the sleigh alongside the lodgepole barn. Winter roses bloomed in her cheeks, in stark contrast to her pale skin. "Are you all right?"

"Yeah. You?"

"I felt better talking to you in the back yard, but on the drive over I started to feel a little sick." The witch held up her hand. "And before you ask, I don't think it's morning sickness, not at this late date."

"Would you like to go back?" Dazzler tensed. No way would she drive the sleigh. Even with her magic, she always crashed them. Her stomach knotted.

"You're not getting out of testing your magic that easily. Besides, I sense a peace about you now." Lonnie looped the reins around the brass rail. "And we're here, so let's do this, and then I can go home and nap."

"A nap sounds good." With Todd next to her and...

Peppermint scented the air, and a twinge centered in Dazzler's chest. Her nose twitched at the familiar cloying scent. Funny. For so long she'd believed all winter elves smelled the same. Now she knew that scent belonged to one in particular. But who? Candy cane bars blocked her access to the memories.

Climbing out of the sleigh, she planted her feet on the soggy ground. Her boots sank in the mud. She frowned. Where was the newly sown grass?

"There's only two reindeer left to treat." Lonnie swallowed hard as if the words were sour eggnog. "Both are yearlings with sprains from trying to fly after too much magic corn."

"A common enough occurrence." The young always wanted to grow up so fast. Dazzler flexed her fingers, and her toes inside her boots. No magic spilled out to create wildflowers. Her magic was under control. First step done. Now to check her casting skills.

"So, you know how to treat them?" Lonnie hooked her arm through Dazzler's and dragged her through the access door inside the barn's bigger one.

"It's the first thing we learn as elflings." And one of the first spells that had gone awry when she'd banished all her painful memories. Without the strength of her pain, she couldn't heal others. Sweat beaded her forehead; her chest tightened. But that was all in the past, right?

"Good. Then we should be out of here in no time." Lonnie released Dazzler's arm and led the way down the aisle between the stalls. The witch seemed to be doing better.

Too bad Dazzler couldn't say the same. The barn reminded her of home, Santa, the North Pole. Of burned and salt-filled cookies. Of sizzling reindeer hair when her magic failed. Lead filled her boots as she walked between the empty stalls. She crushed straw and hay with every step. The sour stench of past failures underscored the sweet scent of the magic corn upstairs. She struggled to breathe. She could do this. She had her memories back. She had her magic back. Everything would be fine.

"In all honesty, if Candance hadn't taken so many pictures of you, I would have believed Todd created you to keep other women at bay." Hinges creaked as Lonnie shoved aside an interior set of doors. Leather and oil perfumed the tack room. The Edison bulbs gilded a cherry-red sleigh waiting for new runners.

"Other women?" Dazzler tripped over her boots. He'd dated others? Could someone do that when they loved someone? And why had he never said? Shouldn't he have said? They'd talked and emailed nearly every day. For years. She'd told him about her outings with Cheddar.

"Nothing serious. And there was never a second date." Lonnie winked. "In fact, I believe blackmail was used to get him to go on those initial blind dates."

"Oh." *That's* all right, then. Mostly. Dazzler rubbed her chest. The ache didn't ease.

"We keep the young ones back here." Lonnie opened a small door and ducked under the jamb.

Dazzler stepped onto the dirt floor, and the door slammed shut behind her. A sense of age surrounded her, and Christmas magic blanketed her. Bare bulbs hung from the low rafters. Eight narrow stalls crammed the interior. She stroked the knots in the nearest pole. Her body hummed the Song of Ages, and she breathed easy.

"This is the original structure." She traced her family crest, burned into the stall door. Her family had once been builders, now they made toys. Not a bad trade but...

She shook off the disquiet. "Elfmade. Probably from when the way station began."

Color bloomed in Lonnie's cheeks. Her shoulders straightened. "Old magic. I can feel it every time I enter. If any place could cure me, this is it. It's one thing to have a hovering husband, and another to have the whole clan trying to take care of you. Judging by the look in Todd's eye, that's something you'll discover yourself. Probably before Christmas. "

Marry Todd. Warmth flooded Dazzler's limbs. And a whole family to look after her. To accept her, no matter what. That would be the best Christmas present.

A wave of glee washed over Dazzler. The murmur of yearling conversation filled her head with static as the two injured reindeer dreamed of pulling the sleigh during Santa's midnight ride. She smiled. Soaring over a wintry landscape was so much better than a dream. She hoped these two experienced it for themselves once they were older.

Lonnie opened the stall door. The hinges squeaked. "These are my patients."

Pain washed away the reindeer glee. Softly whimpering, the two huddled close together. Large brown eyes stared at the witch.

She paused. "I'm afraid they associate me with their accident. Maybe you could...?"

"Of course." Dazzler let out her breath slowly and closed her eyes. This was it. Doubt and fear weighted her. She giftwrapped the thoughts and unearthed memories of Todd—the laugh lines at the corner of his cobalt eyes, the wicked smile before he'd kissed her that afternoon, the gentle caress as he'd washed her back, then other places.

"Oh, my." Lonnie whispered.

Dazzler opened her eyes. She'd done it. No spells. No incantations. Just happy thoughts aimed toward those who needed it.

The reindeer hovered above the ground. Tiny chortles and squeaks gurgled from their throats, and their injuries glowed with red-and-green light. Their bandages fell away, revealing whole and healed limbs. Then, their hooves touched the packed earthen floor.

Her magic was back. Fully back. She was whole. And happy. Everything was going to be all right.

The reindeer stumbled forward, nuzzling Dazzler's hand. She rubbed their heads between their small antlers before they moved on to Lonnie.

"Feeling better, I take it. I guess you can join the others. But no more practice flying." The witch laughed before opening the outside door.

A cold wind snaked inside. Dazzler's limbs shook. She sagged against the side of the stall; nails dug into the pole for support.

"I was afraid they'd end up with a fifth leg or lose their antlers." She shivered at the memories. And the remembered laughter of the other elves.

"And you didn't need me at all." Lonnie dipped her fingers in her pocket and dug out her phone. "I'll let Todd know, so he can stop worrying." She swept her thumb over the screen then frowned. "My phone's dead."

Dazzler tucked her hands into her jacket. Her fingers brushed the lining of Todd's jacket. Empty. "I didn't bring mine."

"I'll use the one in the tackroom." Lonnie scratched her stomach as she walked. "At least, I hope they didn't get rid of the landline."

Dazzler followed her from the stalls. Her steps felt sticky, as if she walked on warm taffy. Her magic faded on pungent notes of peppermint. Exhaustion caused her knees to wobble. She kept hold of the stalls and remained on her feet.

"I think I may have overdone it."

"You can rest in the sleigh on the ride home." Lonnie shoved open the door.

Another blast of cold air slammed into Dazzler. She stumbled back a step and swallowed bile.

"You feel it, too, right?" Lonnie covered her stomach with her hands. "Something isn't—"

Her eyes rolled back, and she collapsed.

Dazzler caught her before she banged her head on the floor then eased her down. Her attention flew around the room. Halters, harnesses, and leads. Jingle bells and leatherworking tools. Spare parts glistened in plastic bins. No phone in sight. Hands shaking, she removed the phone from Lonnie's pocket. Magic prickled her skin, charged the phone. She thumbed it on. It came to life.

Then the battery went from fully charged to dead in a blink.

Dazzler's scalp prickled. She needed to get help for Lonnie. She kicked off her boots and dug her feet into the mud. Pulling magic through the soles of her feet, she enhanced her strength and lifted the unconscious woman. She crossed the tackroom with ease and entered the original barn. The lights dimmed. Her chest tightened. She stumbled to the open door. Cold air stung her cheeks. Ice crusted her toes.

Her magic had a leak.

Had she used it too soon after regaining her memories, or was this malfunction because they weren't all back? Sweat stung her eyes as she glanced down the long building. The sleigh was her only hope.

She mimicked Santa's low whistle. Reindeer heads perked up. Two leaped as if trying to fly, but remained on the ground. Several trotted over, including the two pulling the sleigh.

Dazzler laid the witch on the back seat and tossed the blanket over her. Her own limbs shook, and her lungs labored for oxygen. Sweat soaked her back and pooled under her arms.

Groaning, Lonnie curled around her stomach. "Take me home."

"I will." Dazzler climbed into the sleigh. The cushion dipped under her weight. Nausea roared up her throat. She dry-heaved then crawled closer to the reins. Something sharp stabbed her palm. "What in the world?"

Blood beaded on the fleshy part of her hand, and she sucked it off while groping under the cushion. Her fingers brushed hot metal. Hissing through the pain, she tugged out a metal snowflake and tossed it to the side.

It plinked against the floorboards.

"Why would someone put an ornament there?"

Dazzler bent forward. Her skin prickled. Ice banded her chest. "I'll deal with you once I get home."

A plume of frost-smoke rose from the center of the glowing crystal. The sleigh lurched forward. Reindeer hooves dug into the ground, spraying mud inside. Dazzler slammed against the seat and collapsed against the cushions. The flash of silver caught her eye. She felt the tug of magic, but couldn't move. Todd. She had to get to Todd.

The sleigh took the turn from the pasture to the street on one runner and careened toward town.

CHAPTER 20

Hands on his hips, Todd glanced around the town square. Perfect. Everything was perfect. Not just for the upcoming holiday but for the rest of his life. He inhaled the scent of pine and cinnamon and detected the sweet notes of chocolate and the bitter hint of coffee. His stomach clenched for a moment. Now, if only his sister-in-law helped Dazzler work her magic.

Christmas lights outlined the Grecian courthouse in the center of the square, and the gingerbread gazebo on the right. Twinkling red, green, blue, and yellow lights draped the towering pines. Spotlights shone on Santa and the town's founder, Helga Holly, with her hand on the first pair of reindeer. Families tweaked their animated dioramas depicting the fantastic lives of elves and the Clauses at the North Pole. Laughter drifted on the night.

Mayor Browning slapped Todd's back before offering him a mug of coffee. "Everything is going well."

"No reason why it wouldn't." Todd just hoped his antimagic vibe didn't extend to Dazzler. His fingers brushed the talisman in his pocket before checking his phone. No text message from Lonnie or Dazzler. They'd been gone at least two hours. Was that a good sign or bad?

"What's with the frown?" Browning blew steam off his mug before sipping it. "I thought you and your dark elf had finally realized you were made for each other."

"She loves me." Even after he'd broken her heart. He wouldn't question it. Not when he needed her more than the air he breathed. Todd peered inside his mug. Black, like he preferred. He took a mouthful. Bitterness rolled over his tongue. His stomach bucked. Cheeks bulged as he debated spitting out the poison. What had the Hutchinses done to their famous cup of joe?

The mayor arched a brow. The politician would never let Todd live down spewing the bakers' coffee. By Dickens, they might even withhold their pastry at the insult. He swallowed quickly then opened his mouth to purge the foul taste.

"You deserve a scalded mouth for gulping hot coffee." Browning chuckled. "I only bought it for you because I thought you might be cold standing out here without a jacket or hat."

Todd shrugged and carefully set the mug on one of the tables near the bakers' cart. "It's a warm night."

Browning snorted and adjusted his fur collar against his neck. "You've been hanging out with winter elves too long. This is the coldest Thanksgiving week on record."

"Obviously, someone needs to keep better records." Todd rechecked his phone. Where was she?

Browning sighed heavily. "I guess this means you win the bet. And get to keep your sleigh."

"Never doubted I would." Todd wiped his sweaty palms on his jeans. His heartbeat drummed in his ears, and he labored to breathe. Why was he panicking? His fingers bit into his silent phone. Should he call Dazzler? Cold misted his skin. He couldn't call her if her magic didn't work. She didn't have a cellphone like a normal person.

Rocking back on his heels, Browning tilted his head. "So, where *is* your elf?"

"Tending the herd." Working her magic. He hoped.

Walking to the edge of the square, he peered into the darkness. He could have sworn he'd heard the glide of sleigh runners over cobblestones.

"You got her doing your job." Browning barked a laugh. "Next, is she going to have you making toys and using magic to make your ears pointy?" He reached for the tip of Todd's ear.

Todd batted the hand away. "Magic doesn't work on me."

"Sure, and—"

A shout cut the mayor off. The crowd near the town Christmas tree turned to stare down the road. Horror slackened their features. Hooves clattered against cobblestones.

Fear weighted Todd's limbs, his boots rooted to the spot. Dazzler's cry scratched his ears. He lurched forward, then ran, arms and legs pumping. Faster. Faster. She was going to collide with the tree. His chest heated; his legs burned.

"Who's driving that sleigh?" the librarian shouted and pushed her readers higher on her nose.

"Get out of the way." Todd waved to the crowd to clear a path. His stomach condensed into a hard knot.

They stood transfixed. The air shimmered near the tree. Willa materialized in a flurry of snowflakes.

"Move," Todd shouted.

One by one, the crowd shifted to the side but stayed close to have a first-hand view of the impending disaster. Willa wove a shield spell of shimmering silver to protect them.

Which left Dazzler for him. Todd sprinted on an intercept course. He would jump in, take the reins, avoid the tree, and stop the sleigh. Maybe conjure a little world peace while he was at it.

Dazzler pulled herself up in the driver's seat. Her face was Casper-white under the tangle of dark hair.

He cupped his hands around his mouth. "Take the reins. The reins."

She fumbled along the rail. The reins dissolved in a firework of sparkles. She fell back. The reindeer strained in their traces. Streamers of gold trailed behind them and fizzled out each time their hooves touched the ground.

"Why aren't they flying?" The librarian asked no one. "Shouldn't they be able to fly by now?"

Todd's heart wedged in his throat. The reindeer had flown earlier. In fact, these two were his best flyers. What had changed? Him. He had dared to accept Dazzler's love. Had he broken the reindeer, too?

The traces binding the two reindeer to the sleigh snapped. The animals veered to the left, heading back to their pasture. How was he to stop the sleigh now? There was only one way.

"Use your magic. Magic."

Dazzler raised her hands. Nothing happened. Not even a twinkle. "It's gone."

Gone. Because of him. Todd stumbled. A weight slammed against his side. He collided with the road, solid bone ramming against hard stone. Pain rattled up his body.

The sleigh raced past; the swish of the runners sprayed sparks over him. It slammed into the Christmas tree with a loud bang and the scream of wood.

Silence rang for half a heartbeat.

He rolled onto his belly. Untangled his legs from the mayor's grip.

"Dazzler!" He stumbled forward. Where was she? Why couldn't he see her?

Branches devoured the front half of the sleigh. Splintered wood showered the ground like confetti. Ornaments clinked together before they dropped to the ground in miniature explosions. People covered their heads with their hands but didn't move. The lights on the tree fell dark; then the bulbs popped in bursts of sparkles.

"No. No. No!" Todd tripped over the curb and landed on his knee.

A cascade of failure raced through the park. The candy cane lights lining the sidewalks fizzled and smoked. Displays arced with light then caught fire. Paint bubbled and streaked the backdrops. The figurines shattered; limbs, heads, and torsos rocketed in every direction. The crowd gasped. A child squealed.

The Christmas tree groaned and swayed.

It was going to fall. On Dazzler.

He leaped to his feet. Branches cracked and twisted to the side.

Dazzler held up one hand. A gold shield swirled in front of her. She was doing it. She was working her magic. Yes! There was hope for them.

Todd reached the back of the sleigh.

"Get her out of here." Dazzler's voice cracked.

"Her?" He glanced into the back seat.

Lonnie crawled toward him. "Something isn't right."

And that something was him. This was his fault.

"Hold on. Just hold on." Todd scooped up his pregnant sister-in-law. "I'll be back."

"Don't worry about me." Dazzler's body shook. The shield dissolved in a vortex and drained onto the floor beside her. Her body jerked, and she slammed against the seat back.

"I've got this." Willa set one hand on the front seat then raised the other. Her silver shield sparkled with gold. She hissed through clenched teeth, and the air heated.

He turned. Right. Lonnie first, then Dazzler.

His brother met him before he covered five feet. He jerked his wife from Todd's arms and held her tight to his chest.

"Damn your stubborn hide."

A whoosh sounded behind him. Flames engulfed the Christmas tree. Sap popped like gunfire. A siren wailed. The crowd fell back. A half-dozen citizens raced for the firehouse across the street.

The fire died, and ash drifted on the air. Coughing, Dazzler groped along the seat back and pulled herself up. Tears left trails on her soot-stained cheeks.

"Christmas is ruined."

Willa pulled one hand out of her pocket. Her lips twitched as she smoothed away the gray spotting her white dress.

"Wherever she goes, disaster follows."

Todd's fingers dug into his palms. He wanted to wring his ex-wife's neck. This was his fault. Dazzler's magic started acting up when she met him, fell in love with him.

"Please." Dazzler coughed then reached for his hand. "Once I get my memories in order, I'm sure I can fix this."

The most powerful elf in six generations couldn't weave magic.

He'd broken her.

Because she loved him.

If he touched her, took her hand, he'd never let her go. And it would kill her. His sister-in-law had said it—elves were magic. Pure magic. Without it, she would die.

And he would have killed her.

"Do something." Browning poked his shoulder.

"You better fix this mess," Old man Henderson shouted from the curb.

The townspeople nodded and glared at him.

"Fix it," the librarian shouted.

"Todd?" Dazzler stared at her extended palm then at him.

Pain speared him, splitting open his chest. His heart splintered, piercing his lungs, and he floundered for air.

"You need to leave. Go."

As far away from him as possible. Maybe once she got away from him, her magic would work again. Saving her would kill him, but he'd pay that price. Any price. He turned his back to her.

"But I love you." Dazzler's voice cracked. "And you—"

"Go. I don't want you here. No one wants you here." He moved his right foot. Then his left. Two steps. Three. Four.

The townspeople shuffled out of his way.

It didn't matter. Nothing mattered. He should never have risked it. He should have been content to have her as his friend. He'd ruined everything.

But if she said his name just one more time, he'd run to her. He didn't have the strength to refuse her again. He half-hoped, half-feared she would.

Cold blasted his back. He winced and stumbled but kept going. One foot in front of the other. He'd been right. Her magic would return once she escaped his influence.

Too bad he could never put enough distance between himself and the wreck he'd made of his life.

And hers.

CHAPTER 21

Dazzler struggled to sit up on the bench seat of the sleigh. Ashes swirled through the air like dirty snow. She'd lost Cheddar. She'd lost Todd. She'd lost her magic.

She'd lost everything.

Her empty hand dropped onto her lap. A scrape of a shoe caught her attention. Sweat beaded her lip as she turned her head.

"Now you know what it's like to lose everything." Willa smirked at her before disappearing.

Dazzler sucked in a breath.

Candance burst through the gathered crowd. Her jaw dropped open at sight of the smoldering remains of the town's Christmas display.

"Auntie D?"

Embarrassment prickled Dazzler's skin. "I can explain..."

How she'd ruined Christmas. How she'd ruined everything.

Clamping her lips together, Candance scanned the crowd. A few pointed to the path where Todd walked away from the mess in the town square, from the town, from Dazzler.

"Dad!" Ignoring Dazzler, Candance chased after her father.

Dazzler sagged in her seat. Frigid air washed over her. *Frost.*

"Time to go." He smirked.

Smug jerk. Her skin zinged with a spell to hit him with, but Todd had told her to go. What was the point in fighting anymore?

The air turned incandescent as a bubble of magic surrounded her. She blinked. Todd, Candance, and the town and populace of Holly disappeared. Her stomach cramped as the lodge-pole buildings, gumdrop streetlights, and candy cane picket fences came into view. She was home.

Anger fueled her. She still had a month until the hearing. Anything could happen in a month. A sharp twinge cramped her chest. She pushed thoughts of Todd aside. Her heart would never mend, but maybe, given all she knew, she could fix her magic.

She rose onto her knees and pressed her palms against her prison. The spell was cold and unyielding. Frost towed her down the icy main street, trapped like an exotic animal in a balloon cage.

Doors opened and closed. Elves in evergreen and crimson, sunshine-yellow and ice-blue left their shops to stand in the street. Adults shielded the young elfling's eyes. Teens threw snowballs at her. She flinched as the ice hit her prison and shattered. She kicked at the slushy remnants. Why did they hate her so? Why?

Willa materialized next to Pepper and whispered in her ear. Pepper nodded, sidled left, and spoke to a dumpling elf in purple robes. The purple elf stiffened then turned to the human next to him.

Willa was behind the animosity? The door to the closet holding her memories rattled but didn't yield the reason. Screw the reason. Dazzler pressed against her prison. She had lost Todd.

No one was taking her magic, too.

The Clauses' log cabin overlooked everything from atop a small knoll. Hard-candy swirls lined the sidewalk, and smoke puffed from the stone chimney. Sugar cookies scented the air. Below the Clauses' house, the toy-factory workshops huddled like rectangular shadows. Icicles reflected the colorful lights outlining the eaves and climbing the bell tower. On her right, lights blazed from the lattice windows of the two-story common meeting room.

Frost paused in front of the building. He wrapped the magical tether tighter in his fist before mounting the steps. His icy blue eyes blazed in his pale face.

"If you'd just agreed to marry me, none of this would have happened."

The placard of the North Pole Review Board glittered in the upper windows.

"I don't love you." Dazzler swallowed despite her dry mouth.

A klaxon peeled from the steeple of the toy factory signaling the end of the shift. Snowy winter elves and dark-haired humans filled the street. Many drew up short after spying her bubble prison. Mothers scooped up their children and hustled by, avoiding her eyes. Instead of heading to the cocoa houses, most of the rest lined the street to stare.

She stared back until they looked away. She'd done nothing wrong. Nothing. Her gaze locked with Sterling's.

"I will never love you."

He shrugged. "What does love have to do with it?"

"Everything." She pushed on the magic barrier. It warmed under her touch but didn't move.

"Do you think your human will rescue you? Didn't he tell you to go away?" Frost smirked, flashing sharp incisors. "Is that love?"

Dazzler sank onto her heels, wrapped her arms around her chest to stop it from splitting open. Todd's jacket enveloped her, held off the cold while hollowing her out with his woodsy scent. Todd *had* told her to go away. Was human love so fickle? Or did he love his town and Christmas more than her?

Maybe she was just too different for anyone to love.

The double doors to the communal building opened. Wrinkled elders in jewel-toned robes glided out. Santa ducked under the honey-colored jamb as he followed. His eyes widened at the sight of her.

"Illustrious elders." Sterling placed his hand over his heart and bowed slightly at the waist. "I have retrieved the renegade elf and demand we move up the trial to prove her unfit for magic."

Dazzler inhaled deeply then opened her mouth. No words came out. What was the point in begging for more time? She had nowhere to go. And no one to spend her life with. Without love, her magic would never work properly. Perhaps it was better to get it over with now, rather than later.

Sterling pointed to the stairs. "As you can see, her magic is already starting to affect the integrity of the North Pole. Ice that has stood for centuries is disappearing in seconds. What will happen when it reaches our houses or tears down our wards and exposes us to the rest of the world?"

Water trickled along the cobblestones. Was she responsible for that? She set her hand on her prison wall. The hard surface was now tacky, sticky. Energy flowed through her. She felt the sap moving in the evergreens. The plink of a cardinal's heartbeat.

"She endangered the humans who gave her sanctuary, ruining their Christmas by destroying their displays." Sterling opened his arms wide. "Her very presence is putting Christmas at risk."

The crowd gasped in horror. Many moved away, widening the area around her.

The elders stared impassively. Santa studied Dazzler and stroked his beard.

What did he want from her? She'd put herself together, and her magic was still broken. She glared at Sterling's back.

"No elf is powerful enough to ruin Christmas. Have you so little faith in the holiday?"

Santa's eyes twinkled. Sterling's narrowed.

"You ruined Christmas for Holly, one of our most important way stations."

She glared back. Christmas was still a month away. And it was more than decorations and animated dioramas.

Fabric rustled. The crowd shifted. Her parents pushed through and rushed to stand next to her bubble.

"We need more than a day to organize our daughter's defense," her father protested. His frost-white hair stood up in swirls instead of being neatly combed, and he had cookie crumbs on his tunic. "Everyone knows the penalty of removing magic from an elf."

Death. Her death. Dazzler bit her bottom lip. Death would be easy, just like taking her pain and creating a scarecrow to contain it. So, how could she fight these charges?

Her fingers tingled. Magic glittered in the air. Her magic was returning, but could she control it? She pressed a finger against her prison wall. It poked through. She quickly tugged it free. Maybe...

Sterling turned his back on her father. "No one would ask this price be paid if the risk to all of our kind were not so great."

Fancy words. But it wasn't *his* magic on the line. Dazzler scanned the crowd. No one met her gaze. She turned her attention to the elders. One by one they returned her stare. She felt the tingle of their power.

A crop of goosebumps grew atop her arms. Her insides heated. She unbuttoned Todd's jacket and raised her chin.

The elder closest to the door nodded. "If Santa has no objection, we will convene tomorrow at first light."

She gasped. Dawn was just hours away. Could she be ready by then? Maybe her parents could help.

Instead of looking at her, her parents trembled and held each other. No help there. They didn't believe in her.

Santa stroked his snowy white beard. "Look at me, child."

Dazzler turned her attention to the fat man. Her heart tripped a beat. Santa's blue eyes were warm, but not the same cobalt shade as Todd's.

"Did you complete the task I sent you on?"

A murmur rippled through the crowd. Sterling's mouth opened and closed. Santa had just given her a gift—she hadn't fled like a name on the Naughty list, she'd been on a mission. One she'd completed. All was not lost.

Dazzler nodded then cleared her throat. "Yes, Santa, I did."

She'd found her hidden memories. Too bad the jagged edges of her heart threatened to cut her to ribbons when she should be delighted.

"Good." Santa hooked his thumbs through the black belt holding his red jacket closed. "Let it be known Dazzler Spitfire did not run from the charges, nor did she try to allude Elven justice, but was on a mission. A secret mission commissioned by myself."

The elves glanced at each other. A few glared at Pepper. Willa was nowhere to be seen. Her parents' features slackened in shock.

Dazzler sat up straighter. Santa believed in her. If she believed in him, then she should believe in herself, too.

"I am ready."

"Good. Then I suggest we meet back here tomorrow morning for a magical demonstration by Dazzler." Santa winked at her.

"But—" Sterling protested.

Santa interrupted. "If the demonstration goes as planned, the board's decision will be much easier. Removing an elf's magic is serious business."

Sterling's teeth clicked together when he shut his mouth. His lips compressed into a thin blue line, and red tinged his ears.

"Now, I suggest Mr. and Mrs. Spitfire take their daughter home. I am sure they would like to spend this time together." Santa shooed them off with his hands.

Dazzler's prison dissolved into slush, and she landed on her feet. Her parents rushed to her side but stopped short of touching her.

"Enjoy your last night." Sterling's compressed lips twitched into a smile.

She shook her head. She'd deal with him later. Right now, she had a magic test to prepare for.

"Let's go home." She held out her hands for her parents to take. They trembled while she waited. One heartbeat. Two. Would they reject her, too?

Her father latched onto her first. "Of course, sugar plum. I have several spells I think you could perform to wow the judges."

Her mother looped her arm through Dazzler's. She sniffed, then kissed her cheek. "I cleaned your place just today, so your bedding is fresh."

Her parents seemed to be grieving her loss even though she was still here. And she grieved for Todd, for what should have been. If she survived the test—no, *when*—she survived the test—she would see him again.

"I'll be fine."

She almost believed it.

"Of course." Her dad squeezed her hand.

The villagers waited until they'd walked by before going about their business. Instead of heading down the road to her parents' place, however, they turned off onto the winding path to her cottage on the border of the woods.

Her mother's sniffles broke the silence. "Will Cheddar be joining us?"

Images of him filled her mind. The scarecrow might not be with her physically, but he would never be far from her thoughts.

"He's always with me." She tapped her chest.

Her mother paused on the welcome mat in front of Dazzler's door. She smoothed the dark hair out of Dazzler's eyes.

"Perhaps he can speak on your behalf to the board."

"Perhaps." Dazzler opened her door. The peppermint scent of her mother's magic washed over her. "Would you like to come in for cocoa?"

"Naturally! We have a defense to plan." Her father strode into the sitting room and stopped.

Framed pictures of Dazzler, Todd, and Candance covered nearly every surface. Trinkets of their vacations filled the nooks and crannies of her round cottage. A t-shirt she'd borrowed from Todd lay at the foot of her bed near the door to the tiny bathroom. Boxes covered the granite counters in her kitchenette. Hundreds of boxes of exotic cocoa.

Her mother frowned. "Those were not here when I cleaned up earlier."

No. No, they had been safe in Todd's house. Did he really want nothing more to do with her? Or...?

Hope rioted in her chest.

"Pumpkin spice and cocoa?" Her father wrinkled his nose. "What could humans be thinking to mix good ol' plain cocoa with spices?"

Dazzler rushed forward. On the counter beside the shiny Theobromator, her snow globe lay dark. No message.

She covered her mouth to contain her scream. He really didn't love her.

The air twinkled around her. In a blink of lights, cups appeared on the counters; dark cocoa bubbled from the depths.

They exploded. Shards of ceramic and splatters of cocoa covered everything.

Her mother sobbed.

Her dad patted her shoulder. "Now, sugar plum…"

"Don't. Just don't." Brushing aside his hand, she ran into the bathroom and sealed herself inside. She couldn't even make a simple cup of cocoa. How could she survive tomorrow's demonstration in front of the board?

CHAPTER 22

*Dazzler leaned against the bathroom wall. The silence in-*side her small cottage made the storm of memories all the louder. Stupid little memories of childhood slights and teenage angst overlaid the dance of the red-and-green northern lights outside the round window.

The content of the snippets changed, focusing on one person: Willa.

Swallowing the bile rising in her throat, Dazzler used the door to crawl to her feet. She couldn't take images of Willa and Todd together, not on an empty stomach. Cocoa would make everything better. Cocoa understood.

The memories slowed: Willa at school, daring Dazzler to use her magic on advanced spells. The pain of the magic flood-ing through Dazzler's young limbs, and Willa's laughter. For-bidden transfer spells that left Dazzler curled in a fetal posi-tion while Willa flew on the wings of "borrowed" magic. Willa urging Dazzler to pour all her troubles into an iron cup. The gleam in Willa's blue eyes when Dazzler agreed, and the smack across her face when Dazzler created Cheddar as her reposito-ry.

Had she ever really been friends with her cousin?

Opening the door, she staggered at the rag rug spiraling out from her knotty-wood side table. Parchment crinkled under her feet. Dad's spells. The ones she was to perform tomorrow in front of the Board. She pinched the papers off the floor, holding them between her index finger and thumb.

The warmth of her parents' magic infused the parchment and trickled into her fingers. Tears stung her eyes. They had loaned her their magic to perform spells she now saw were the sort any three- or four-year-old elfling could do. They really didn't have any faith in her.

She tossed the papers onto the crazy quilt covering her bed as she walked by. With a flutter, they landed in a neat stack.

Did she believe she could pass the Board's test?

She paused just outside the kitchen and leaned against the island serving as her table and prep area. Cocoa boxes covered the surface and stood in pillars on the floor nearby. Todd's gifts to her. Thoughtfulness thrown aside to evict her from his life. Her muscles twitched, and she forced herself to breathe. Pushing the packages off and stomping on them would just waste good cocoa.

And wouldn't fix her broken heart.

Turning her back to them, she planted her palms on the granite and hung her head. Her fingertips brushed the Theobromator. She moved her hand back. She would magic up her cocoa. Her stomach growled. Her mouth watered. She imagined the rich chocolate rolling across her tongue. The dark shavings on a cloud of whipped cream.

The air twinkled. A reindeer mug appeared, antlers tipped jauntily toward the ceiling. A fountain of cocoa bubbled at the bottom. Heartbeat by heartbeat the brown liquid approached the rim. She was doing it. She could do it. She rose on her tiptoes.

An icy hand seemed to punch her gut. The cup exploded. Shards of crockery and droplets of liquid sprayed her kitchen.

Slow applause sounded from behind her. Ice spiraled down Dazzler's spine. Her stomach cramped, and bile rose in her throat. She turned just as a wave of nausea hit her.

"Willa."

"Oh, you poor thing. It looks like your magic messed up again." Dressed in pristine white, Willa leaned against the entrance door jamb. Snow swirled around her, and the yellow and blue lights outlining Dazzler's house painted swaths of color on her ivory hair.

Dazzler stiffened. "Why are you here? We aren't friends."

"Aren't we? Don't you tell everyone that we're the best of friends? As close as sisters."

The truth was bitter on Dazzler's tongue. "You don't even like me."

Willa shrugged. "A little friendly sibling rivalry and all that."

"A real sister would have helped me by offering me cocoa and cookies, not urging me to give up my memories." Dazzler froze the image of the iron cup in her head. Those glyphs hadn't been for memories but power. "Or stealing my mate like I owed you."

"So, your memories have returned. I had wondered." Willa entered the cottage and slammed the door after her. "Not that it will do you any good." She ran her hands down her robes. A golden glow emanated from her pockets. "But I'm glad I don't have to spend your last night on Earth explaining why this had to happen to poor old you. Why you had to be humiliated then punished. Why you had to suffer."

"There's more?" Dazzler collapsed against the kitchen island. Let Willa think she was defeated. That was the key to recovering the last bit of her memories.

"I can't believe you've forgotten. You got off too easily. As usual." Willa flicked her wrist. A new reindeer mug materialized on the granite. Instead of cocoa, marshmallows filled the interior.

Dazzler pushed the mug aside. Marshmallows were Willa's treat, and Dazzler needed her wits about her.

Like old movie clips, the last of her memories replayed. Snippets at a time, but enough to form a tale. A tale that began with the death of Willa's true mate.

"Blade."

The name slipped past Dazzler's lips. The smirk slid off Willa's face. Her eyes narrowed, her nostrils flared, and her lips twisted.

"Don't you dare say his name. You killed him. You did it."

Images unrolled within Dazzler's mind. Willa sneaking Blade inside while babysitting her. The couple telling horror stories of powerful ogres stealing elven magic. Odd knocks on the door, growling in the attic, grotesque shadows on the wall. Willa urging Dazzler to pour her magic into a pendant, to keep it safe from the ogres. And a ten-year-old Dazzler, shaking with terror of the monsters at her door, had obeyed.

But there hadn't been monsters. Only Blade's magic, Willa's deceit, and an elf-child's trust.

"You tricked me."

Willa's hands dipped into her glowing pocket. "I did. I did trick you, and stole your powers. And it was wonderful." Her fingers curled into fists. "Amazing. Such power didn't belong to someone as pathetic as you. I should have had it. As the first-born of our generation of the Spitfire clan, I deserved to be the most powerful elf. Not you. Never you."

Dazzler flinched. The transfer of power had drained her, and she'd passed out. When she'd awakened, she'd been alone in the house. But still afraid. Afraid of ogres. She'd gone looking for her babysitter to protect her.

"You two were dancing on the frost smoke over the ice." They'd ignored the Board's warning of thin ice. Willa always knew better. They had invited Dazzler's classmate and friend Pepper to join them but had left her behind.

"You should have slept all night, leaving me alone to have fun with Blade," Willa snapped.

Dazzler remained in the past, reliving the memories. "I called out."

The magic had broken free of the pendant around Willa's neck. The couple plummeted toward the ice. It shattered when they hit, and they disappeared beneath the water.

Her freed magic had returned to her, slamming her back against a tree. She'd hit her head, vaguely heard the screams for help above the buzzing blackness inside her skull. She'd tied her magic to Pepper's, allowing her friend to save one elf. Just one—Willa.

"You blamed me."

"It was your fault. And the town knew it." Willa waved a hand, and the boxes of cocoa turned to ash. "I told them, I told everyone. But your parents didn't believe it. They convinced the elders to cast an integrity spell on Pepper, and she blabbed every-thing.”

Dazzler’s hands curled into fists. Magic blistered her skin. She couldn’t fight her cousin with her magic acting up, not if she wanted to win. Besides, she still had Todd’s gift of the Theobromator. It was enough. For now.

“That’s why you want the Review Board to take my magic.”

To punish Dazzler’s parents.

“The board stole my magic from me and sent me away to that stupid school in Flagstaff.” Willa snagged the mug off the counter and drained it of marshmallows. She dragged the other hand across her mouth before slamming it down. “I could never forget living with those wretched humans. Then you showed up, reminding me of everything that had been taken from me.”

And Dazzler had rear-ended Todd’s vehicle then disguised herself as Willa.

Willa bared her teeth. “But you handed me the best way to get revenge. Since you had stolen my mate, I stole yours.”

Dazzler shook her head. “I wasn’t responsible for Blade’s death.”

“But Todd never loved me,” Willa went on, as if Dazzler hadn’t said anything. “He couldn’t stop thinking about those two stupid dates you shared. Two.” Willa waved her arm again. A fire blazed in the stone fireplace. Her hair crackled with static electricity. “And you didn’t give me your magic like you were supposed to. A fair exchange to stop your suffering.”

Hope flickered in Dazzler’s chest. Todd had never stopped thinking about those dates. He had to care, just a little, didn’t he? And if he cared, then maybe, just maybe, she could find enough magic inside her to convince the board to give her a second chance.

“The only reason Todd isn’t suffering right now is because of Candance. When I became pregnant, the board had no choice but to give me back my powers. And I could finally escape the humans.” Willa’s twisted features smoothed out, and she sighed. Snow buried the flames in the hearth. She smoothed her hair then shook out her robes. “You did have me worried there for a moment. Todd’s loyal to a fault. But you’ve screwed up again and lost. I knew all those years of me telling him he was the reason my elven powers didn't work would eventually pay off. And here you are." She laughed.

Dazzler's skin tightened. Willa was the reason Todd believed magic didn't work on him? Was the man idiotic enough to think he was the reason *Dazzler's* magic didn't work? Yes, of course he was, and her broken magic had aided and abetted the stupidity. The fool had sent her away to protect her. By Kringle, how she loved him.

"Too bad your suffering won't last as long as mine." Willa dipped her hands in her pocket. Silver flashed in her palm before it vanished. "But I do have some compensation."

She disappeared in a firework of glitter.

Dazzler dropped to the floor. She knew everything. But what was she to do about it? Regaining her memories hadn't solved anything. Loving Todd hadn't fixed her...

A tendril of warmth curled inside her. Photographs of the two of them together over the years stared back at her from her walls. Knowing he cared enough to send her away hadn't taken care of her problems, either.

Well, not all her problems.

But he had always believed in her, urged her to help the sick kids, to build a fantasy world. He'd trusted her to teach Candance magic and to watch over his daughter.

She huddled around the vision of the warmth of his smile, the softness of his caress, and the music of his laughter. And she *had* taught Candance. She had watched over her. She had done everything she could because she loved the little girl.

Like she loved Christmas.

Like she loved her parents.

Like she loved helping those kids in the hospital.

Like she loved Todd.

Magic stretched Dazzler's skin. She tapped into the flow of water under ice. The polar bear's heartbeat in its cave. The snores of the reindeer in their barn. She rolled onto her feet then stood up.

Steam swirled above a mug of cocoa sitting on the counter.

"I'll need more than one mug before this problem is solved."

Three more mugs appeared in a swirl of glitter. She glanced around the small cottage. She was alone.

This was her. All her.

Someone scratched at the door. Picking up her mug, she licked the whipped cream then snapped her fingers. The door eased open. Nice and controlled. Her magic was back.

The ornaments she had crafted as a child flew in. Twirling stars, dancing snowflakes, and waddling penguins circled her. She raised her hand, and they brushed her fingertips before forming an inverted vortex in the corner. A Christmas tree materialized by her hearth, ropes of red garland settled on the boughs, and candles marked a spot near each ornament's place. A stocking burst into being and hung itself on the mantle. Red and white berries decorated swags of holly. Gold ribbons finished the look.

The ornaments left the tree, surrounded her, and urged her toward the door. They paused on the threshold. She drained her cocoa, then magicked the other mugs into a Thermos. Following the ornaments, she stepped into the night.

The ornaments cavorted in the air along the path, dipping and swaying. The soft glow of lights appeared through the pines. Instead of entering the town, her guides zagged left and hovered over an empty lot.

A hollow thud sounded under Dazzler's feet. Crouching, she brushed away the powdery snow. Ice-blue letters proclaimed the Frost-Spitfire Tech Center was coming soon. A crack ran the length of the rendering of the crystal cathedral Sterling had envisioned.

Dazzler held the sign up, comparing the drawing to the flat piece of land rolling down to Crystalline Lake. She would never create such a colorless building, and who wanted flying buttresses? Technology was sleek, with clean lines, and vibrant with the palette of nature.

She could see it.

She could imagine it.

She could build it.

She crumpled the board, changing it into a flock of white doves. They swept away the snow, clearing room for the foundation. She sank to the ground. Her heart changed tempo to the pulse of magma deep under the earth's crust, and the fine hairs at her nape stood on end from the charge of the magnetic field.

With a thought, she tapped into the iron ore veins, mixing it with other raw materials until tempered steel vines grew. They thickened and soared high, forming walls three stories high, then bent to create rafters and joists. Like an orchestra conductor, she weaved her hands back and forth, high and low. Metal branches fractured into wisps of filigree delineating poinsettias, holly, and pine boughs on the side walls. Gift-wrapped boxes filled the façade and nestled in curling spools of ribbon and spongey bows.

She looped her hands to the left, creating a bump-out for a break room. Silver outlined a design of oversized mugs and gingerbread men along the walls.

Tapping into an ancient seabed, she dredged up sand and heated it, then poured the liquid onto the metal framework. Fossils shimmered inside the triple panes, and magic painted vibrant colors in a stained-glass mosaic. Fairy lights glowed inside. With a thought, she transported the wood-and-stone workbenches to the new building. Elves didn't need cleanrooms and sterile suits to create tech.

The hum of old magic vibrated inside her. She arranged the spaces just so, allowing the power to harmonize, amplifying the effects.

With the inside finished, she focused on the outside. A flick of her wrist pulled stones from under the permafrost to create sidewalks and patios where workers could enjoy the midnight sun. Peppermint candy lights lined the walks, while gumdrop lights matched those on the streets of the North Pole.

She dropped her hands to her sides and stepped back to admire her work. The building was missing something. She tapped her chin, then smiled. A glass-and-metal spire formed an icy Christmas tree at the apex of the roof. Ribbons of metal formed script over the front doors: *Spitfire-Dugan Annex: Sharing dreams with the world.*

Sterling Frost could suck sour eggnog.

Rising, she dusted her hands on her pants. She had another Christmas to fix.

She flicked her wrist, opening a portal. The elders' magic lashed out at her, trying to bind her to the North Pole. She sliced through the wards. She wasn't running. She would face the Board in a few hours.

She would defend her magic and save her life.

And she would win.

CHAPTER 23

Todd stared at his blaring alarm clock. Three-thirty-two in the morning. He yanked the blankets up to his neck. He'd gotten a whole two minutes of sleep. Just what he deserved. His tongue stuck to the furry roof of his mouth. Seven cups of coffee and half a bottle of bourbon were a poor sedative substitute for eggnog and brandy.

His stomach bucked at the thought of eggs.

Shoving aside his blankets, he stabbed the alarm button on his cell phone. Silence caused his eyes to ping-pong in their sockets. He squeezed them closed for a second and rolled into a sitting position. The room settled on an even keel. Bracing for the cold, he set his feet on the wood floor.

Nothing.

He raked his fingers through his hair. Why had he expected to feel anything? His heart was with Dazzler.

And it wasn't coming back.

Plucking his jeans off the floor, he sniffed them. Clean enough. Stepping into them, he buttoned the fly while padding down the runner in the hall. His footsteps slowed by Dazzler's room.

Keep moving. Don't stop. His traitorous body opened the door. The scent of sunshine and sugar cookies surrounded him. Dazzler. His knees buckled, and he grabbed the door jamb to remain on his feet. Pain filled his hollowed-out chest.

Sending her away had been the right thing—the *only* thing —he could do. So why did he feel like he'd just received a sack of coal at Christmas?

Holding his breath, he eased the door closed. He tromped down the stairs, avoiding the second step and its creak. No sense in waking everyone else and ruining their Thanksgiving.

He snorted. The townspeople's displays were charred rubble, the Christmas tree a stick with a skirt of ashes. He flicked the switch by the front door. And no electricity. Thanksgiving was definitely already ruined.

But maybe if he worked hard, he could salvage something for the visitors seeking a town devoted to Christmas.

He stepped into his boots, tied the laces, then slammed into his coat and threw open the door. His shoulders sagged. Not even a speck of frost to cover up the carnage. Easing the door closed, he crossed the porch and rushed down the stoop. Dead grass crunched underfoot. A breeze moaned through the bare branches of dark trees and tumbled a paper cup and napkins down the empty street.

The atmosphere would be just right for Halloween. Too bad it was Thanksgiving. The eve of the Christmas season. A season he'd ruined because magic didn't work around him. Why had he thought he could make this the best holiday season yet?

"Why are you slowing? We got work to do." Candance jogged to his side, a Thermos tucked under her arm and a steaming plastic cup in her hand. "I made coffee."

She shook the metal container.

He yawned and scraped a hand down his face. Coffee was human magic. At least that worked on him. He held out his hand for the Thermos.

"You don't have to help, you know."

She offered him the cup. "This is partially my fault."

Shaking his head, he sipped the coffee. The tastes of sugar and creamer hit his back molars, but he downed the contents. Caffeine slogged through his veins.

"It's my fault." He was a magic repeller. "Only me, sweetpea. Why don't you go back to bed? I'm sure your grandmother will be calling in a few hours to ask for help preparing Thanksgiving dinner."

Candance hooked her hand through his arm and dragged him toward the town square. "I don't think this is the Thanksgiving any of us pictured. But we'll make the best of it. We always do."

They reached the end of the street without saying another word. At the corner, they turned right. Two more blocks and another turn before they could see the destruction. Todd hoped it wasn't as bad as he remembered.

"We might be able to salvage strings of lights from the dioramas to hang from the trees and outline the courthouse and gazebo. Then we'll return home and collect the displays in our yard and ask others to donate what they can."

"Christmas isn't about the decorations, you know." She rested her head against his shoulder. White highlights streaked her brown hair.

Smiling, he kissed his daughter's head. "I know. It's about being with the ones you love."

And he loved his town.

His family.

His daughter.

But all the fancy lights and decorations wouldn't distract him from Dazzler's absence. Or erase the fact that, for one brief moment, he'd almost had it all.

"I'm sorry, Dad."

"Don't be." His baby girl was all grown up. Soon she'd head off for her career at the North Pole, and he would be alone. Perhaps he deserved it.

She bit her bottom lip. "I truly believed magic was for everyone. That you just had a hang-up because of your divorce from Mom."

"I'm just thankful I never affected your ability to perform magic."

"Yeah. It doesn't make sense, does it?" She scrunched up her face, looking more like Dazzler than she did her mother, Willa.

Todd looked away and turned onto Main Street. He stopped. Candance tugged on their linked arms before skidding to a halt.

"What?"

He blinked then rubbed his eyes. His hand shook as he raised it.

The words *Merry Christmas* danced like northern lights in the air. Luminous candy canes, peppermints sticks, and lollipops lined the walkways. Animatronic elves, humans, and animals depicted life at the North Pole. Poinsettias adorned cafe tables draped in red and green tablecloths. A new Christmas tree stood where the old one had been. Loops of craft paper garland and strings of lights highlighted the otherwise undecorated boughs, waiting for the village children to hang their ornaments. A mug-shaped booth advertised cocoa and cookies from the foam of a whipped cream roof.

He smiled through his pain. Only Dazzler would think of cocoa and cookies.

The Hutchinses stepped out of their bakery. Mouths agape, they stared at the displays. A rock skittered across the cobblestone street, and Nick and his wife hustled across the street. Cradling her swollen stomach, Lonnie oohed and aahed over the displays.

Candance danced by his side. "Look at Mrs. Claus taking cookies from the oven. It looks just like her, even to the flour on her cheek." She clapped. "And Blitzen is showing his normal attitude about the size of his carrot." Rushing forward, she stared at the gleaming star on top of the tree. "Is it taller than the other one?"

"Probably." Everything thrived around Dazzler. And her magic thrived without his presence to hinder it. Sometimes being right sucked.

Stepping out from behind the Christmas tree, Willa brushed needles from her ivory robes. "It's nice work, if I do say so myself."

His brother and sister-in-law paused near the curb.

Todd's insides clenched. Not Dazzler's work? He could almost feel her presence in the happy, warm scenes.

"And apparently you do say so, Willa. As I'm sure you'll tell everyone."

Candance eyed the dioramas. "You did this, Mom?"

His ex-wife gloated. "I would never let you down, sweetie."

He ground his teeth. Willa only used endearments when she wanted something.

Candance bit her bottom lip before she asked in a somewhat disbelieving tone, "You did this for me?"

Yeah, he couldn't believe his ex had done a Scrooge-like transformation either. Todd rocked back on his heels.

Willa's nostrils flared, and anger splashed red on her pale cheeks. "Your aunt isn't the only one who can perform magic." She smirked. "In fact, when I last left her under house arrest, your precious Auntie D couldn't even make a cup of cocoa."

Todd struggled to breathe. Dazzler under house arrest. Dazzler unable to magic up a cup of cocoa. Would she be able to overcome his effect before her trial?

"Thank you, Mom, it's the nicest gift you've ever given me."

Nick ushered Lonnie closer, aligning himself by Todd's side. "Such generosity is so uncharacteristic of you." He sniffed the air then leaned closer to Willa. "Funny how I smell gingerbread when normally your magic stinks of mint."

Willa's glare encompassed the couple. Lonnie's fingers twitched. Todd recognized the subtle protection spell. He didn't need a magic battle leveling the decorations.

Turning his back to his ex, he faced his brother.

"What brings you out so early?"

"We thought we would help restore the display." Nick waved at the square. "Obviously, you don't need our help. And I can see no reason for her to stay." He pointed at Willa. "Don't we have custody of Candance until Christmas break?"

Todd pushed his brother's hand down. Being rude to Willa only hurt his daughter. Leaving his brother to fend for himself, he went to stand next to Candance and nudged her. She rolled her eyes and nudged him back.

"I suppose I *should* be going." Willa shook out her robes then paused and tapped her finger against her chin. "With D safely locked up, I should take that protective medallion back. We can't have Elven magic loose in the human world. Even if it is Christmas."

Nick snorted and jerked his chin toward the square. "You mean this isn't elven magic?"

Todd's fingers curled into fists. Why was Nick antagonizing Willa? His ex could simply snap her fingers and whisk everything away. Then they'd really be screwed. It was one thing for him to suffer, another for the town and their annual flood of visitors to have their holiday ruined. He patted his jeans pockets. If giving the amulet would make her leave faster, he'd give it to her.

Her eyes narrowed. "Don't tell me you lost it?"

"I didn't." His hands stilled. "Besides, I don't think you have to worry about the Review Board coming after you. The amulet didn't work."

Willa's lips twitched.

"What amulet is this?" Lonnie edged closer to her husband.

Candance tugged the necklace from under her sweater. The silver snowflake glowed in the Christmas lights and the crystal in the center blazed brightly.

"Mom gave Dad and me each one to protect us from Auntie D's magic."

Willa snatched it from her daughter's hands. "Perfect."

Candance yelped and stuck her cut finger in her mouth.

A wave of nausea rolled over Todd. He tasted again the sickly-sweet coffee he'd drunk.

"There is no malice in your aunt." Lonnie set her hands on her back, pushing her belly forward. Her cheeks lost their ruddy color. "Why would you or your father need protection from her?"

"Mine was to protect Dazzler from me." Not that it worked. Good riddance to bad rubbish. His fingers tingled when they brushed his pocket. Found it.

Candance wiped her finger on her pants. "Auntie D nearly crushed Dad with hay bales, nearly poisoned him with bad cocoa, and you were there when the Christmas tree nearly fell on him."

"Three times. You know what that means." Nick grinned.

Todd shook his head. His brother was always a little slow, but laughing at near-death experiences wasn't side-splitting comedy.

Lonnie nodded. "The curse works."

Todd swore under his breath. "Not this again."

"Curse?" Candance's attention bounced from him to her aunt.

Lonnie nodded. "My family cursed yours so that when a Dugan finds his mate, if he doesn't admit to it right away, his action can cause his true love's death."

His daughter's mouth opened. "Why have I never heard of this curse before?"

Nick laughed. "Because you haven't met your true love."

"She better not have." Todd growled, then pinned his sister-in-law with a "shut up" glare. He'd had enough of this nonsense.

Lonnie went on regardless. "Your Auntie D has so much magic, the curse is reflected back onto your father."

"And it's proof that your dad is a big, fat idiot." Nick smirked.

Todd rubbed his eye with his middle finger, turning so his brother could see.

Willa cleared her throat. "As an elf, I don't have time for fairy tales." She held out her hand, palm up. "The medallion."

He dipped his fingers inside his pocket. A spark of static electricity bit his finger. Shaking off the sting, he tugged it out. The snowflake swung from the chain, the crystal at its heart glowed bright red.

Willa reached for it, but Lonnie snatched it away. The witch turned so her body shielded it from Willa.

"This isn't a protection amulet; it's a magic sink. Small wonder Dazzler's magic acted up. This would cause anybody's magic to go haywire."

Todd tried to process the thought. Did that mean he wasn't the root of the problem?

Candance rounded on her mother. "You sabotaged Dad and Auntie D's romance? And you...you tricked me into helping?"

Willa raised her hand. A stream of glitter shot from her fingers, knocking the amulet from Lonnie's fingers. She dove for it.

Todd stomped on the amulet. The crystal shattered. Magic wrapped around his foot. Electricity jangled up his leg, tightened his chest, and paralyzed him. He struggled to breathe.

"You hit my wife." Nick lunged for Willa.

She disappeared in a spray of flurries.

Stars twinkled in Todd's peripheral vision. He struggled to remain alert. His heartbeat thudded loudly in his ear. Ten. Twenty.

Twenty-three heartbeats later, he gasped for air. His thoughts firmed up in the silence. Hope blossomed within him. Dare he ask?

Candance dug her nails into his arm. "You mean it was the amulet that stole all of Auntie D's magic, not my dad?" she asked Lonnie. "And that he isn't immune to magic?"

"Let's find out." Lonnie rubbed her hands together. With a wicked smile, she flashed her palms at Todd.

A blast of compressed air slammed into his chest. He stumbled back. Fudge, that hurt. But it was a good kind of hurt, because maybe, just maybe, he could be with Dazzler.

If she forgave him.

Candance bounced on the balls of her feet before throwing her arms around his neck. "Magic *does* affect you. You and Auntie D can be together. We can be a real family."

"I have to get to the North Pole." He would help Dazzler tame her magic. He would promise to never send her away again. He would love her forever if only she forgave him.

Candance's cell phone vibrated against his hip. Releasing him, she thumbed it on. "Oh, no. The North Pole Review Board is meeting this morning to decide Auntie D's fate."

No. No, he wouldn't lose her now that they finally had a chance to be together. He set his hands on his daughter's shoulders. "Open a portal."

Tears shimmered in her eyes. "I never learned how."

"And she couldn't even if she wanted to." Lonnie pursed her lips. "That amulet drained her magic, too."

"What do we do?" A tear trickled down Candance's cheek. "How do we save Auntie D?"

"She created a portal at the house to bring her clothes." Spinning on his heel, Todd sprinted for his house. His muscles burned. His lungs heaved. A stitch throbbed in his side. The door banged against the wall as he slammed inside and raced up the stairs. Panting, he opened the bathroom cupboard.

Nothing but towels.

He raced from room to room, throwing open closets and cabinets, even the attic door. None contained a secret passageway to the North Pole. He was stuck in Holly with no way to rescue Dazzler.

No way to tell her he loved her.

Unless...

Unless, he took the reindeer. He'd feed them as much corn as they could eat. He raced down the stairs and ran into the night.

"Hold on, Dazzler, I'm coming."

CHAPTER 24

Dazzler scooted her knotty pine chair closer to the marble table. Silence filled the lobby of the Magical Review Board Meeting Center. Rubbing her eyes, she gave in to the yawn stretching her jaw.

She'd had no time to sleep. She still hadn't found the answers she needed for her defense. That she had control of her magic was easy enough to prove, but she still had to defend the theft of a Christmas ornament by her human guest. She selected a scroll from the pile closest to her, hoping it carried a precedent that would work in her favor. Old magic prickled her skin.

A bell tinkled as the door opened. A cold breeze whisked in the scent of peppermint. Wood creaked as she turned. A young elfling rushed inside and froze when he caught her watching him. A blush crossed his face and tinged his pointy ears. From the corner of her eyes, she spied more faces pressed against the mullioned windowpanes. Someone had lost a dare.

Unrolling a scroll, she used magic to translate the ancient script. "The sugar cookies are fresh," she told the elfling without looking up.

A floorboard squeaked. "May I...May I have one?"

"Of course." She scanned the document then sighed. Another case involving a love spell. The elders had been right to ban their use. She rolled the parchment.

The elfling had reached the sideboard. Chubby fingers danced over a star-shaped sugar cookie with red icing before selecting a round ornament-shaped one from the mound. He bit off the knob at the top. Lips smacking, he eyed the carafe of cocoa.

"Cocoa's fresh, too." Dazzler waved her hand, returning half the scrolls to their proper shelves. "It does have a touch of cinnamon in it."

"I like cimanom." Crumbs clung to his lips. His missing front teeth made a gap in his smile. Holding the cookie in his remaining teeth, he poured the tan brew into a mug decorated with holly leaves.

The bell rang again. A dumpling of an elf waddled in. Gray hair tucked under her green cap, she hustled to the elfling at the sideboard.

"Twink, you were not to enter the lobby." The old one smiled at Dazzler but didn't meet her gaze. "The new tech center is amazing."

"Thank you." Dazzler trailed her fingers over the remaining scrolls. *Help me find what I need to know.* She willed her magic to solve her problem. Cold burned her skin. A red wax seal flaked off yellowed vellum. Her heart rate sped up. Had she found the answer? "I hope it serves everyone for a long time."

"Oh, it will. I'm sure of it." The newcomer tapped her foot while Twink finished his cocoa. "And it *is* magnificent. I'm glad the humans didn't affect your design. They're always changing our legends. By Kringle, we don't want any more rockets on Santa's sleigh."

Dazzler blinked. Rockets on Santa's sleigh. Could that be the answer?

"Can I work there when I grow up?" Crumbs splattered the elfling's vest and a rainbow of cocoa coated his upper lip.

"You can do whatever you want, Twink." Dazzler ruffled his hair then magicked away the debris of his snack. The bell tinkled again as the pair left. The light outside brightened, heralding the dawn.

She tapped the scroll against her chin. Elves had knowingly invited humans into their culture when the Kringles arrived. Humans had taken the stories as their own and changed them. It could work as a defense.

Shuffling sounded from beyond the closed doors of the board chamber. The elders were arriving. Her trial would start soon. The defense would have to work.

When she leaned forward to set the scroll with the others, a small envelope tumbled out. Odd. The parchment unfolded before she touched it. Her magic automatically repaired the cracks in the folds. Ink flowed across the page in a cramped script.

Another love spell. She raked her fingers through her hair. Combing it over her right shoulder, she checked the color. Still dark brown with honey highlights. No white strands to be seen. She would never fit in here. Would Todd mind them living in Holly?

He'd have to come to his senses first.

She blew her bangs out of her eyes. One problem at a time.

The air thickened with the scents of pine and poinsettias, of hope and goodwill. She glanced up from the love spell. The vellum crinkled in her grip.

"Magnificent job with the expansion." Standing beside her chair, Santa smoothed his white beard before straightening the jacket of his red suit.

"This hearing was always just a means to get two stubborn beings to see reason." Mrs. Claus set a tray of gingerbread men on the sideboard next to the assortment of cookies Dazzler had created. "And now that you have, things will proceed as they should. And you even made cocoa. You are such a thoughtful child."

Dazzler straightened. The Clauses approved. Now she just had to get Todd to go along.

"I could use some cocoa." Santa collected a mug then held it under the spout. The dark brew filled the cup. He sniffed the contents before taking a sip. "Just the right amount of cinnamon."

His eyes twinkled.

Mrs. Claus filled a plate with a selection of cookies. "I think these should do for the hearing. It is always nice to have something sweet to chase away—"

Santa cleared his throat. Dazzler, however, leaned forward in her seat. Mrs. Claus was known for her gift of precognition.

Mrs. Claus blinked. "It's always nice to have something sweet."

"And cocoa to wash it down with." Santa held up two full mugs. He pulled out his readers and set them on his nose. "And our Dazzler will finally close the scroll on an event nearly twenty years in the making, won't you, Dazzler?"

He stared at her. Her skin prickled with the magic inhabiting him, compelling her to do his bidding.

"Yes, Santa."

The doors to the chamber opened.

"We shall see you inside." Santa set his hand on the small of his wife's back and guided her through them.

Dazzler sighed. She wanted a love like that with Todd. Maybe she shouldn't be so quick to dismiss love spells. She scanned the spell. The words changed halfway down. This wasn't a love spell. This was a binding spell. And not a passive one, either. This siphoned magic from anything in its vicinity. Including elves, humans, and objects.

The receptacle was a snowflake with a crystal center.

Her heart fluttered in her throat. The kind that Todd's mother had hung in his kitchen. The kind that had been on the sleigh when her magic acted up and Todd's witchy sister-in-law had become sick.

"Willa." Dazzler's hand shook. Her cousin was still stealing magic. She'd demand a demonstration while having a snowflake nearby so Dazzler's magic would fail.

She scanned the paper again, looking for a way to break or block the spell. Nothing. *Think, Dazzler. Think. If I can't break the spell, Willa will win.*

"Dazzler Spitfire." The elder stared down at her. "We're ready to begin your trial."

Todd rushed outside and across his front porch. His family's herd of flying reindeer could take him to the North Pole. He'd give every Christmas future if they could get him there before Dazzler's trial. Boots pounding on the stone walk, he reached the gate in the picket fence just as his father arrived.

Burl Dugan blocked the opening. Todd shifted left then right but his father shadowed him, blocking his escape.

"Dad, I'm in a hurry."

"I know, son."

He clamped his hands on his father's shoulder, holding him in place. "Stay."

Burl wrapped his hands around Todd's wrists. "It's no use. The reindeer aren't flying."

Todd gritted his teeth. He knew all about the flying ban that began on Thanksgiving Day. Heck, he had even come up with the plan, to prevent any injuries that could damage the team.

"This is an emergency. Dazzler's life depends on me."

Burl shook his head. His shoulders bowed. "The reindeer *can't* fly. Not because of our rules, but because the herd is grounded."

What nonsense was this? Todd's gut clenched. There had to be a way around it. There was always a way. Magic corn. He still had the magic corn in the barn.

"Then I'll give them magic corn."

Stuff them to the gills. It might delay his departure for fifteen minutes, but surely Dazzler's trial would last longer than fifteen minutes.

Burl rolled his eyes. "I checked the barrel. There *is* no magic corn."

"What do you mean there's no magic corn?" There was always magic corn. The barrel never emptied of the glowing yellow nuggets. That was magic. Unless...

Stars twinkled in his peripheral vision. Unless the talisman Willa had given him had stolen that magic, too. His knees threatened to buckle.

"How am I to get to Dazzler?"

He couldn't fail her. His mind flashed him an image of her pale and scared face when he'd told her to leave.

Burl threw his arm around Todd's shoulders and guided him through the gate. "Don't give up hope, son. Lonnie thinks she and her coven might be able to help."

"They can create a portal?" Todd stumbled beside his father. They didn't head across the street to his parent's house but turned down the street heading toward the town square.

Burl shrugged. "I don't know. I know whatever was in that amulet drained Lonnie's magic. I'm afraid you're going to owe your brother for any help she can give."

"As long as I can get Dazzler back." Todd didn't care, would pay any price. His skin tightened. "Do you think she'll forgive me?"

Burl glanced at the stars in the sky. "You've been friends for a long time. I'm sure she's seen you act like an idiot before."

Todd's skin heated. It was one thing to think he'd been a fool, another to hear it. "Thanks, Dad."

"But have a good speech as a backup plan." Burl scratched his chin. "Lots of groveling and apologies. Consider it practice for the future."

Todd opened, then shut his mouth. Dazzler had come to him for help, trusted him to work with her to solve her problems. Instead, he'd shut her out. Groveling was the least he could do.

They reached the end of his street. Doors had opened and shut as they walked. Homes emptied as bundled-up residents hurried to the town square. Excitement tinged the air. A few children *oohed* and *aahed* at the wishes for Merry Christmas hovering in the night sky switched from English to French to Spanish, and some languages he didn't recognize.

Mrs. Crumbie hustled by. Tugging down the muffler wrapped around her neck, she beamed at Todd. "Nice job with decorations."

"It wasn't me. It was Dazzler." No way would he give Willa credit for the decorations. Despite her claims, he could feel Dazzler's presence in the magic.

"It's your love for her that made it all possible." Mrs. Crumbie wagged an arthritic finger at him. They turned the corner and she gasped upon spying the Sugar Plum Fairies dancing around the Christmas tree. "I don't even mind losing the bet on how long it would take you to come to your senses."

"Bet?" He raised his voice but spoke only to the old woman's back. "What bet?"

His father blushed. "Now, son, don't let your cookies crumble."

Todd's cookies were scorched. Could the whole town have colluded to bring him and Dazzler together? What could they have been thinking to risk Christmas? Didn't they understand how important the magic they generated was to keeping the spirit alive?

"What bet, Dad?"

Candance fell into step beside him as they reached the curb. "Everyone knew you and Auntie D are supposed to be together, but you were just taking your own sweet time. Yammering on and on about how magic didn't work on you and making excuses."

Yammering? Todd's seventeen-year-old daughter didn't say *yammering*. No self-respecting teen had since long before he was born. Who was behind the plot? Who would risk Christmas?

"And just how did they learn about Dazzler anyway?"

His father snorted. "Anyone with ears heard about her after you return from your vacations. And then there are the photos. Pictures of the three of you." He nodded to Candance. "Every wall, tabletop, and refrigerator has photos of you guys. By gumdrops, you even have a picture of the two of you embracing on the beach on your nightstand."

Todd mentally smacked himself. He really was an idiot. He just hoped his sister-in-law could provide him with the opportunity to spend the rest of his life making it up to Dazzler.

People fanned out in the square, stopping to marvel at the dioramas while sipping hot drinks and nibbling on pastries. The Hutchinses kept the line at the oversized cocoa stand moving.

The librarian dabbed at the cherry filling on her cheek as she met them by the tree. "Where is that little elf so I can congratulate her for getting through your thick skull and making you take a chance on love?"

Todd's father cleared his throat. "We're working on that."

The librarian pushed her glasses higher up her nose. "Well, you best get cracking, young man. You've wasted enough time."

She left to help the schoolteachers pulling a wagon with the homemade ornaments toward the tree.

Todd's muscles twitched. Time. Dazzler's time was running out. "Where's Lonnie and her coven?"

"Here." Dressed in his sheriff's uniform, Nick guided the sleigh to the curb. "The others will be here shortly."

That was something, at least. Todd eyed the curved lines of the sleigh, familiar but gleaming like new. "Is that...?"

Nick nodded. "Apparently, your little elf fixed everything. Even the sleigh."

"Too bad she couldn't have brought you to your senses earlier." Mayor Browning smoothed his leather gloves around his fingers. "I would have won the bet if you'd stopped being an idiot between four and five p.m. yesterday."

The bet again. Todd was beginning to hate the word. "Did everyone in town participate in this bet?"

"Not the children." Burl eyed the line at the cocoa stand. "We do have some standards."

Browning nodded. "The trick was to get you to participate. Hence our wager that the lights would go out and I would take away your sleigh for the season."

Todd blinked. The whole town had not only manipulated him but had planned to profit from it. "You all deserve to be on Santa's Naughty List."

Browning smacked Todd between the shoulder blades. "Do you *want* to be just friends with your elf?"

Darned stockings. Todd hated that his friend was right. Not that he would ever tell him. He would grovel to Dazzler, but not anyone else.

"Isn't that like a politician, always taking credit when they haven't done anything?"

"You're welcome." Browning grinned.

A red SUV turned on to the Main Street. Todd counted three heads. "Isn't a coven supposed to be seven witches?"

Lonnie frowned at him. "Covens can be any number, but I don't know who that is."

Nick hitched the equipment belt of his sheriff's uniform. "Our first guests aren't supposed to arrive until tonight. The spell to disable cars won't be in effect until after dinner."

The SUV coasted to a stop in front of the Christmas tree. The engine died. Doors opened. A family of three stumbled onto the sidewalk. The doors slammed closed.

The townspeople focused on the trio. Nick stepped toward them. Todd stopped him with a hand on his arm.

"They look familiar."

Leaving his family behind, he approached the visitors.

The mother's cheeks were hollow; the circles under her eyes a dark purple. The father stared blankly, seeing something that wasn't in the square. A preteen walked between them, her hands clasped in prayer in front of her.

Todd's heart lurched in his chest. He knew that look, those actions. They had lost a child. Recently, if the red tearstained eyes were anything to go by.

"They're some of Dazzler's people."

"They're elves?" Nick, who had followed him, cocked an eyebrow.

"From her work at the children's hospital." How many nights had she shared the highlights of her work with terminally-ill children? How many times had he offered to go with her? "And they're humans."

Todd pointed to his ears then at the family. Obviously, idiocy was a family trait.

The tween opened her hands. A dark ball lay in the center. It stretched, then stood. Dazzler's stolen reindeer.

Todd rushed over to them. "May I help you?"

The mother swallowed hard; her finger shook as she stroked the wobbly animal in her daughter's hands. Tears shimmered in her eyes.

"We had an experience, you see."

The father shuddered as he returned to the present that no longer contained all of his children. "We thought we'd made it up. Like a dream that we all shared. Then we found him in Rich's things after..."

His voice broke.

The little girl raised her hand. "I don't think he's doing well. He used to fly and do tricks. But then he stopped eating."

The reindeer looked at Todd with dull eyes and a dusty coat. The tether that had once attached him to the Christmas tree at the North Pole was tarnished.

Poor guy *wasn't* doing well at all.

Todd let them talk, empty out the ever-refilling well of grief. They would have to give him the magic ornament. He wouldn't take it until they were ready. Dazzler wouldn't want him to add to their pain, not even to save herself. And he wouldn't fail her again.

The mother looped her arm around her daughter's shoulders. "We knew he didn't belong to us, But he was our last link to Rich."

She turned and buried her face against her husband's chest. He embraced her with one arm but kept the free hand on his daughter's shoulder. "Our son had been sick for so long, you see. And we prayed for a miracle."

"Especially when we knew the end was near." His wife straightened, turned, scrubbed at her tears. "Just one happy memory to remember our boy. Not the way he was that last year, but before...when he smiled and laughed."

The girl kissed the reindeer's head between his missing antlers. "I found him in Rich's baseball mitt. He'd nibbled on the price tag. I knew then it wasn't a dream. Santa gave us a present."

The mom nodded. "Not Santa himself, you see, but one of his elves. She was beautiful and sunny and always smiled."

"Dazzler." Todd's gut clenched.

"Dazzling, indeed. We saw dinosaurs and unicorns playing in cotton candy fields." The father laughed then covered his mouth as if he'd betrayed his son's memory. "Things only little kids dream of. She made it all come true."

The mom lowered the dad's hand. Her smile wobbled before collapsing. "It was amazing. It was like before. We were so happy. Rich didn't cough once as he ran around. He even led us through the fields as we rode unicorns."

The girl tilted her hands, setting the reindeer into Todd's palm. "Like Rich, he can't live in our world. I fed him everything I could think of, but I don't want him to die, too."

The reindeer shivered. Todd stroked his head then ran a fingertip down his spine. He wagged his heart-shaped tail.

The father let out a shaky breath. "We thought maybe because this town is devoted to Christmas that you would know what to do. How to heal him."

"Of course." Todd leaned closer to the family and lowered his voice. "I manage one of Santa's herds of reindeer for his midnight ride."

The girl clapped. "I knew it. I knew you did."

"I think a little magic corn might make him all right." The area around Todd's palm twinkled. Miniature magic corn materialized in his hands. The little reindeer snuffled it before starting to eat. What in the world? How had the corn appeared?

Candance nudged his shoulder. "You smell like Auntie D. Why would you smell like Auntie D?"

Lonnie tugged on his sleeve. "Because she gave you some of her magic. Apparently, elves share everything with those they love. It's why they can only have one soulmate."

Todd raised his palm. It also explained why he wasn't affected by the cold anymore. Would one lifetime be enough to make it up to her?

"Auntie D?" The girl tilted her head to the left. "Who is Auntie D?"

Candance thumbed on her phone and flashed a picture at the family. Dazzler pressed her nose against a cookie display case in a bakery; her pointed ears visible through her dark hair. "Dazzler is going to be my mother."

Todd smiled. Thankfully, they'd been in California that trip. No one had looked twice at her ears, but her enthusiasm had snagged everyone's attention. Especially the men. He'd bought her one of every kind of cookie that day just to get her away before one of the creeps made a move on her.

The little girl squealed and bounced around her parents. "That's her. That's her!"

Rusty chuckles escaped her mother. "I can see that."

The reindeer launched from Todd's palm and buzzed his head before hovering in front of his face.

"If only you were bigger," Todd said, "I'd ride you back to the North Pole."

A golden halo surrounded the reindeer. He grew from the size of a kiwi to a watermelon in the blink of an eye. Turning in a circle, he doubled in size again and again until a full-size reindeer stood in front of Todd. He tossed his rack of antlers and presented his back.

Burl, who had also joined them, nudged him. "What are you waiting for? Go get your elf."

Todd didn't need to be told twice. He climbed on the animal's back and leaned over his neck. "Take me to Dazzler."

The reindeer shot forward then left the ground. The family cried out in wonder. The townspeople cheered. Todd hung on as they climbed higher and higher. Clouds gathered overhead, forming a vortex. The center cleared and opened. A portal. He'd opened a portal.

"Hang on, Dazzler. I'm coming."

He just hoped he wasn't too late.

CHAPTER 25

Dazzler folded the instructions for the snowflake power amulet and tucked them into her pocket. Four steps carried her into the North Pole Review Board chamber. Fairy lights twinkled high in the star-studded ceiling. The aurora borealis veiled the seven elders waiting to decide her fate. She strode down the sloping flagstone floor to the defendant's table. Vines of silver and gold held up the sheet of glass. Sapphire velvet upholstered the ornate seat waiting for her.

The packed observation gallery on the floor above her remained silent. To her left, Mr. and Mrs. Claus finished their plate of cookies as they waited to provide evidence on her behalf. Her parents sat beside them, their hands clasped in a white-knuckled grip, but their faces devoid of emotion.

Benches reserved for those giving evidence for the prosecution were on her left. Sterling Frost watched something on a snowball in his hands, his face set in hard lines. She hoped he was annoyed by her name for the new expansion. Willa glared at her.

Instead of sitting, Dazzler stood beside her chair. She was ready.

The witnesses rose. The seven judges, representing the seven clans of elves, recorded their presence with a spectral signature.

The trial officially began.

Elder Misty Moonlight glided to the front of the judges' balcony. She had registered as the presiding judge and spoke on behalf of the others.

Dazzler braced her hand on the glass tabletop. Misty Moonlight had been a fair but stern instructor at North Pole Academy. She'd also failed Dazzler for spell work, preventing her from graduating.

"We are present today to hear four cases in which Dazzler Spitfire of the Sylvan clan will provide testimony. You may all be seated." Four rings of fire hovered along the judges' platform.

Four cases? Dazzler had only prepared for three. A scroll appeared on the table. Only three charges were listed. What was this fourth one? Her attention returned to her cousin.

Willa smirked. She knew something. But what?

Dazzler pushed her questions regarding the fourth case to the side. She had to be vindicated on charges one through three before she could worry about number four.

Elder Misty raised her slim hand but didn't tap any of the fiery rings in front of her. "Before Dazzler Spitfire presents her defense, does anyone wish to add anything to their testimony regarding the charges?"

She glanced around the room. The witnesses shook their heads.

Writing magically appeared on the scroll in front of Dazzler—a summation of the evidence filed inside her head. The process took two minutes to review. Nothing had changed since Santa had briefed her, then sent her away to "pull herself together".

"The testimony of Dazzler Spitfire may begin." Elder Misty glided back to her throne. The aurora borealis curtain shrouded her again.

Dazzler straightened. "We all know about the bloodshed that occurred shortly after humans and elves met for the first time. A simple misunderstanding between cultures led to a war that lasted centuries and brought both our species to the brink of extinction."

She inhaled, waiting for a rebuke of her history lesson. Nothing. So far so good.

"In the Starlight Treaty, we agreed to share our story with the humans through their dreams. We hoped this would eliminate any misunderstandings should they ever rediscover our existence."

She licked her dry lips and glanced at her parents. Their shoulders had relaxed, and their clasped hands rested between them. Chewing a sugar cookie, Mrs. Claus nodded and snapped her fingers. A mug of cocoa appeared on Dazzler's table near the scroll. Santa tapped the side of his nose in encouragement.

Dazzler propped a hip against the table. "Aside from a group of humans who devote themselves to the spinning of tales, it is human children who remain our primary source of contact. Children are the future. And it is in the future that once again the magical beings of Earth will reunite with humans."

Willa nudged Sterling. Dazzler heard her whisper, "I didn't realize we were here for a history lesson."

Dazzler sipped her cocoa. Her cousin's attempt to distract her would not work, not this time. She focused on Elder Misty.

"One of our greatest success stories and most enduring connections is of Santa Claus and Christmas. A celebration that evolves every day." She paused a heartbeat. "It is about this evolution that I wish to testify."

Willa snorted and popped a marshmallow in her mouth. "I wish you'd get on with it," she muttered.

Frost shifted away from her on the bench. She glared at him, then shrugged and patted her pocket. Dazzler spied a flash of silver. Her cousin had brought the snowflake amulet to the hearing. She was either confident of having the upper hand, or foolish. Dazzler bet it was a little of both.

Whispering, she cast a spell that let her visualize the lines of magic in the chamber. Streams of it bent like arrows toward Willa then flattened as they contacted her cousin's pocket. The snowflake amulet was ready to explode—and a protection spell shielded Frost. The rat knew.

Dazzler's heart danced in her chest. Perhaps all was not lost after all. Perhaps she could expose them both.

"Per the provisions in the treaty, we give our stories as a gift to the humans. And as an act of good faith, we allow them to control those stories. Our stories. It is in the spirit of this trust that the Board allowed me to bring terminally-ill children to our sanctuary."

The elders glanced at each other before nodding.

She paused to sip her cocoa. Now for the hard sell.

"The removal of the ornament from our sacred Christmas tree is not a crime but an extension of the treaty. From that one encounter, the recipient shared the ornament with first his companions at the hospital, then later his family. Both events triggered a spike in magic, a ripple that brightened our world as well as the human one."

Elder Misty ran her fingers along the aurora borealis. The air shimmered as she searched for the data to confirm Dazzler's testimony.

Dazzler didn't wait. "I submit as my defense in case one that the disappearance of the ornament from the tree in no way risks our exposure but instead provides another avenue to maintain contact with humans, in keeping with the spirit of the treaty."

Elder Misty swept one hand through the aurora. "We concur with this interpretation."

Willa yawned.

Dazzler released a shaky breath. One down, three to go, each one increasing in severity. But a victory was a victory. She would take it.

"Regarding case two—the creation of my dream world—I humbly submit that this world is also in keeping with the Starlight Treaty."

She scanned her judges. Elder Misty nodded once.

"Explain."

"I created the world as a means of providing a respite for the terminally-ill children. To give them a place free of sickness where they can experience health and movement free of pain, some for the first time in their lives. I never intended to leave it operating without my presence, and indeed, when I returned to shut it down, I discovered other children present. Ones I had never met, but who needed the world." She cleared her throat.

"It seems those children who had visited the world talked about it. Shared it with their friends. It was no longer my world, but a shared world, composed of magic and of human imagination and a desire for sanctuary." Dazzler sniffed, touched that her gift had been so readily accepted. And that dying children would be happy to give back and help others in their situation. "Thankfully, none of them had altered it the way the adult humans did when they strapped a rocket to Santa's sleigh."

Her parents smiled slightly. Santa barked a laugh. Mrs. Claus pinned him with a look over her glasses.

"That rocket was not amusing, dear," she murmured. "You could have broken an arm."

Elder Misty parted the aurora borealis once again to stand at the judgment balcony.

"As it is in keeping with the spirit of comfort and joy which we promised humans, the world created by Dazzler Spitfire and enhanced by the spirit of childhood and sharing shall remain accessible to those who need it."

Dazzler resisted the urge to fist-pump. Two down, two to go. She still didn't know what the fourth charge was about, but the next one was a doozy.

Elder Misty waved away two of the rings. "Case three regarding Dazzler Spitfire's ability to control her magic."

Willa leaned forward, lifting part of the snowflake amulet from her pocket but keeping it out of plain sight. It siphoned off the Elder's magic, except they were so powerful it would take far longer than Dazzler's trial for them to feel the impact. The crystal bulged.

Santa rapped his knuckles against the railing. "I do not believe we need any demonstration of Dazzler's abilities. It is clear from the new technology annex she created that Dazzler Spitfire has perfect control and use of her magic."

"No. No!" Willa's objection echoed through the chamber. "With all due respect to Santa, Dazzler Spitfire's parents are powerful elves. They could have created the building, hoping the Elders would jump to exactly that conclusion."

Dazzler's father sprang to his feet, and he pounded the railing with one fist. "We would never interfere with the Board's inquiry. The insinuation is insulting to both our clan and our personal integrity as elves."

Dazzler held her breath and waited for her cousin to bait her trap.

Willa pressed her point. "Given that everyone denies any involvement, I propose a simple test. Have Dazzler cast a spell. I'll even allow my dear sweet cousin to pick it herself. Something simple, like conjuring a cup of cocoa."

Dazzler's nails dug into the glass desktop. The snowflake in Willa's pocket tugged on her magic, siphoning it from her body. Dazzler wanted to vomit. Thankfully, hers was not the only power affected. The Elders were also being drained. And that was the key.

Straightening, she threw back her shoulders. "As much as I appreciate my cousin's consideration, I do not believe that to be a fair test. In fact, I would humbly request Elder Misty choose a spell and demonstrate it first, so that all may judge *my* execution of said spell."

Willa opened her mouth, no doubt to object.

"Agreed." Elder Misty waved her hand. Her emerald sleeves slid below her slim wrists. "I have always favored spinning tops."

The air swirled. A ball formed then flattened before adding a point at the bottom and top.

Willa's amulet pulled on the magic threads, first one, then two, then ten. Soon, more of Elder Misty's magic fed the amulet then went into creating the top

Elder Misty's forehead wrinkled. She snapped her fingers. A lump of crimson metal plummeted to the floor. The clang reverberated through the chamber. She squinted at Dazzler.

"Can you explain that?"

Willa jumped to her feet and pointed at Dazzler. "Her lack of ability to control her magic is infecting everyone. As much as it pains me to say it, Dazzler must be neutralized before she ruins us all."

"We object," Dazzler's mother cried, jumping to her feet.

Mrs. Claus inspected the bottom of her mug. Santa's blue eyes twinkled at Dazzler. He knew about the amulet and was trusting her to handle it.

She glanced down. The fourth charge had appeared. Power glitches at the North Pole. He'd sent her away to prove she wasn't responsible. Too bad Willa had followed her. Now the burden rested on Dazzler.

The parchment with the spell lay heavy against her chest. "My magic misbehaved because I hid the truth in my heart from myself. I have since pulled myself together, as instructed by Santa."

Willa snorted. "So you say, but there is no evidence of that, only of your contamination of our home."

Dazzler smiled at her cousin. Was she doomed to be on the Naughty List for enjoying this? "In my search, I became aware of other, similar aberrations of magic. A spell that explains the Honored Elder's top."

Willa gripped the railing. "I object. She's just trying to deflect blame."

Elder Misty frowned. "I would be interested in hearing what she has learned."

Dazzler tied her magic to the elders' and prayed it was enough to block the power of the amulet. Her hair stood on end. Her skin prickled. *Here goes everything.*

She snapped her fingers. The snowflake shot out of Willa's pocket to hover before the judges. A protection spell now bound its ability to steal magic.

"What is this?" Elder Misty touched it. An arc of blue light zapped her finger.

Willa throttled the railing. "It's just a trinket. Nothing more."

She glared at Dazzler.

Pulling the folded note from her pocket, Dazzler balanced it on her fingertips. A current of air carried it to the Elders. "That snowflake is designed to harvest the energy of other elves without their knowledge. It enables the elf who wears it to use the stolen magic for their own purposes."

Elder Misty unfolded the parchment and held up the drawing beside the snowflake. She blinked twice, and all the lines of magic in the room became visible, as did Frost's shield spell. He quickly waved it away, but the damage had been done.

Dazzler's mother gasped. Dazzler looked down. The strength of her magic matched the combined might of the elders. O Holy Night, no wonder everyone was afraid of her.

Willa hissed. Elder Misty pinned her with a glare.

"Do you have an explanation for your possession of this amulet, Willa Sparkles?"

Dazzler focused on the desk. She couldn't look at her cousin. She might give away the trap she'd laid.

Willa raised her chin. "I found it. And thought it was pretty, so I kept it."

Elder Misty tapped one foot. "Is that the extent of your defense?"

"I am not in any need of defense. I've done nothing wrong."

Dazzler's skin prickled. She took a chance, glanced up, and caught her cousin's glare.

Willa flashed her standard smirk. "Dazzler had the spell, and I found the amulet at her house. She must have created it. That would explain why she is so powerful."

Dazzler rolled her eyes. Willa was usually better at lying than this.

Elder Misty wove glyphs in the air. The parchment fluttered in the throes of her power.

"Show me all who handled you within the last hundred days."

Dazzler's face shimmered in the summoning-mist. Willa pointed at it in triumph. "See, I told you. My cousin created the amulet to frame me."

Dazzler's image faded. Willa's took its place. The spell even showed her cousin creating six copies of the amulet.

Elder Misty wiped away the images then turned to Dazzler. "Do you have any questions for your cousin?"

Dazzler nodded. She knew the exact words to break the spell; she just had to get her cousin to say them.

"Willa Sparkles." She refused to allow her cousin any association with Todd. "Are you willing to testify that you never wanted the magic contained within the amulet?"

"No." Willa leaned forward. "I mean, I never wanted anyone's magic but my own."

The metal snowflake tarnished and dropped to the floor. The crystal shattered, releasing its contents. Magic ricocheted around the chambers.

Dazzler braced her feet and held her breath. The magic would return to her soon. She hoped it didn't sting too much.

It blew a hole through the roof. There was a loud yelp. Someone dropped from the sky.

She blinked. "Todd?"

In front of her, a magic net caught him before he crashed to the floor.

CHAPTER 26

Todd gasped for breath. Magic may have stopped him from splatting on the floor, but the sudden stop at the end had still knocked the breath from his body. He glanced up.

Dazzler stared down at him. Love and happiness brightened her brown eyes. Did she still love him, or was she happy about his falling at her feet? Then again, maybe he was in heaven. He didn't care where he was as long as they were together.

She knelt beside him. Her green robes draped around her, and a crown of poinsettias circled her brown hair. "Are you all right?"

Other presences made themselves known. Willa looked like she'd sucked on a lemon. Frost glanced at him then at the exit. Seven very old, very annoyed elves peered down at him.

If his entrance had irritated them, their heads might explode at his next words.

"I object."

Black boots pounded across the stone floor. Red velvet trimmed in white encased large thighs.

Santa Claus. Great, just what I need. But Todd wouldn't back down. Dazzler's life was at stake.

"I object."

Santa crouched beside him. "Just what is it you are objecting to?"

"Dazzler is innocent of the charges." Todd pointed to the miniature reindeer now circling his head.

"We've already dealt with that charge, son."

"Oh." Todd swallowed hard. The trial was over? He was too late? Obviously, Dazzler had won, since she was still alive. Maybe she didn't need him after all.

Santa stroked his beard and rose to his feet. "I'd like to request a five-minute break to deal with this newcomer's arrival."

"Five minutes. But the doors will be locked. No one escapes justice this time." The elderly she-elf at the railing disappeared behind a curtain of red-and-green light.

Santa tapped his nose then pinned Todd with a stare. "Don't waste a second more."

The fat man rose and intercepted Dazzler's mother and father, turning them back to their seats.

"Will you get up, or do you wish to remain on the floor?" Dazzler held out her hand.

He traced his fingers over the life and love lines on her palm. They were long, so very long. He wanted to travel that path with her, at her side always. His skin tingled as energy flowed from her to him and back again. His heartbeat synced with hers; her perfume filled up his senses.

She tugged on his arm. "Todd?"

The reindeer ornament buzzed her ear before touching down on her shoulder. His small muzzle snuffled her ear, then his tiny tongue licked the lobe. Giggling, she scratched him under the chin.

"You need to join the others. They've missed you."

The reindeer circled them once before soaring toward the hole Todd had punched in the ceiling. Smiling, she watched the ornament fly away.

Todd squelched a spurt of jealousy. Dazzler was never stingy with her affection. He just didn't want to wait any longer to have it lavished on him, so he could treat her as she deserved.

"Ready?"

"Just a minute." He held her wrist tight and didn't budge. They'd been separated for an eternity. He had to see if the separation had affected her as it had him. He scanned her from

flowery crown to slippered feet. She was beautiful, kind, wonderful. "I wish we were in Maine, surrounded by fall leaves, a
campfire to warm us, and you a little tipsy from s'mores."

"You said I wouldn't get drunk because the marshmallows
were toasted." She rubbed her temple. "I had such a hangover
the next morning. We didn't go hiking until noon, and Candance
didn't get to see that rock formation she'd wanted to photo-
graph."

"You made it up to her, though, turning Cheddar into a
Sasquatch made of blueberries. She got an A on her essay." Todd
shook his head. Dazzler always made the best of what she had,
but he wanted to give her the best of everything. For the rest
of her life. The speech he'd practiced on the ride here surfed
inside his head. Despite the setting, he didn't want to wait
another second to make them official. "I'm an idiot."

He blinked. That wasn't quite the way he'd phrased the
proposal inside his head

Chuckling, she sank to the flagstones and slid close. Their
knees touched, and her thumb stroked the sensitive skin inside
his wrist.

"An idiot, huh?"

"I never should have asked you to leave. We're a team.
When troubles visit you, I should be there to help you through
them. I *want* to be there." He replayed his words. That didn't
sound quite right, either. "Not that I want you to be troubled,
but—"

She pressed her index finger against his lips, then traced
the curve of his bottom lip. "I know you were just trying to
protect me."

"I'll do better next time. And every time from now on. If
you let me." Bitterness rolled across his tongue. Frost had used
the opportunity to kidnap her. He vowed never to have a pity
party for one again.

Dazzler sighed. "The real blame falls on me. I was the one
who disguised myself as Willa. Instead of having a cute meeting story to tell our offspring, I messed everything up from the
beginning."

Offspring. She hadn't given up on him. Was she really willing to forgive him so easily? Did he deserve it?

"It's not your fault. Things with Willa never felt right, but I charged ahead. I should have known better and trusted my instincts. You were young, but I was old enough to know better."

She patted his hand then pulled free of his hold. "Since females of both our species mature faster than males, I think technically we were about the same age."

He opened his mouth to debate the issue. What was he doing? It was enough that she was willing to give him another chance.

"Do you think we can start again?"

"No."

His heart condensed into a tight knot and dropped to the floor. No? But he loved her, and she loved him, didn't she?

"I'll apologize every day for the rest of our lives. Twice on Sunday. Ten times on Christmas. I'll do whatever it takes." He raked his fingers through his hair. "Just, please, let me love you."

"Let you? You couldn't stop loving me any more than I can stop loving you." She cupped his cheek. "I don't want us to go back to who we were nearly twenty years ago. We've had too much fun, too many amazing shared memories. Why would we want to pretend that none of them happened?"

His brain took a moment to process her words. She was giving him a second chance. He'd take it. He'd take anything she'd give him. Forever and always.

"After we're married, we can live here. We can live anywhere. As long as we live together."

He rolled to his knees, then up to balance on the balls of his feet, then held out his hand. Would she accept his proposal?

She placed her hand in his. "Holly seems to be a nice place. We should live there at least for the first couple hundred years."

They rose together.

"Couple hundred years?" He knew elves were long-lived, but hundreds of years?

She stepped closer to him and turned her face to his. "Don't look so afraid. We'll probably live another two hundred years at the North Pole."

"We? Me, too?" He should probably be paying attention to their conversation, but it had been an eternity since he'd kissed her.

"I shared my magic with you. Our mating bound us." She brushed her nose against his. "So, you only need to spend the first hundred years apologizing to me every day and ten times on Sunday."

"If that's what it takes to get to happily ever after."

Her eyes fluttered closed.

He tilted his head. His lips touched hers, soft as a petal and as sweet as cocoa.

Her mouth opened.

He'd accept that invitation.

Someone banged on wood. Loudly.

"How quaint, but let's return to the matter at hand."

Willa. Todd groaned in frustration. What did a man have to do to kiss his betrothed?

He opened his eyes. Dazzler's attention shifted to the side. Todd glared at his ex-wife then Frost. He must have arrived before the magic part of the test.

Ducking his head, he whispered in Dazzler's ear, "Willa has a vampire snowflake that sucks magic. Your magic. Everyone's magic."

She kissed his cheek. "I already found and destroyed it." She jerked her chin toward a tarnished lump of metal and glistening bits of glass on the floor.

She really didn't need him. But she wanted him. That was a good thing.

He wrapped his arm around her waist. "I love you."

Her lips parted. "I—"

"Dazzler Spitfire." The old she-elf leaned on the railing as she stared down at them.

"Yes, Elder Misty?" Dazzler leaned against him. "I—"

Todd cleared his throat and caught her eye. She nodded once.

"We are ready to begin."

"Then, in the matter of Dazzler Spitfire's ability to manage and control magic—"

"If I may interrupt." Todd tightened his grip on Dazzler. "Dazzler has given me the gift of not only her love but has also shared her magic. Whatever judgment you pass on her, I, too, will share that judgment."

"You see?" Willa pounded on the railing in front of her. "You see? Dazzler cannot control her magic. It's seeping into humans."

Todd flinched. He'd meant to help, not hurt, Dazzler's defense.

Elder Misty's white hair crackled with static electricity. "Magic was designed to be shared with those we love. Dazzler Spitfire's magic is behaving exactly as it should." She smoothed her hair then her robes. "In the matter of Dazzler's magic, it is the opinion of the Elders that she is in complete control. And since the human, Todd Dugan, has accepted his role as her mate, we bless their union and are relieved they both came to their senses."

Chills ran down Todd's spine. They knew his name. How did they know his name?

He turned toward the door. "Let's leave before they turn me into a toad."

Elder Misty speared him with a look. "You will know when it's time for you to leave, human."

Todd froze. It might have been better when they called him by his name.

Dazzler squeezed his hand. "It's okay."

"In the matter of the fourth charge Dazzler Spitfire provided evidence for, the elders are in agreement as to the consequences. Willa Sparkles, this is not the first time you have appeared in front of the Board for stealing another's magic using the dark arts."

Willa was in trouble. It couldn't happen to a more deserving elf. Todd shifted so he stood between his ex and Dazzler. If Willa wanted revenge, she'd have to go through him first.

"In the first instance, we believed that the loss of your chosen mate was consequence enough, and that the loss of your magic would reinforce the lesson."

Todd blinked. The North Pole Review Board had taken her magic? He had never been cursed? He'd spent years...If he'd known, maybe he and Dazzler...

She tugged on his sleeve. "It doesn't matter now. We made so many good memories, we raised Candance to be a grown woman, and we have the rest of our lives to be together."

Todd shook out his fingers. Dazzler was so forgiving. He didn't deserve her.

"The world doesn't deserve someone as kind as you."

She rolled her eyes. "She blamed me for her soulmate's death. That's why she married you. If you think I didn't imagine sending her someplace hotter than Hades, you'd be mistaken."

"Right." Message received. She'd turn him into a toad if he was an idiot again.

Magic sparkled around them. Elder Misty tapped her fingernail on the railing.

"In imposing on you no serious consequences for meddling with the dark arts, we erred. Willa Sparkles, you are hereby sentenced to the coal mines until all your magic has been absorbed—"

"No!" A shout echoed around the room.

Todd turned. Candance stood in the open doorway, his mother and old man Henderson bracketing her. He opened his mouth and shut it. How had they gotten here?

"Santa, please." Candance stopped before the fat man. "I know I've asked for Auntie D to be my mother."

Santa waved his hand. A dozen letters appeared in his hands. "I'm happy to be able to give my favorite halfling her Christmas gift, a little early."

She juggled the cards. "But I don't want Mom to die."

Todd recognized his daughter's wishlists from Christmases past. All this time, she'd never asked for a bicycle or tablet, just for Dazzler to join their family. She was truly an amazing woman, much like her Auntie D.

Dazzler squeezed his fingers. "She's remarkable, thinking of others before herself. She loves you."

"Willa die?" Santa set his hands on his belly and rocked back on his bootheels. "No one said anything about dying."

"But...but, if you take Mom's magic..." Candance sputtered. "She'll die. Elves are magic. No magic, no elf. Everyone knows that."

Todd nodded and tugged Dazzler closer. He wouldn't lose her now. As for his daughter, he shifted so he partially concealed her. If the Elders became upset, he'd whisk them both away.

Santa stroked his beard. "I've never heard of such a thing."

Elder Misty stared at old man Henderson. "Do you have an explanation, Ole?"

Ole Henderson rubbed the back of his neck as he blushed. "I may have embellished the story of my wife and I just a bit. But, well, they were being stubborn, and I wanted to hurry things along. Make them understand the seriousness of their obstinacy."

Todd blinked. Old man Henderson was married? "Your wife?"

"Fern of Leahway." The old man's ears shifted from rounded to pointed.

Candance rounded on him. "Fern of Leahway died when they took her magic from her for misbehaving. Everyone knows the story."

Mrs. Claus caught her laughter in her hand.

Santa laughed. "Fern of Leahway was a human. A sorceress who threatened to take away Ole's powers if he didn't marry her before their son was born."

"I was always going to marry her." Ole crossed his arms. "I loved the daft woman, and as soon as this business is wrapped up here, I aim to join her."

The old reprobate. Todd almost liked him. Almost. Still, The old man had made up everything and let them think Dazzler faced certain death.

Elder Misty cleared her throat. "So, that is cleared up. Willa Sparkles—"

Willa made a break for the door with Frost one step ahead. Elder Misty raised her hand, freezing them both in place.

"Willa Sparkles, you are hereby sentenced to the coal mines until all your magic has been absorbed, at which point you will be banished from our community. Your memories, except those of your daughter and your love for her, will be taken from you, and you will be released into the human community which you hold in so much contempt."

Willa squirmed in the older elf's hold. "You can't do this to me. You—"

Her shout bounced around the chamber, but she was gone.

Todd whistled under his breath. He'd thought coal was punishment for humans. Seems elves had a reason to fear it as well. Maybe being a toad wasn't so bad.

"As for you, Sterling Frost..." The elf judge used magic to spin the ice king around so he faced her. "Your job is to usher in the cold, not to be unfeeling. Until your heart is thawed, your magic will be bound, your memories removed, and you, too, will be sent to live among the humans."

Frost grunted. "I already lost my name on the expansion, and I—"

He disappeared in a flurry of snowflakes.

"Dazzler Spitfire." Elder Misty turned her attention to them.

Todd straightened beside Dazzler. They would face her punishment together. Candance moved closer. He and Dazzler linked hands with his daughter.

"As you are an expert on the Starlight Treaty, the elders are certain that you know what comes next."

Dazzler straightened. "I am to leave the North Pole and live among the humans."

"Wait. Why?" Todd stepped in front of her and his daughter. "You said she'd been cleared of any wrongdoing. Why is she being punished?"

She tugged on his shirt. "Todd."

He remained in place. He'd go wherever Dazzler wanted to go, but no one would force her to anywhere. Not without going through him first.

In a spiral of glitter, Santa and his wife materialized next to Todd. "Dazzler is not being punished. She is the chosen one. According to the terms of the Starlight Treaty, our most powerful elf must mate with a chosen human. Your union maintains the connection between our species, in the hope that peace will remain when we reveal ourselves and all the magical creatures to the human world once again."

Spinning on his heel, Todd faced Dazzler. Amusement danced in her eyes.

"You can't weasel out of marrying me now. Santa, the universe, and everyone knows we were made to be together."

"Well, that's all right, then." He clasped her hands. "And I don't plan to let you weasel out of marrying *me*. As much as I treasure our friendship, I look forward to being something more for hundreds of years to come."

He waggled his eyebrows.

Dazzler blushed. "Just remember that I loved you first."

He knew the perfect way to stop her facts from ruining his perfectly good story. He leaned in for a kiss. She rose on tiptoe.

Santa shoved his hands between them. "Not until you two make this official. The world has waited long enough."

"That's right. Humans have a funny way of weaseling out of the terms of treaties." Dazzler's father tugged Todd away from her.

Martha Dugan stepped in. "I have something to say to Dazzler."

"Mom," Todd whispered. His mother better not hurt Dazzler.

"This is important, son." Martha Dugan patted his cheek then fished in her apron pocket. A string of pearls dangled from her fingers. "Dazzler, dear. I know I wasn't very pleasant when we first met, er, as us, not you as...as..." She waved her empty hand. "Well, I apologize for my behavior."

"You were just protecting Todd." Maintaining her grip on Todd's hand, Dazzler hugged his mother. "I was angry when Michael broke Candance's heart, and don't think I could have been as pleasant if I had met him then."

Todd stared at his daughter. She wasn't supposed to have boyfriends, so how could her heart get broken?

"When was this?"

Candance studied the hole in the ceiling.

Martha pressed the pearls into Dazzler's hands. "My mother gave these to me to wear on my wedding day. I had intended to pass them down to my daughters, but well, I had sons, so I decided that the wife of my oldest should have them. For luck. Will you?"

Dazzler turned around and raised her hair out of her way. "I'd be honored."

Martha's hands shook as she fastened the clasp. "I know you two will be very happy together, but if he ever steps out of line, I'm just across the street."

"Oh, hey!" Todd set his hand over his heart. He was going to be a great husband. He knew exactly how lucky he was.

The women ignored him.

Dazzler's mother pulled her toward the exit. "I think a wedding is the perfect way to christen the new tech center."

The elves, Todd's mother, and Mrs. Claus disappeared.

Todd stepped into the center of the fading twinkling lights. This couldn't be some elven ploy to stop the wedding, could it? Maybe he should call in reinforcements of his own. Since his mother and Candance were here, his dad should be, too. Maybe it would be all right if his brothers showed up, provided they didn't start boasting about making the wedding possible. He eyed Santa.

"Do I have to write a letter to marry her by tonight?"

Santa laughed and strode to the door.

Dazzler's father, Tobin, slapped Todd on the back. "Knowing my wife, she'll have everything ready by the time we walk over there. And that's if we walk fast. She's been planning this day for a long time. Although, in truth, after we listened to Willa regarding your unsuitability as a husband, we did not think this day would come."

"I know what you mean." Todd had experienced a lot of those moments in the last day.

"Which garb would you prefer? Human or elf?" Magic sparked between Tobin's hands.

"Which do you think Dazzler would prefer?"

Tobin snorted. "She doesn't care. But her mother would prefer elven."

Todd's skin tingled. A green tunic molded to his chest. Leggings outlined his calves. Gold stitching bracketed the embroidered pine cones on his cuffs and collar. He eyed the door.

"Can we go now?"

"Santa is arranging the rest of your family's arrival, but I believe it is customary to have someone stand up for you." Tobin rubbed his hands. "Who would you prefer?"

Todd considered and dismissed his brothers and father. They'd been there for him from the beginning, but only one being had been there for Dazzler. She deserved to have him here for the celebration.

"Cheddar."

Tobin's hands stilled. "You know she gave him up for you?"

Deer droppings. Todd hadn't known, and she wouldn't tell him.

"Can we get him back?"

"Well..." Tobin tapped his chin then pointed to the corner. The air thickened. Snow flurries swirled. A human-sized gingerbread man twinkled into existence.

"Took you long enough to bring me back. But at least I won't miss the wedding." Cheddar adjusted the icing of his bow tie, then examined his gumdrop buttons. His licorice lips pursed. "I don't know if I'll be safe as a cookie at the North Pole. Elves can be cookie fiends, especially when they're celebrating." He flexed his arm. "I hope these regrow."

Todd slapped his back. "Let's go."

Ten minutes later, Todd entered a cathedral of electronic toys. Dazzler's and his names scrolled across the front of the building. Elves occupied rows of seats, while others took turns exploring.

He searched the open space for his bride. His family sat clustered at the front. Ole Henderson was beside them. The old man morphed into an elf. An ancient elf. One who'd fulfilled his part in the Starlight Treaty before Todd. He nodded once in acknowledgment.

Thanksgiving dinner for thousands filled the sideboards, including his great-grandmother's rhubarb-cranberry sauce. From the front of the room, Candance waved over the crowd. The wedding march started.

The elves sat, but his family stood. Then the elves stood while his family sat.

Laughing, Santa set his hands on his belly. "Everyone can sit. The groom isn't planning to run."

Cheddar looped his arm through Todd's and dragged him forward. "This way."

Dazzler wore a simple white gown that brushed her ivory slippers, a bouquet of daffodils blossomed in her hands, and a chain of daisies wove her dark hair into a sleek knot on top of her head.

Candance waved from behind her. She flashed a stack of letters addressed to Santa.

"Best Christmas ever." The letters turned into a bouquet of poinsettias. "Auntie D's going to be my mom."

"She's always been your mom. We're just finally making it official." Todd stopped in front of Dazzler.

She swiped at a tear on her cheek. "You brought back Cheddar for me."

"He's family." Todd leaned forward to kiss her.

Santa tsked. "Vows first."

"Right." Now was the time for that speech he'd practiced. Todd opened his mouth.

Dazzler spoke first. "Todd Dugan, I knew you were the human for me the moment I tried to kill you."

His family chuckled. Aurora and Tobin Spitfire shifted on the front seat. Todd tightened his grip on her hands. He better not wake up and find himself alone.

"We were the biggest obstacle on our way to true love. But we got here. And you were worth whatever trial we endured. I know that even when I breathe my last, I will never stop loving you. Or the life we create together. Thank you for being my best friend as well as my soulmate."

A ring of tender vines wrapped around his ring finger then hardened into platinum.

Crap. He'd forgotten a ring. He had to have a ring. Silence filled the space around them. What was he thinking? He had magic. He could create a ring worthy of her.

She squeezed his hand.

Right. His turn. "I suppose I should get used to you always knowing the right thing to do and to say."

His father gave him a thumbs-up.

Todd focused on Dazzler. They would celebrate with his family later. This moment was theirs.

"For so long, I thought I was broken, smashed beyond repair. But your patience and kindness healed the cracks. Your laughter shined a light into the darkness that had taken over my soul. I promise I will never take you for granted. Every day we spend together will be Thanksgiving because you're at my side. I never thought I could love someone as much as I love you, Dazzler Spitfire, but tomorrow I will love you even more."

Delicate vines twined around her ring finger until they hardened into platinum. Their rings matched. Perfect.

Santa's voice echoed around the room. "By the power vested in me and blessed by the Starlight Treaty, I now pronounce you one and inseparable."

Finally. How long did these ceremonies have to last anyway? Todd bent down to kiss his soulmate. Rising on tiptoes, Dazzler met him halfway.

Despite having centuries of tomorrows, he wanted this moment to last forever. How long did one have to kiss to make up for nearly two decades of missed kisses?

Someone cleared their throat. A hand tugged on his coat.

Maybe he didn't ever have to stop.

A zing of electricity zapped him. He leaned back, touching his throbbing lip.

Santa arched one white eyebrow. "May you love happily ever after."

Todd would make sure they did.

END

About The Author

LINDA ANDREWS lives with her husband and three children in Phoenix, Arizona. When she announced to her family that her paranormal romance was to be published, her sister pronounce: "What else would she write? She's never been normal."

All kidding aside, writing has become a surprising passion. So just how did a scientist start to write paranormal romances? What other option is there when you're married to romantic man and live in a haunted house?

If you've enjoyed her stories or want to share your own paranormal experience, she'd love to hear from you.

About The Artist

CHARLES BERNARD is an illustrator and graphic designer who has worked for Columbia House and the Famous Artists Schools in Westport, Connecticut. He has created cover art for various publishers, including story illustrations for *Analog Science Fiction and Fact* magazine.